I0541173

Wing Tip

SHERRY BOAS

Caritas Press, Arizona, USA

Wing Tip

Sherry Boas

First Edition

10 9 8 7 6 5 4 3 2 1

ISBN 978-0-9833866-4-3

Published by Caritas Press, Arizona, USA

For reorders and other works by Sherry Boas, visit LilyTrilogy.com

For the Good Shepherd
and all the shepherds of our day
who lead us to truth and beauty.

Acknowledgements

Heartfelt thanks to Bishop Thomas J. Olmsted for his support and encouragement. To Father Paul Sullivan, Father Kyle Schnippel and Father John Lankeit for their invaluable feedback and guidance. To my beautiful mother and my wonderful friends Liz Schiavone and Cindy Troiano for the prayers and pep talks and for enduring my rough, rough, rough, rough, very rough drafts. To Father Doug Lorig, Father Sergio M. Fita and Father Juan Miguel Cano, whose lives are a constant reminder of what it means to walk humbly and love deeply. And to my friends and family, for their patience, love, kindness and coffee.

Contents

1

The Voices of Roses

He held the gift in front of her overcast gaze, longing to fly past the stratus of cataracts into the deep blue comfort of her eyes. He was sure it was still there somewhere, beyond the hazy veil. Her hair descended in muddled strands of silver straggles over the top pillow in a stack of three. This was the farthest she had sat up in weeks. The abundance of pillows was, the priest imagined, responsible for the overwhelming smell of laundry disinfectant. It was an odor that forged unwelcome distance between him and the frail old woman, a smell foreign to the sweetness that had always lain between them. Its sterile unfamiliarity threatened to erase all that can be remembered about growing up in the care of a woman who understood that all the hurts of the world could be allayed by a soft pressing of a small, tear-streaked face into a lightly perfumed embrace. All his life, his mother had smelled vaguely of Prince Matchabelli's Cachet. He could not remember a day when she hadn't.

The thought of her leaving frightened him, maybe every bit as much as if he were a boy. Ever since he was ten, ever since his father's death, he had dreaded this moment. And now that the moment was here, it was exactly as he had lived and relived it in his fears. It wasn't that he lacked faith. He knew he would see her again. It was the living without her in the meantime. It was the being orphaned for this flash of time before the start of eternity.

"The Body of Christ," he said.

She stared at the small white circle, her milky eyes motionless and intense, her thoughts seemingly plumbing the depths of her own soul, as if there were nobody and nothing else in the room but those two – just her and the unleavened host that held promises unfathomable to the human mind.

"Mama?" He was kneeling by her bedside, holding the food of angels between their two faces. He moved closer. "The Body of Christ."

This was bread for the journey, strength for her passage from this earthly life into eternity. And he felt grateful to be able to give it to the person he loved most in the world.

"No," her voice grated, and her eyelids fell.

"What is it, Mama Dulce?"

"I can't," she said. "I haven't made a good confession."

"Mama, I just heard your confession. Don't you remember? Look, here's my stole." He pinched at the strip of purple cloth folded on the foot of the bed.

"No," she said. "It was not a good confession. There is something else."

"Oh, Mama," he smiled. "Don't let scruples rob you of your peace. God has forgiven you. Even for the things you forgot to confess."

"No, no," she said. "I did not forget. I withheld."

"OK, then," he said, slowly placing the host back in the gold pyx hanging around his neck from a leather cord. "Let's hear it, and I will give you absolution again." He draped the stole around his neck, took his mother's hand, bowed his head and closed his eyes.

"Bless me, Father, for I have sinned." Her voice was shaky, as if she were riding in a very old jeep over a gravelly road. She covered her eyes with her veiny hands. "Oh, Dante, why don't we wait until tomorrow? I am so tired."

"No, Mama, it won't take long. Then you can receive our Lord in Holy Communion. And He will give you strength. He is waiting for you."

"Can you come back tomorrow, Dante?"

"Well, of course I will come back tomorrow, Mama, but—" Tears threatened his eyes. "But it's best not to leave the unburdening of our souls for another day."

"Don't worry, Dante. I am not going to die tonight."

"No one knows the hour or the day, Mama Dulce. Besides, I have brought you Communion. I can't very well leave without giving it to you."

"There is something I cannot confess to you. I need another priest. Can you call another priest, Dante?"

"Well, of course I can, Mama. But you don't need to be afraid to tell me. After ten years in the Confessional, believe me, I have heard everything."

She closed her eyes and breathed heavily. He could see the life slipping out of her, as if by drops, draining into the vast whiteness of the hospital.

"OK, Mama," he said, stroking her forehead. "I'll get you another priest. Don't worry. I'll get one right away."

"Dante? My rose. Did you bring me a rose?"

"I'm sorry Mama Dulce. There just wasn't one beautiful enough for my Mama today."

"Tomorrow, Dante. Just bring one tomorrow. Maybe there'll be a red one. They have the prettiest voices. Look for a red one, Dante."

၈ဝ၌ၜ၌ဝ၌ၜ၌ဝ၌ၜ၌ဝ၌ၜ

In the hospital corridor, outside his mother's room, Dante pressed his sister's head into his chest. She had been, so far, successful at damming a torrent of sobs back behind her dark-ringed eyes. But the second her cheek touched the starched black cotton of her brother's cassock, she could manage it no longer.

Sylvie was six years his junior, and Dante had played this role many times. For instance, the first day she rode with him to the park without her training wheels and wiped out on the curb at the intersection of Eighth and Citrus, sustaining a bruised knee and a skinned elbow and (much worse than that) the agonizing embarrassment of having taken such a spill in front of "big kids," a pair of eight- and ten-year-old ferret-eyed brothers, whose unabridged laughter snarked out in snide belches past their enormous front teeth. Dante had it all under control because he knew everything there was to know back then, including how to take a small, demoralized young girl under his arm and convince her, while gently brushing pea gravel off her magenta corduroys, that there is not a single cyclist in the world who hasn't wound up horizontal under his or her own wheels.

He wanted to be the strong one now, but he wasn't. He couldn't help trying to imagine what his mother could be confessing to Father Francis on the other side of that faux wood door. After so many years in the confessional, Father Dante knew no sin can withstand the power of God's mercy, but he worried that his mother might lack peace in her final moments.

He grabbed Sylvie's cold hand and squeezed it tight. "Do you think Mama had any secrets?" he asked.

"Secrets?"

"Things she kept from us."

"Of course," she sniffed.

"How do you know?"

"Every parent keeps secrets from their children, Dante." She pulled a tissue from her sweater pocket and wiped at her nose.

"Like what kind of secrets would our mother keep?"

"I don't know. If I knew, they wouldn't be secrets."

"Have you?"

"Have I what?"

"Kept secrets?"

"Sure."

"Like what?"

"You really don't understand the concept, do you?"

"I mean, from your children. Have you kept secrets from your children?"

"Of course. I'm not going to tell them everything I did when I was young and stupid."

"Oh, you could not have that much in your youth to hide."

"You have no idea, Dante, because you were never young or stupid. Mom used to say you were a wise old man of 84 when you popped out of the womb."

He turned his mouth into a half smile and shook his head.

"Fun, but old," Sylvie said, smiling up at him.

"Mama said I was fun?"

"No, *I* said you were fun."

ಬ⁕ಚಬ⁕ಚಬ⁕ಚಬ⁕ಚಬ⁕ಚ

Father Dante walked home to the rectory that night in sheets of rain, without an umbrella or a coat. He could have taken a train, but he chose to walk. He was nearly an orphan now, with no one to tell him he was going to catch cold. Frankly, he didn't care if he did. His mother had lapsed into a coma right after Father Francis left the hospital. Dante had knelt at her bedside for more than four hours, praying the Rosary, Divine Mercy Chaplet, Litany of the Saints, the St. Michael prayer, the Memorare and every other prayer he had committed to memory.

Father Dante was normally a highly considerate roommate, but at 11:30 p.m., standing in the hallway panting and dripping, he gave a commanding knock on the door. Father Francis had been asleep for more than two hours because he had to rise early the next morning to celebrate 6:30 a.m. Mass.

"Dante." The startled priest blinked hard into the sight before him, making certain he was awake and not dreaming. "Is she-- is your mother-- has she gone home, Dante?"

"No," he croaked through a throat thick with sorrow. "Father Francis, what do you think is the state of my mother's soul? Do you think she's at peace?"

"All of us would like to know that about our loved ones, Dante, and none of us does, fully. Here, come get a towel. You

11

are drenched. Why don't you get changed?" He took Dante's arm and walked him to the bathroom. The elder priest's shiny bald head, pale blue eyes and gray beard afforded him an air of time-honored wisdom. He put a towel around Dante's shoulders and took a quick survey of his face, finding there a brokenness that he would have given anything to fix. He placed his wrinkled hands on Dante's arms and looked him square in the eye. "We must put our full trust in the mercy of God, at the same time that we pray with all diligence for the souls of the departed. But, Father Dante, I think you know all of that. There's something else troubling you."

"I just can't imagine what it was my mother could not tell me."

"I understand how you must feel. But don't fret. You know that she confessed it. That should be enough to ease your mind."

"It should. But it's not. I can't stop thinking about it."

"I have a feeling there will come a day when you will find out what it was. Until then, you will have to ask the Lord to free you from your obsessive thoughts and grant you peace."

"I don't see how I will ever know. The doctors say she will never regain consciousness."

"If the Lord grants it, you will know. As for your mother, I think she is as ready as any of us can be, Father Dante. She received the Sacraments. And I doubt there's any way she can possibly have committed any more sin after that. If I were a gambling man, I would bet my last nickel that she will fly straight into the arms of an angel."

⁞❳❲❳❲❳❲❳❲❳❲

On a warm sunny day, sweet with the scent of orange blossoms, Elina De Luz was buried beside her beloved Mateo. Per her request, Mateo's right wing tip shoe was buried with her. The left had been buried with Mateo twenty-five years before. Those shoes had always been a symbol of their union. During the couple's years together, Elina stored them with her simple satin wedding dress in a generations-old cedar trunk, which

Mateo's mother gave them as a wedding gift. Every year on their anniversary, Elina put on that dress and Mateo would wear a suit and bow tie and, of course, the wing tips, and they would go out for dinner while Mateo's mother stayed with Dante and Sylvie, bringing pop-up books about Scottish castles, U.S. and world map puzzles, Twister and Dominoes. On their tenth wedding anniversary, their last one together, the couple hired a limo for their date and came home talking, with great glee in their melodious voices, about how the driver that night wore the very same shoes as Mateo.

Dante knelt on the cemetery ground between them, folded himself over at the hip, and wept. He loved his parents as much as any mortal son has ever loved. Maybe even more. And that fact was a reflection on *them* more than on *him*. They were not perfect people with the perfect lives. Money was always a bit of a difficulty. But love was not. Those two people knew how to love.

Dante blotted his eyes with his hanky, looked out across the brilliant green and wondered if he would ever possess the happiness of green again. And then she appeared -- the twirling child with shining raven hair, bare feet lightly touching the ground -- or maybe not touching at all. She came in times of sadness or confusion, whirling amidst large white volumes of georgette crepe. Sometimes she smiled at him. This time, their eyes didn't meet. She just danced to inaudible music and Dante watched, wishing he could hear it, but knowing he could not enjoy it anyway. He couldn't imagine there would ever come a time when he would enjoy music again.

And then he was suddenly aware of a hand on his shoulder. Father Francis had knelt beside him.

"Your mother wanted you to have this after her passing," he said giving him a sealed white envelope. "You should take it to a quiet place, maybe, and read it. The things you will find in the letter are likely to be difficult for you. I'm going straight back to the rectory if you need to talk." The priest squeezed Dante's shoulder, gave him a smile and stood.

Dante felt a lump grow in his throat as he struggled to his feet. His knees were shaky. He was off balance for the first time in his life.

೮ೱೲೱ೮ೱೲೱ೮ೱೲೱ೮ೱೲ

Father Dante blessed himself with holy water, walked down the center aisle and knelt before the tabernacle. After several minutes, he moved to the front pew and sat staring straight ahead, watching the flicker from the candles at a Marian shrine to the right of the altar. He grasped the envelope in his hand. His name was written in blue ink in simple handwriting. "Dante." It was not his mother's handwriting. His mother's handwriting had a pronounced forward, almost unnatural slant. He knew it well because he spent a great deal of time studying it in his youth. He had, on several occasions, forged her signature.

The first time was in third grade when he had forgotten to have her sign a field trip permission slip. He really meant no harm. He knew his mother would have had no objections to an outing to the science museum. The permission slip was just a technicality, he reasoned, and should not hinder him from participating. In fact, his mother would be upset if he missed it. And she would have used the incident as yet another occasion to lecture him on the wisdom of keeping his important things organized and not stuffed and crumpled in the bottom of his backpack. The forgery may have worked if it wasn't for the fact that his teacher had, on her lunch break, made a reminder phone call to the three parents whose signatures she had not yet received, only to have Dante materialize his mother's just before the dismissal bell. When Dante's mother found out, she announced to him that she would keep him home on field trip day. The crime of forgery deserved nothing less severe, and Dante knew it. He retreated to his room in tears and emerged an hour and fifteen minutes later with a written discourse on the turpitude of defrauding someone you love. Seeing his complete repentance and full understanding of the wrongness of his deed, Elina put her arms around her son, kissed him on the top of the head and told him how proud she was of his humility. She told him he could go on the field trip if he promised to help clean the garage on Saturday for his penance. Dante agreed, as long as there would be time for confession on Saturday afternoon. Elina assured her son that his father would take him. Although she was not Catholic, she somehow understood that the Sacraments were forming her son and informing his conscience, which she considered well developed for a boy his age. She felt sure it would be the last time he ever signed anyone else's name.

And he didn't do it again for eight more years. Despite his genuine repentance, he forged his mother's signature again, this time on an algebra mid-term that parents had to sign if their children didn't pass it. His mother seemed worried about many things at the time, and he didn't want to add to her burden. She was working during the day as a publicist for a radio station and taking care of an ailing neighbor in the evenings -- grocery shopping, cooking and cleaning for her. Elina never found out about the sixty-six percent on the mid-term and Dante ended up pulling his grade up to a C by the time report cards came around.

Then, when he was a senior, he brought a signed note to school to request an early release for a doctor's appointment. He himself had authored it and signed his mother's name. He was headed to the beach with his friends. As the waves leapt around his ankles and the foaming surf carried ever more ground away from his sinking toes, he stood still like an Italian statue, muscular and vacant, his mind as far away from all his friends' frivolity as was the golden afternoon sun. He could find some justification for the other two times he had forged his mother's signature. But this one, he could not. It was born of completely selfish motives. And it was deceptive. And he couldn't live with that between him and the person he loved most in the world. So, he went home and told her about it.

Her reaction was not what he had hoped for, but it was understandable. She felt grateful for the eventual honesty, yet betrayed by the initial lie.

He knew that the reason he was able to act with such

disregard for her trust is that this same sin, practiced in lesser degrees in the past, had diminished his sensitivity to its ugliness. From then on, he resolved to do everything in his power to avoid even the smallest sin.

Father Francis cautioned him on more than one occasion on the very real dangers of scrupulosity. But Dante wholesale denied any tendency toward being too hard on himself.

And yet seventeen years after the forgery, Dante still had a knotted stomach when he thought about it. The small envelope, grasped in his two hands now, was plain white and unremarkable, and there was nothing to fixate on, except for his name, which he theorized had been written by Father Francis. He turned the envelope over and slid his finger under the flap. His hands were not shaking, but somehow unsteady and tight, not fully responsive to the wishes of his brain. His brain wanted desperately to know what was inside. The rest of him, apparently not.

With his finger just about to the midpoint under the seal of the envelope, he felt a hand touch his shoulder and turned to see a gray-haired woman he recognized as one of his parishioners, though he did not know her name. She had, at some point, slipped into the pew behind him.

"Hello," he whispered. "How are you tonight?"

"I am not well, Father. I came here to pray, but I really don't feel like praying."

"Well, what do you feel like doing?"

"I feel like screaming."

"Well, we've all had those moments," he said with a smile. "What do you feel like screaming about?"

"My husband just decided it would be a good idea to tell me that he had an affair. *Twenty-five years ago.*"

"Oh, I'm so sorry."

"Twenty-five years ago, Father."

"Why did he tell you now? Was he seeking your forgiveness?"

"Yes."

16

"Were you able to give it to him?"

"I don't know."

"You don't know?"

"I'm not really that angry at him for having the affair, Father. It was such a long time ago. I'm angry at him for telling me. What purpose does it serve to tell me something like that 25 years later? I am 63 years old, Father. I could have gone to my grave happily believing that he has always been crazy over me. But he ruined it for me. For that, I cannot forgive him."

"You really would have rather not known?"

"I absolutely would have rather not known."

"Well, I'm sure he told you because he thought you had the right to know."

"Bull. He told me to get it off his chest."

"But not to hurt you."

She drew a long breath and fixed her eyes to the left of the altar, where a statue of St. Joseph stood within a niche adorned with gold carvings of lilies.

"Is your husband in good health?"

"Yes."

"So, why do you suppose he told you now?"

"I think it's been eating at him for 25 years."

"How long have you been married?"

"Thirty-six years."

"Has it been a good marriage?"

"I guess the first 11 were good."

"But not the last 25?"

"I thought they were good. But I guess they weren't what I thought they were. Turns out I was married to an adulterer and didn't even know it. Those years made a fool out of me."

"So, it's not the affair that bothers you, but the fact that you didn't know about it until now?"

"I wish he hadn't told me at all."

"Then your pride would not have been wounded."

"My pride? The Sacrament of Marriage is holy, Father. He betrayed that."

17

"Yes, it is a betrayal. But you just said the affair is not the part you are having trouble forgiving."

"I'm having trouble with all of it, Father. But, I wouldn't be having this trouble at all if he had kept his big trap shut about it." She punctuated her statement with a swift chop, as if trying to slice through a thick slab of air, and then folded her arms to rest over her large belly. "That's my point."

Dante silently stared at the altar for several minutes. He glanced over at the woman. She was doing the same. "You never suspected there was a secret he was keeping?"

"I guess there were times when it would cross my mind and I would wonder. But suspecting is much different than knowing."

"You know, there is a secret my mother has kept from me. I suspect I will find it inside this half-opened envelope." He gazed again at his name. "I have no idea what it is, but I do know that knowing it will be better than not knowing it."

"Don't be so sure, Father."

"Even if it's the worst possible thing that I can imagine, I want to know. It was part of my mother's life."

"Well, it may be worse than you can imagine. You like your life, Father? You have a pretty good life, don't ya?"

"Sure. I have been abundantly blessed."

"Then you would be wise to throw that thing in the trash," the woman said, waving her hand at the envelope with a look of disgust. "Open it, and your life may never be the same."

2

Thumbs of Angels

The voice glided smoothly like blades over ice.

"Good morning. Crenshaw Enterprises, President's office. How may I help you?"

"Yes, I would like to speak with Mr. Crenshaw please," said Father Dante, sitting straight and a little stiff in his low-backed secretarial chair behind his oak laminate desk, tapping his fingers on a pile of baptismal certificates awaiting his signature.

"He's not available. May I take a message?"

"Yes, I've called several times and left messages. It's really important that I reach him."

"What is it regarding?"

"It's of a personal nature. But it's very important."

"He is semi-retired. He doesn't come in very often. Can someone else help you?"

"No. They told me they'd get a message to Mr. Crenshaw at home."

"Then I'm sure the message has been delivered."

"It's very important that I speak to him."

"If you'd like to leave your name again, I'll pass the message along."

"Dante De Luz." He closed his eyes and implored heaven for direction. *Jesus, son of the living God, have mercy on me. Do I tell her I'm a priest?* "Father Dante De Luz."

"Is this about donations? All of that is handled through our community relations department. I can connect you, if you like."

"No, it's not about donations. Please, it's very important. Please see that Mr. Crenshaw gets the message."

"Your last name again?"

"De Luz. Two words. Capital-D-e-capital-L-u-z."

"Thank you Mr. -- Father De Luz."

"And what is your name?"

"Roberta."

"Will you see to it personally, Roberta?"

"He will get the message, Father."

"Thank you. God bless you. I will remember you at the altar of our Lord."

"No need, Father. I am a recovered Catholic. Haven't been to Mass in seven years."

"Then I will pray that you find your way home."

"Have a nice day, Father."

⊱✠⊰✠⊱✠⊰✠⊱✠⊰

After stopping at the rectory chapel to pray a Rosary for the abatement of Roberta's anger at God, Father Dante googled Lawrence Crenshaw and learned that he was named one of the top 100 most successful businessmen in American history, making his fortune as the CEO of three companies, including the world's largest in the electronic gaming industry. Among his notable philanthropic causes was a foundation to provide scholarships to inner-city kids and another dedicated to the preservation of endangered species in South America.

Father Dante had known enough kids in dire need of help with higher education to fully appreciate Crenshaw's generosity toward scholarship funds, but he scoffed internally at the decision to sink money into trendy environmental causes. Then he reminded himself that God must have had a reason for all the creatures He created. Even, he supposed, the various varieties of rats that are now on the endangered and threatened list. And yet he found it interesting that people should be so concerned over the demise of the Giant Atlantic Tree Rat of Brazil, the Unexpected Cotton Rat of Ecuador, the Gray-footed Spiny Rat of Columbia, the Pittier's Crab-eating Rat of Venezuela, Torres's Crimson-nosed Rat of Argentina or Zuniga's Dark Rice Rat of Peru. Certainly, no one would lose any sleep over the extinction of the sewer rat of L.A. Not that there's any chance of that ever happening any more than it is likely that a nuclear holocaust would do the roaches in. It seems that entire species of animals can only be eliminated by accident. Extermination is only effective if it is unintentional. Indeed, there can only be one explanation for a highly successful, well-educated, presumably intelligent man spending a portion of his billions on the preservation of rats: Dante's parents were right.

"Your father used to say, it's all about perspective," his mother would tell him. "He'd say 'If you live in a crack in the sidewalk and you think it's a palace, then you are a rich man.'"

Save the rats? Eliminate the rats? It all depends on your perspective, doesn't it?

Not that Dante would want to see any animal go extinct. He had theorized that every species of animal exists, not only to aid in the functioning of the ecosystem, but to teach people something. He never forgot the first time he realized how thoughtful God is. He was just a little boy, watching a nature show about the three-toed tree sloth. The sloth has wrong-way fur, which means it actually falls the right way when the sloth hangs upside down from a tree. That proves those creatures were made by an obliging Creator. One who tends to every last detail, including the fact that the sloth would be hanging upside down a good portion of its time and therefore should have fur that cooperates with gravity.

৳৵❁৳৵❁৳৵❁৳৵❁৳৵❁

Father Dante stood at the intersection, waiting for the "walk" sign as the cars buzzed past. A woman in front of him spewed curse words into her phone. She was tall with large curves

21

poured into dark blue jeans, secured with a broad gold sequin belt, as if there was some chance her pants could fall off.

She dropped her phone into her purse and shook her head. Father Dante touched her arm. She whipped around with a glare, which immediately dissolved into a soft gaze when she saw the person who dared put his hand on her was wearing a long black cassock, carrying a very large duffle bag.

"Peace be with you, Sister," he said softly, with a wide smile.

"I'm sorry, Father," she said, "if you heard any of that."

"Sounds like this day has brought you some trouble."

"It's my boyfriend. Every day with him brings troubles."

"There's one who never disappoints." He placed a card with the Our Lady of Joy mass times into her hand. "Come find out sometime who He is."

On the corner of Fourth Avenue and Rose, Father Dante set up a stool in front of a small easel, amidst the fumes and dirt of blighted beach-town gloom. There's money and fame in Venice Beach, but certainly not here in the Oakwood neighborhood, infused with a long history of the usual dysfunctions that accompany poverty and resentment. The neighborhood, just a few blocks inland from the tourist trap shoreline, is called "the pentagon" because of the shape marked out by its border streets.

This is where Father Dante often set up shop, dressed in his trademark slate-colored beret and black cassock. Always his cassock. A very apparent cassock, so long, it nearly brushed the ground as he walked – a silent reminder to a Godless world that God exists and that there are still a number of people willing to cloak their entire bodies in testimony to that fact.

Father Dante's backdrop was a faded pink low-profile building housing a coin laundry and dry cleaning establishment. In the window, a bright yellow sign with bold black letters declared "Internet Access." The marquis said "SUITS $999." Never what anyone would call "accomplished" at math, Father Dante did, at least, grasp the importance of decimal points and smiled to himself at the thought of a clerk holding a suit hostage (in the interest of truth in advertising) until its owner materialized a cool grand.

Father Dante parked himself, his easel and an empty collapsible lawn chair next to the *Los Angeles Times* news rack, dented in three places, most likely by someone's rage. A small box of assorted trash sat next to it. The empty chair never stayed empty for long. Many of those who filled it were repeat "customers," some of whom would drop a dollar or two in the coffee can covered with baby blue construction paper marked in black Sharpie, "Donations for St. Vincent de Paul," some of whom didn't have a dollar to drop.

The man in his early 20s who sat there on this particular day was not a regular. Father Dante held a felt-tip pen, head cocked, looking intently into the eyes of his subject, seemingly trying to determine what trait to accentuate in the caricature he was about to create, but more likely trying to assess what demon has blocked the channel for supernatural grace.

The priest frequented the corner of Rose and Fourth so often, that he showed up on the street view of Google maps. He was the only artist in this part of town. The rest were on the boardwalk of Venice Beach, selling their abstract works resembling private body parts, setting up shop amidst a predictably eclectic collection of characters, including the Buddha peddler, the toe ring vendor, the intriguing guy with long, flying gray hair playing a lidless baby grand and a number of middle-aged women dressed in colorful moo-moos, dripping in gaudy bangles, claiming to be "Venice Beach's original" fortune teller.

Dante took an online drawing course when he was a senior in high school. He settled in on caricatures because it amused all his friends. It's what Father Dante did to break the ice. And because he loved to draw. But mostly to break the ice. If you can break the ice, you can thaw the soul. There are so many frozen over. Within any given person's life here in this part of the city, someone has always left. Either by drugs or death or abandonment. Loss is always fresh and deep. And so, a friendly smile isn't enough, like it often is in the upper middle class suburbs.

The face that sat before him on that overcast afternoon was no exception. It had angular cheek bones, a sharp-edged chin and a forehead with prominent corners. The eyes were deep-set with anger, heavily sunken into some degenerative affliction.

"Draw me with a smile," the expressionless man requested. "I'm going to give this to my mother. It's her birthday."

"Nice present," Father said, moving his marker across the paper. "I'm sure she will like it. But if you want me to draw you with a smile, you will have to smile."

The man just stared.

"Well, I can't draw it if I don't know what it looks like."

"Just draw me regular then, man. It don't matter."

"How old is your mama?"

"Sixty-four. She may not see sixty-five." His eyes softened slightly. "She's real sick."

"I'm sorry. What's her name?"

"Matilda."

"Matilda. That's a pretty name. I will pray for her."

The man nodded, still expressionless.

Father Dante began to hum as his felt-tip filled in details of his subject's face – the upside-down "U" on his chin, the lines that led out from the outer corner of his eyes like tributaries on a map. Then he began to whistle the song he had been humming, still adding more detail, working on the body now, the arm with the skull tattoo, which of course, had to be drawn as a caricature as well. He once had to wonder: *How do you draw a caricature of a skull?* But he had now perfected it. Then the priest began to sing. He got through the first three verses of *Waltzing Matilda* and then paused to concentrate on the hollows of the skull's cheeks.

"What's the point of that song?" The man simultaneously hung his head and shook it.

"Catchy, isn't it?"

The man rolled his eyes.

24

"You know I always thought that song was about a woman named Matilda who liked to dance," Father said, still sketching. "Then the 2000 Olympics were held in Sydney and Slim Dusty sang that song, which is actually the unofficial national anthem for Australia, and one of the news commentators explained it's really about a homeless guy who tried to steal a sheep."

"A sheep named Matilda?

"No," Father Dante chuckled, "Matilda is the name the lyricist gave his hobo bag that is carried by the swag man -- that's a vagrant. And one day as he sat by the billabong -- that's a lake -- a sheep came wandering by -- they call it a jumbuck -- and he stuffed it in his food bag."

"And that's the national anthem?"

"I know. The patriotism, huh?"

The man raised his eyebrows and said nothing. Father Dante sketched in silence for a few minutes.

"What's her favorite food? Your mother's?"

"Shrimp."

"What kind of shrimp."

"I don't know. Just shrimp. The pink kind."

"Fixed how, I mean?"

"I don't know. Just any kind of shrimp."

"Father Francis likes to cook. Why don't you bring your mother by the rectory tomorrow night. We'll cook her a birthday dinner. Shrimp scampi, maybe. That's my favorite way to eat shrimp. Aw, heck. We'll make her some shrimp cocktail too. I've got a bottle of wine a parishioner gave me for Christmas last year. We'll celebrate."

"Celebrate what?"

Father Dante turned the board toward his subject. "We'll celebrate the completion of a fine work of art."

The man smiled, for the first time showing his teeth, and shook his head. "You're some kind of a crazy dude."

"You don't think I'm serious? I'm serious. You bring the salad." The priest handed him an Our Lady of Joy card.

25

"OK." He hung his head, shook it and looked at the ground, still smiling slightly.

"Don't stand us up, now. Father Francis will be miffed at me if I make him go through all that work for nothing."

"OK, man. OK. We'll be there. We wouldn't want to miff Father Francis."

ᔆᕽᔆᕽᔆᕽᔆᕽᔆᕽᔆᕽᔆᕽᔆᕽᔆᕽ

Father Dante googled Lawrence Crenshaw again and found a CNN interview. He was a very thin man with tailored hair -- salt intermingled with pepper like the weave in the acrylic scarf Dante's father wore and Dante clutched onto when he would throw his arms around his father's neck at the end of a work day. Lawrence Crenshaw had a number of well-defined and distinguished lines in his tanned face. You wouldn't call them wrinkles. They were lines.

The report showed footage of his two-story garage, which housed 52 exotic cars (one for each week of the year?) and his 33,000-square-foot mansion -- complete with nine bedrooms, two luxury kitchens, a movie theater and twenty televisions, including one in the bathroom mirror.

"I'm not going to apologize for my wealth," he told the reporter. "I give a great deal of money away every year. The rich, the ability to get rich, the desire to get rich, it's what drives the American economy. If American's don't like the rich, they ought not have capitalism. It's the system we have and it's a damn good one. I challenge anyone to find a better one. No, I won't apologize for my ability to benefit from a good system."

Father Dante logged off and picked up the phone.

"Roberta?"

"Yes?"

"This is Father Dante."

"Hello, Father."

"Did you give Mr. Crenshaw the message?"

"Yes. Has he not returned your call?"

"No, he hasn't."

"I'll give him another message."

"Oh, thank you."

"Sure. You're welcome."

"You have been very patient with me, Roberta. I'm sorry to make such a pest of myself. It's just that I'm desperate. I have to speak with him."

"I understand, Father. But Mr. Crenshaw is a very busy man."

"Yes, well, God bless you, Roberta for passing along another message. You are in my prayers."

"Can you hold just a minute please, Father. I have another call."

"Sure."

The line clicked over to on-hold music from the 80's. *Thank You for the Music.* Father thought probably by Abba. Roberta returned right after the chipper duo chirped the thought-provoking question, "Without a song or a dance, what are we?"

"Hello, Father. I just wanted to let you know, I know you're a priest, but some people may be offended by your insistence on bringing prayer into every interaction."

"Are you offended?"

"Not exactly. I'm only saying, Father, that not everyone shares the same belief system you do. I don't believe in prayer any more than you believe in voodoo."

"Oh, I see."

"So, you know, it would be kind of like me telling you I'm going to be practicing voodoo on you. You'd feel kind of uncomfortable, wouldn't you?"

"Well, yes. All those sharp pins and everything. But my prayers don't have any chance of hurting you, do they? Especially if there's no God, they really can't do anything to you at all."

"OK, Father. Pray for whomever you please. Meanwhile, I'll give Mr. Crenshaw your message. Again."

"Thank you, Roberta. May God reward you for your kindness."

Father Dante was sure that Roberta was his one way to Crenshaw. And he knew that she was going to be quite a hindrance. And he was sure that she would one day relent. This he knew because his mother taught him a certain virtue.

"Nothing will get you farther than perseverance," she would say. "Intelligence, education and prestige – these things are valuable. But perseverance is invaluable. Invaluable, Dante, means you can't live without it."

Probably ninety percent of the English-speaking population cannot spell perseverance. But Dante was among the elite ten percent by the time he was six years old. He couldn't spell "have," "what," "they," "walk," or nearly half of the words on his first grade spelling test. But he could spell *perseverance* because his mother saw to it. She taught him an awe and an admiration for the word and she supplied many examples. Any one of those examples or a combination of all may have been responsible for the fruitfulness of his vocation. He has not once ever given up on a soul. This is why, on the first Friday of every month, armed with a stack of Sacred Heart holy cards and a rare penchant for finding words that resonate within the human heart, he will walk to the darkest corner of the wretched, squalid, seamy city, in search of the most miserable people he can find. Not every priest has the stomach for this. But Father Dante has seen what even a narrow beam of light can do to lance a festering boil.

After his ordination, Dante liked to, in his mind, change the quality of perseverance into a Christian virtue: one of the big three. Hope. Not because it was easier to spell. But because he knew it meant so much more.

And so he would employ this virtue against the likes of Roberta, and three days later, find himself standing in front of her desk, unannounced, with a humble countenance only possible for a man who fully grasps the undeniable fact that he is a beggar before God and receptionist.

"Roberta?"

"Yes?"

"I'm Father Dante De Luz."

"Really? I wouldn't have guessed. Except that it is a bit too early for Halloween, so that wouldn't go very far to explain the priest costume."

"Well, my nun costume is at the cleaners."

"They didn't tell me you were coming up."

"I told the receptionist downstairs I was surprising you."

"Oh, so the rose is not for Mr. Crenshaw?"

"Oh, no. This is for you." He stretched his arm straight out and held it there, until she took the coral-colored rose. "For all the pestering you've put up with. It is from Our Lady of Joy. There's a beautiful garden there that our former pastor put in the care of the three archangels."

"Archangels."

"Yes. Gabriel, Michael and Rafael. Gabriel specifically is in charge of the roses because he is the one who announced to Mary that she was to be the mother of our Lord."

"Uh-huh?"

"And roses are Our Lady's flower."

"Oh, OK. Gotcha." She put the bud to her nose. "It smells like Pez candy. It's a beautiful rose, Father. Thank you." She laid it gingerly on the Brazilian cherry desk and picked up her pen, poising it to write, though there was nothing to write on but a pristine black leather desk blotter.

"You should see the ones that got away. You'll have to come to the church sometime. The Rose Society actually wrote us up in their quarterly. They wanted to know all of our horticultural secrets. I don't think they believed us when we told them our roses thrive on human neglect. It's very hard to convince anyone that angels have green thumbs."

"Yes. I wasn't aware angels had thumbs at all."

"Nor was I. But you know, some people say they can hear angels singing in our rose garden. You really must come by."

Roberta held the rose to her ear and shook her head.

"Don't hear anything?" Father asked, with a smile and raised eyebrows.

29

"Nope."

"Oh," he said, reaching into his pocket. "I also brought you this." He put a small plastic box into her hand. She opened it and pulled out a string of beads.

"A rosary from a pilgrimage to Fatima I went on a couple years back," he informed.

She put the dangling blue glass beads back in the box. "Oh, Father, you should give this to someone who will appreciate it more than I would. I don't pray the rosary."

"Well, someday you might," he said closing her hand around the box. "Keep this in your sock drawer until then."

"What will that do? Bless my feet?"

"I don't know about that, but you will always know where it is. Things in sock drawers are never forgotten."

"Did you come here for a specific reason, Father?"

"Yes. I came to ask you if Mr. Crenshaw can see me."

"He's not in today."

"Tomorrow?"

"I don't know. He doesn't have a set schedule."

"Can you call him so I can talk to him?"

"He checks in for his messages. I'll make sure he knows you came by."

"I mean can you call him now?"

"You mean from here? Right now?"

"Yes, if I could just get him on the phone, I know he will want to talk to me."

"He says he doesn't know you."

"He doesn't. But it's important I see him. Could you just call him and ask if he will talk to me?"

"I'm sorry, Father. I can't do that."

"Please, Roberta."

"Look, Father. I know he would not be happy with me if I did that."

"How do you know?"

"He's been trying to avoid you. He says you must be a kook."

"Well, now that you've met me, maybe you can convince him I'm not."

"Let's see, how would I go about that? Hello, Mr. Crenshaw? The gentleman you've been trying to avoid is here and he's no kook. Really. Just to prove it, he brought me a singing rose and a strand of beads for my socks."

"I never said the roses sing. I said the angels sing."

"Sorry. The angels. The green-thumbed angels."

"If Mr. Crenshaw just knew what I was calling about, Roberta, he would want to talk to me."

"Look, why don't you tell me what you want with him?"

"I just want a minute of his time."

"For what?"

"To hear me."

"About what."

"Something of a personal nature. I can't go into it with anyone but him."

"Why not?"

"It's of a personal nature to him."

"I'm sorry, Father. I will tell him you came by."

"What happened seven years ago, Roberta?"

"Seven years ago?"

"You said you haven't been to Mass in seven years."

"I saw the light."

"And what did the light tell you?"

"I'll give Mr. Crenshaw the message, Father. It's the most I can promise."

෴⚜෴

3

A Limo to Far Away

The young man who sat before Father Dante was skeletal, with visible joints in his knees and elbows. He wore khaki shorts and white crew socks pulled halfway up his sharp shins. In contrast to his stick-like legs, his athletic shoes, which may have only been a size 10 at the most, looked huge and clubby. The man, who was probably in his early twenties, sat with curved posture, nearly swallowed by the oversized brown leather chair in Father Dante's office.

"Thank you for seeing me, Father," said the man, who pushed his words out in a slow, dragging drawl, his tongue limp and thick, bathed in an excess of saliva. "I've really been needing some spiritual direction."

"Great. Why don't we start with you telling me what's on your heart and mind?"

"Well, on my mind, is a question. And on my heart is the answer."

"And the question is?"

"How do you know if God is calling you to the priesthood?"

"And the answer?"

"He is."

"And how did you come to that answer?"

"Like I said. It's from my heart."

Father Dante nodded and smiled.

"I know what you're thinking, Father. I'm actually wondering the same thing. How is someone like me going to be able to carry out the duties of the priesthood. I mean, with my speech impediment."

"Well, yes, I was thinking that. And then I remembered Moses."

"Yes, although he had Aaron. And I doubt Moses' speech impediment was as severe as mine."

"I guess we don't really know, do we?"

"No. Well, mine stems from brain damage. I was in a bad car accident when I was 18. I was in a coma and nearly died. The doctors tried to convince my mother to let them pull the plug. But she refused. They told her that, even if I were to regain consciousness, my life would mean nothing. I would be in an institution the rest of my life. She believed them, but she still couldn't give up on me. One of them even told her she was being cruel and selfish for not letting me go."

"She is quite a woman."

"I owe everything to my mother. She took care of me and helped me with my therapies. I wouldn't be able to do anything without her."

"Does she know of your desire to become a priest."

"Oh, yes."

"Is she happy?"

"Ecstatic. She prayed all her life for vocations. Taught me to pray too. I never felt called until after the accident."

"How did the accident happen?"

"A young teenager was sitting next to his girlfriend, driving and kissing at the same time, and ran a red light. And then he fled the scene."

"And how do you feel towards that driver today?"

"I have forgiven him."

"Have you?"

"Yes."

"A priest, if he is to be holy, cannot harbor any grudges."

"It was not easy, but I think I have put aside my grudge. My mother helped me. She went in front of the judge and pleaded for leniency. I figured, if she was going to do that, after he had brought such harm on her only son, I would have to try to forgive too. My mother was so grateful to God that I had lived, she couldn't refuse God's call to forgive."

"So you say, you *think* you have put aside your grudge."

The man glanced down at his oversized feet. "Truth be told, Father, I still have moments of, you know, resentment."

"Anger."

"Yes. Anger, I suppose."

"That young man took something very precious away from you. But he gave you something too."

"What?"

"That is what I want you to contemplate. When you have figured it out, come back and we'll talk some more about the priesthood."

When Dante was a kid, he liked to imagine he could see things that no one could see. Like when his mother made pinto bean soup, he would try to picture all the spiral noodles and cubes of carrots and minces of celery and onions, dancing around in the bubbles, as if he had special eyesight to see, not only through the scratched yellow enamel of the stock pot, but also through the murk of opaque brown broth.

He liked to pretend he could see the cutaway view of an underground wasp's nest -- the busy goings-on inside the intricate chambers and crannies, the winged creatures making their way through the maze of elbow-to-elbow crowds (if bees have elbows), to bring prized gifts of spiders and caterpillars to their queen, seated majestically on a throne of eggs.

As he got older and began to understand the world on a molecular level, he would spend a fair amount of time, staring at a table, pretending to see particles of matter which make up the atoms therein -- the protons and neutrons joining together, the electrons orbiting the nucleus.

The practice of all this, he imagined, primed him for the ability to see the unsettled, swirling contents of human souls.

ೞ)✄(ೞೞ)✄(ೞೞ)✄(ೞೞ)✄(ೞೞ)✄(ೞ

Two long baguettes jutted from the plastic grocery sack that Father Dante had placed on the counter just as the phone rang.

"Father De Luz."

"Yes."

"Mr. Crenshaw is returning your call."

"Oh, thank you. Thank you. Thank you, Roberta. May the Lord reward you for your kindness."

"Please hold for Mr. Crenshaw."

Father Dante grabbed the two loaves of bread, laid them on the counter and reached in for the tight bundle of fresh shrimp wrapped in white butcher paper. He propped the phone on his shoulder and put the shrimp in the fridge.

"Father De Luz."

"Yes, Mr. Crenshaw." He walked several paces into the family room, in the direction of his favorite recliner, leaving the door to the fridge hanging open.

"I am returning your call. Actually, your *many* calls."

"Thank you. Thank you, Mr. Crenshaw." He swiveled on his heel and returned to the fridge, shutting the door and leaving his hand on the cold handle.

"What can I do for you?" Crenshaw asked, not in a tone of service, but with a faint air of annoyance.

"I would like to meet with you."

"What about?"

"I can't tell you on the phone." He picked up a plastic grocery bag from the counter, started to crumple it and noticed it still contained a lone garlic bulb. "It is something very important."

"I'm sorry, Father De Luz. That is too vague to warrant my time and attention."

"It is concerning Elina De Luz." He squeezed the garlic bulb gently, laid it next to the loaves of bread, got a handled mason jar from the cabinet and filled it with tap water.

"Who?"

"Well, actually, you would have known her as Elina Peltier."

"Elina Peltier."

"Do you remember her?"

"Elina."

"Can we meet? Wherever and whenever is convenient for you."

"Is she in need of something?"

"No, she is -- she has passed away." He set the mason jar down and picked up the garlic bulb again.

"Then, what is this about?"

"Please, Mr. Crenshaw. When can we meet?" He propped the phone on his shoulder and began to pick at the garlic, using his thumbnail to flake off small pieces of papery skin.

"Tomorrow morning at eight. At my office."

"Can we make it nine-thirty?" His fingers paused their work on the garlic. "I say Mass at eight."

"I thought you said any time that's convenient for me."

"Any time but that, Sir. "

"OK. Nine-thirty, Father De Luz."

There was a click and the line was dead. Father Dante looked at the garlic bulb, still intact despite his unconscious efforts to dismantle it. He tossed it in the air, caught it and placed it in a large crimson-colored, plastic fruit bowl, which up until that moment, held only one lemon. "I owe you, Roberta," he whispered as he shook his head. He gulped at the room temperature water in the mason jar. "I owe you big time."

ಬ⟩⟨ಜ⟩⟨ಬ⟩⟨ಜ⟩⟨ಬ⟩⟨ಜ⟩⟨ಬ⟩⟨ಜ⟩⟨ಬ⟩⟨ಜ

"I had a feeling they wouldn't show," said Father Francis, dipping a shrimp into cocktail sauce and popping it in his mouth.

"I would have been surprised if they did," said Father Dante, using his fork to escort the shrimp around his plate, skating it through the buttery sauce. "Well, at least we didn't open the wine yet."

"That's the pity of it," said Father Benny. He squeezed his words through a mouth full of shrimp. "But at least you had the good sense to invite me to help eat. You two would have had shrimp up the wazoo."

At the age of 87, Father Benny was retired, but he occasionally filled in at Our Lady of Joy. When he did, the sound tech had to be reminded to make sure Father's mic was turned off before and after Mass. He said the prayers beautifully during Mass, even with failing vision to read the missal, but there was no telling what he was going to say to the deacon or the sacristan when the liturgy ended. No matter how many times it had happened that the mic was still hot, Father Benny never learned. And so the congregation learned that the crotchetiness of old age is not reserved for the laity. It was usually the sacristan who received a chewing out – for placing the cruets too close to the edge of the credence table or failing to estimate the right amount of communion bread. Occasionally, an altar server was reprimanded for not pouring enough water over Father's hands or holding the book too low for him to read, though it was a special large print edition. His mind had lost its elasticity, its swift reflexes, its ability to process new information and configure a response, so everything always had to be just so. But his tongue was as sharp as ever, probably even sharper.

On this evening, though, the shrimp were delicious and there was nothing to complain about. So he turned to philosophy.

"On my fifty-fifth birthday, I looked in the mirror and I said to myself, 'who is this wrinkled and saggy old coot that has taken over the exterior of my body? The interior of me is still the same, but it's trapped inside this aging shell.' When I was young, I thought of old people as a different breed. As you grow older, you start to see old people, not as old people, but as young people who have grown old. And you start to see the young as people who haven't grown old yet."

"My mother used to say that I was born old," Father Dante

37

said. "What do you do with people like me?"

"Well, now your body is catching up, my friend," said Father Francis, holding his boney pointer finger in the air. "And one day, it will have surpassed your mind." He pointed to his temple. "Your mind will grow childish, even as your body slips closer to the grave. As the wise Rabbi said, 'Once a man, twice a child.'"

Dante awoke well before 5 a.m. to the darkness of his small bedroom. He knelt and fixed his eyes on the crucifix hanging at the head of his bed. He remained there in prayer for an hour. Then he showered and ate his customary breakfast – a slice of whole wheat toast, several pieces of dried mango and black coffee.

He walked across the courtyard bricks and past the opus of color performed by the choir of roses. He unlocked the church's rounded wooden door, heavy like that of a medieval castle. The light poured in through the timeless shards of stained glass, casting various flavors of luminosity onto the contented stillness of the sanctuary. Dante knelt before the tabernacle, planning to pray a litany to the Blessed Virgin Mary. But a profound, unnamed sadness suddenly sliced through him, as if he had just learned of the death of a loved one. He crumpled to the ground and lay prostrate. The anguish intensified to the point of near desolation when suddenly he realized the origin of his misery, and he was quite shocked by it. Lawrence Crenshaw's transgressions were passing through him in wild torrents of grief.

കു✄ജ✄കു✄ജ✄കു✄ജ✄കു✄ജ✄കു

The receptionist in the downstairs lobby invited Father Dante to have a seat. It was not a full three minutes before Roberta appeared, her stout, squat body pressing hard against her powder blue cotton button-down-the-front blouse and black skirt that hit just above her plump knee. The ample flesh on her feet spilled out over her black pumps. She had strikingly lovely dark eyes rimmed in long thick lashes and near-black hair to contrast her flawless, alabaster skin.

"Father Dante," she said. "Mr. Crenshaw can see you now."

"Thank you, Roberta." He rose from his seat and held out his hand. He fought the urge to stoop as he shook her hand. He hadn't realized the other day, while she was seated behind her desk, how short she was. Without her three-inch spindle heels, she was probably about the same height as Mother Teresa. Few women were as short as Mother Teresa, but Roberta probably was. "I mean for everything. Thank you."

"You're welcome. Right this way." She swiveled on her heel and walked with flawless posture down the polished marble hallway to the elevator, which opened as soon as she pressed the button. Father Dante smiled at her on the way up. She averted her eyes to the numbers progressing above the door.

"This is quite a beautiful building. You must enjoy being here every day."

"It's a living."

More hallway after the short elevator ride and then very large double doors. "Mr. Crenshaw is ready to see you," she clarified before opening them.

Lawrence Crenshaw sat staring at his computer on the credenza behind his desk, his back to the door. "Mr. Crenshaw, Father De Luz," Roberta announced.

Crenshaw gave it several seconds and then whirled his chair around, stood and held out his hand, not warmly, but out of obligation. Father Dante noticed a small scar over his right eye as he shook hands with the man, who made an abbreviated attempt at eye contact before returning his gaze to his desktop and taking a seat in his large executive chair.

"Have a seat, Father." He motioned to one of two red leather chairs facing the desk, which served as a large exotic wood barrier between the two men. The door whispered a click behind Roberta on her way out.

"Thank you."

"So what is this most pressing item of business, Father De Luz?"

"Well, I guess there's no easing into something like this, especially since I can tell you are a man who does not like small talk."

"Not so much I don't like it. I don't have time for it."

"So, I will just-- begin-- then."

"Please." Crenshaw swiped his hand swiftly through the air as if he were motioning someone to go ahead of him through a narrow doorway.

"My mother, who recently passed away, dictated a letter, to be read after her death. I'd like to tell you what's in it. Is that OK with you?"

"That's why you're here, I presume."

"My mother's story, it's a rather long one. How much time do we have? Could we go grab a cup of coffee somewhere?"

"Forgive me for not offering you a refreshment." He picked up the phone. "Roberta, coffee please." He let the phone fall back into the cradle. "Got a tee time at 10:30. Maybe you should give me the Readers' Digest version." Mr. Crenshaw sat tall in his buck-colored zero-gravity leather chair and rocked slightly, his elbows propped on the arms of the chair so that his hands locked together just below his neck. He extended his two index fingers and used them like forceps to grab the skin that hung loose under his chin.

"There was a moment in time when the future of my entire life depended on my mother finding the owner of a size 9 ½ wing tip shoe," Father Dante began.

"I think I've heard this story before. Is there a fairy Godmother in it?"

"Yes, of sorts."

"Oh good. I love a good fairy tale. Abridged versions preferred, of course."

"The story I'm about to tell you is nonfiction. I want you to know I would not fabricate something like this. I am well aware that you could contact my bishop if you thought I was lying about something of this magnitude."

"This sounds serious," Crenshaw said with a smirk.

Roberta came in with a black lacquer tray on which sat a stainless steel cream and sugar set, a number of wooden stir sticks standing in a cut crystal juice glass and two white mugs with a gold-emblazoned Crenshaw Enterprises logo – a fancy E hooked on to a stylized C.

"Thank you, Roberta." Father Dante smiled at her and picked up the mug.

"You're welcome, Father." She placed the tray on Father Dante's side of the desk and handed her boss the other mug, handle side toward him, like a good altar server presenting a cruet to the priest. "Would you like anything else, Mr. Crenshaw?"

"No, thank you."

When Roberta left, Father Dante told Lawrence Crenshaw how patient and helpful his assistant had been.

"She's been with me a long time," Crenshaw said, taking a sip of coffee. "I don't know how I'd do it without her."

"Do you take cream or sugar?" Father Dante rose halfway out of his seat in anticipation of passing him the tray.

"No, no. Just black. Now, Father, your fairy tale."

"It all began with an evening that was designed to launch a beautiful, affluent heiress into happily ever after with the most desirable, wealthiest bachelor that the nation's top millionaire matchmaker could find."

Mackey and Associates had set up a mixer for Elina to meet a selection of eight male clients. Elina had already studied and approved their profiles and was now to gauge chemistry and employ intuition to decide if she would like a date with any of them. The mixer was held at the office of Mackey and Associates, in a fifth-floor lounge overlooking the harbor. The bar was stocked with fine wines. Skinny men in white coats pestered guests with silver trays arrayed with imported cheeses, caviar and exotic truffles. Elina sat in the middle of a white linen semi-circle sectional, holding a glass of sparkling water with a twist of lime. The men gathered around, trying to look casual and confident, one with an arm set lengthwise over the back of

41

the couch, one with his sockless, loafered foot propped on the opposite knee. Some talked of their money. Many talked of their business prowess. One (thankfully, only one) spoke of the women he had managed to please beyond all their wildest desires. Elina could tell from all their gazes that they were appreciative of her chest and legs, though no one mentioned them. Two mentioned her blue eyes – sparkling said one, serene said another. And three commented on her hair – "lovely," "golden," "sexy." One made a general comment about how attractive she was. One told her what a rare combination of beauty and intelligence she possessed and one insisted he was certain he would be her choice, based on how much they had in common. This he knew instinctively the moment their eyes met.

All eight men were strikingly handsome. That fact could not be denied.

Elina found them all repugnant.

So, an early limo ride ensued.

"Good evening, Ma'am." The driver said, opening the door for Elina.

"Hello."

The driver was a man of medium build, dressed in black pants, a white shirt and a red necktie. He slid into the front seat and turned to look at her.

"Where may I have the pleasure of taking you this evening, Miss?"

"Far away from here."

"OK," he smiled in the rear view mirror. "I can do that. Do you have a particular destination in mind?"

"I guess home will have to do. Mapleton Drive, please."

"Holmby Hills?"

"Yes."

"Yes, Ma'am." He pulled away from the curb and glanced in the rear view mirror. "I was expecting to take you and a gentleman to dinner or something." His words had a melodious lilt, owing to his Spanish accent.

"Yes, well, I was expecting the same thing. But it didn't

work out that way." She laid her head back on the head rest and closed her eyes.

"There is some Champagne there for you, Ma'am. In the ice bucket. Compliments of Mackey and Associates."

"Thank you." She did not open her eyes. "That's very nice, but I'm afraid that would not help my queasiness."

They drove in silence for a few minutes. She put her hand on her forehead and squeezed at her temples.

"Are you doing OK?"

"Yes, I'm fine."

"If you need anything at all, just let me know."

"Did you ever have the feeling you were in some kind of a hamster wheel? You just keep running and running. Every day the same as the day before and the day to come. Running to nowhere. Running, running, running."

"I have that feeling a lot. Only for me, it's driving, driving, driving."

"Do you think every human being feels like that?"

"Many, probably."

The limo stopped at a red light. A couple in evening attire, most likely on their way to a play or the opera, crossed in front of them.

"Where would you go?" the driver asked, drumming his thumb lightly on the steering wheel. "If you could get off the hamster wheel?"

"I don't know," Elina said. "I have no idea. I've been to so many places. But I don't know."

A woman with excessively long legs, an exceedingly short, skin-tight, silver spandex skirt and an inordinate lack of grace hobbled across the street in her three-inch stilettos, locked arm-in-arm with a very unremarkable, short man in a gray business suit.

"Look," Elina said. "It's Sonny and Cher."

"Du-doo, du-doo, du-doo, du-doo," the driver sang as he drummed his thumbs on the steering wheel. "I got you, babe."

Elina joined in and somehow the two managed perfect

harmony for an entire verse before a giddy laughter overtook them.

They watched each other's eyes in the rear view mirror until the light turned green.

"Where would you go?" Elina asked.

"If I could go anywhere in the world?"

"Yes. Anywhere."

"Memphis, Tennessee."

"Memphis? What in the world is there? Besides the ghost of Elvis?"

"The St. Peregrine's Cancer Center. My little daughter, she's 8 years old. She's dying."

His statement punched her in the belly and made her next words come out breathless. "Oh, I'm so sorry."

"Without a miracle, she will die. There's only one treatment now that has any hope of saving her life. They only do it at St. Peregrine's."

"Then, why are you driving a depressed, hopeless woman around Los Angeles? Why aren't you and your daughter on a plane right now?"

"I don't have that kind of money. I don't even have enough for the airfare. Much less the hospital bills. We are talking hundreds of thousands of dollars, probably. I've never been able to afford very good health insurance."

"So what are you going to do?"

"Pray," he said. "Pray to find a way. I will never give up on my daughter. Never."

"Of course not."

"I am waiting to hear if they will accept her. They only have fifty-six beds. But I would do anything for her. I will work night and day every day for the rest of my life if I have to. If they say yes, I will find a way. Maybe they have a fund or something."

"Yes, I'm sure they do. They must have a very large charity. I'm sure they will be able to help."

"And who will help you?"

"Help me?"

"You said you are depressed and hopeless. But there is always hope. There must be someone or something that can help."

"I don't know."

"You have a very bright future, Miss."

"Do I?"

"In your life, the best is yet to come."

"What is the best?"

"Falling in love. Building a family."

"My stepmother told me the other day that we all assume we have the qualifications to be parents. We assume there's nothing to raising a kid. And that's because we had parents who made it look possible. Sometimes, they made it look easy. On rare occasions, they even made it look enjoyable. It's not until you become a parent, she said, that you realize how much you have given up in order to hear someone call you Mommy."

"If all parents told their children that, there would be no such thing as grandchildren."

"Do you think she is wrong?"

"I'll bet you will find, one day, that it's not nearly as hard as you think it's going to be. And the next day, you will discover that there's no way you could have imagined it would be so hard. But, you know, even on those hardest days, there is nothing in this world that could make you wish it away."

"That's a beautiful idea. But I think many children would be wished away if wishing away were possible."

"I fear you are right. I was a fortunate boy. We had nothing but beans, but in my family, children were the treasures. And there were lots of them. Some would say too many. Maybe even more than beans." He smiled wide. "But my parents had joy on more than rare occasions. It was only in the odd moments that there was none."

"Where did you learn English? You speak very well."

"Not well enough. You figured out it is my second language."

"Only because of your accent. Not because of your command of the language."

"I am a reader. That is why."

"Really? What do you read?"

"In my native tongue, mostly history. In English, anything I can get my hands on."

"History of what?"

"Mexico mainly."

"What brought you to L.A.?"

"Well, that's a long story. Are you from here?"

"I was born at UCLA Medical Center."

"You must like L.A. You stayed."

"Love the sunshine. And the beaches. I'm not always so fond of the people."

"No?"

"And I met eight men tonight that I can add to that list."

"What exactly was wrong with them?"

"There wouldn't be enough time to go into that, even if you were driving me to Kalamazoo." She looked at his eyes in the rear view mirror and knew he was smiling. She found his emerging crow's feet inexplicably endearing. "Do you know what one of them asked me? He asked me if I had made a plastic surgery schedule, so I could stay ahead of the aging process. What kind of a question is that for the first time you ever hold a conversation with someone? And these are supposedly the crème de la crème. The best the agency has to offer. Another guy told me an off-color joke, which bordered on a racial slur. I gave that so-called matchmaker a piece of my mind. This is not what I signed up for. I've never seen such a collection of tanned and handsome, wealthy losers in my whole life."

"Uh-oh." There was a sudden silence to the engine, which had been idling at a red light. The driver put the limo in park and turned the ignition key. Something in the dashboard let out a dull buzz. "I think she's dead."

4

Lifting Pinkies

There is probably a list somewhere of inadvisable places for a rich blonde woman's limo to break down. Any number of those places would have been better than this one.

It didn't take long before a group of young corner loiterers noticed and craned their necks and squinted like hyenas in a fruitless effort to get a look inside the black windows.

"I'll have this taken care of in no time, Ma'am," the limo driver said to the rear view mirror as he opened the passenger window. "Hey, amigos," he called out to the assembly. "Mind giving me a hand? I need a little push."

They all looked at one another and finally simultaneously burst into smiles.

"Sure, man," one of them said, heading to the back of the car. The rest followed.

With the limo pushed safely into the parking lot of El Ranchito Market, the driver shook hands through the open window with one of the good Samaritans and waved at the others from behind his steering wheel.

"Hey, no problem, man," the spokesman for the group said. "If you ever through here again you can give me and my lady a ride, huh?"

The driver smiled and rolled up the window.

He turned to Elina. "I'll call you a cab."

Although she would never say it out loud, there was only one word Elina thought appropriate to describe an L.A. cab. And its driver. But at this moment, a cab sounded glorious. Her only regret was that she had been enjoying the limo ride and the conversation. It was an abrupt end and she wasn't ready for it. The cab arrived within ninety seconds.

"This is not a great neighborhood," the limo driver said, opening the taxi door for Elina. "I don't want to put you in a taxi alone. I will accompany you to your home." He was about to slide in beside her, but froze before getting his second foot inside the cab. "Wait, just one minute, please," he said to the driver. "I need to grab something."

The cab driver, a white heavy-set man with graying hair and a multitude of folds around his eyes, looked straight ahead, uninterested, while Elina watched the limo driver open the trunk of the limo. He was a compact man with just a hint of a thickening middle section.

"Can't forget these," he said, returning with a pair of off-brand running shoes.

"What are those for?" Elina asked when the cab started to move.

"I try to stop by at some point during my shift and see my daughter in the hospital. They have a gymnasium there and she likes me to take her in her wheelchair to play basketball. But they don't like me to wear my dress shoes on the court."

"Oh, that's sweet."

"I cherish every minute. I'm certain I enjoy it more than she does. Even though she is the one who has the dream of becoming a pro basketball player. Ever since I took her to see the Sparks. A client gave me free WNBA tickets."

"She must love playing with you."

"Do you play a sport?"

"I used to play tennis."

"Not anymore?"

"It's a B.S. sport."

"A B.S. sport? What do you mean?"

"It's a sport you must play if you are wealthy and busy and you are to be a good parent. You pay for eight years of private tennis lessons for your daughter and play an occasional game of mixed doubles with her and your client and his daughter."

In this way, Elina explained, you spend time with your kid and at the same time build inroads into new markets, which in turn helps grow the family fortune, benefiting your daughter even more. In light of this outcome, you can easily convince yourself that your intentions are pure. So, you see, tennis is not really a sport after all, but an activity meant to simultaneously accumulate more wealth for your burgeoning empire and ease a conscience riddled with guilt over the neglect of your loved ones.

"But the game doesn't have to be that way, does it?" the limo driver asked, reaching below his pant leg to scratch an itch on his ankle.

"Notice how in tennis, 'love' means 'nothing.' As is often the case in the lives of those who play it."

"Whew. You do hate tennis. So what is your favorite sport?"

"It's between surfing and horseback riding on the beach."

He chuckled. "Are those sports?"

"Probably not."

"My daughter loves horses."

"Every little girl does."

"Why is that?"

"It's just something about the spirit of a horse. Horses make you feel so free. And you can be alone on a horse and not feel the least bit lonely."

The cab pulled into Wingate Estates, passing through the hand-hewn redwood gates and the stone-stacked walls, past decadent green carpets of rye, along the wide and meandering flagstone carriage lane flanked by willows and poplars, which seemed to never end, until finally there came into view a 1927 English tudor revival with tall chimneys rising from its steeply-pitched, thatched roofs and a trademark triangular half-timbering in-filled with warm herringbone brick. The driver put the cab in park, and the limo driver walked Elina to the pillared porch.

He squinted up at the architecture of the place, as if the sun were in his eyes, but there was, of course, no sun.

Though it might have appeared to the world an extravagant show home, to Elina it meant something entirely different. When her father offered her to live in one of his fourteen "secondary" properties, Elina chose this one because of its quaint disposition (if a $16 million home can be quaint.) He tried to convince her to choose one of his more elaborate mansions, but she liked the English estate for its romance -- its seeming remoteness from everyday life. It was her mother's favorite as well. The two of them once, on winter break, brought all the ingredients for orange-currant scones, baked them in the brick oven and ate them with clotted cream and Earl Gray on a picnic blanket spread on the massive lawn. They lifted their pinkies and spoke in faux British accents while wearing white wide-brim hats.

"This is an amazing home," the driver said. "Beautiful."

"I'm sure that yours is very beautiful too," Elina said.

"Oh, my neighborhood is not known for its beauty. I live in South Central."

"It's not just wealth that makes a home beautiful, is it?"

"No, I suppose it is not. I suppose it's love that makes a home beautiful. And yes, we have a lot of that."

"You're lucky." She reached into her purse and pulled out her wallet.

"Yes, well, we also have a lot of cockroaches, moldy walls and neighbors who like to advertise their gang affiliation with spray paint on the side of our house."

"Thank you for the ride," Elina said, pressing three hundred dollar bills into his hand. "This should be enough for the cab and a little extra for all your trouble. And for enduring cheesy Sonny and Cher songs."

The driver smiled. "For that, I should be paying you. If only I had a million dollars."

"I hope your daughter makes a full and speedy recovery."

"Thank you, Ma'am. I hope everything works out for you. That you find the man who is deserving of you. I have a feeling it will not be easy."

That's exactly what her father had told her on her 27th birthday as she sat across from him at dinner, trimming small strips of fat from her filet.

"That's why I have here the perfect gift for my princess." He reached under his sport coat, into his shirt pocket and pulled out a flat, gold, letter-sized box. Elina slid the red velvet bow off and opened it. Some kind of document, folded in threes, lay inside.

"What is this, Dad?"

"The key to your future happiness. A contract with Mackey and Associates."

"Oh Daddy," she said, unfolding it and skimming her eyes over it. "There are some things you have to do yourself. You can't hire someone to find true love for you."

"For some reason, there are a number of movie stars and other multi-millionaires who think you can. Just take a look at the list of satisfied customers on page two."

Elina shook her head and laid the contract in the middle of the table. "I'm not going to a dating service, Daddy."

"Honey, this is not *The Dating Game*. This is a very exclusive, prestigious program. Look, it's hard for people like us to meet people of the same caliber."

"I meet plenty of people, Daddy. Besides, you know I'm already in a relationship."

"I know you believe it's a relationship, Honey, but I don't think Larry does. You've been seeing him for almost three years and still he can't seem to make a commitment."

"Well, I don't give up easily, Daddy. You know that."

"Just one of the many reasons why you are the apple of your father's eye." He reached across the table, picked up her hand and leaned in to kiss it. "And why you deserve the best life has to offer. Which is why I am giving you this gift." He picked the contract up and placed it back in front of her.

"And what makes you think a dating service has anything to offer that would be considered the best?"

"All the men have been well-screened, Sweetheart. These men are not out to get your money because they have plenty of their own. They are handsome and accomplished or they wouldn't be allowed into the program. It just takes a lot of the work out of it for you. You need to start thinking of your future."

"I thought you'd be happy to see me with a man like Larry. How can any dating service top him, Daddy? Really. Accomplished, wealthy, charming, handsome enough to give you gorgeous grandchildren."

"I don't think he intends to give anyone grandchildren."

"And how do you know this?"

"I know my daughter. I know that you would have married him two years ago. And I know you're still not married to him."

"Aw, Dad, I had no idea what an old-fashioned guy you are."

"Well, at least I haven't gone so far as an arranged marriage for my princess."

"Just short of it, though, apparently." She picked up the contract and playfully tossed it toward him.

"You are lovely enough to have your choice of all the men in the kingdom," He placed the paper back in front of her.

"I have already chosen." She put the paper back in front of him.

"Look, Honey, what have you got to lose? If you don't like any of the men they come up with, don't go out with them. But you'll never know if you don't try." He placed the contract back on her side. Elina picked it up and thumbed through the pages.

"Look at this questionnaire, Daddy. They can't be serious."

Which best describes the type of nose you find attractive: Long and straight, wide and short, Roman, pointed, hooked, small and upturned.

What are your favorite eye colors? Blue, brown, green, hazel, gray.

What complexions do you prefer? Light, ruddy, medium, dark, extra dark.

"Are they trying to find my life-long mate or favorite coffee roast?*"*

"Oh come on, Sweetheart. They're just trying to get it right. To make you happy."

What hair colors do you prefer? Light Blonde, medium blonde, brown, dark brown, red, auburn, gray.

What percentage of body fat is acceptable to you? 6-13, 14-17, 18-25.

What skin traits will you accept? freckles, moles, birth mark, scars, none of the above.

What facial hair do you prefer? beard, mustache, gotee, beard with mustache, none.

How much does your ideal mate exercise? Three to five hours per week, five to ten hours per week, more than ten hours per week."

Minimum annual income of the perfect mate:

Minimum value of assets of the perfect mate:

Is your perfect mate famous or an unknown?

In the perfect relationship, sexual encounters would occur at least daily, three to five times a week, twice a week, once a week, less than once a week.

Children desired: none, one, two, more than two

On the first date, I prefer a man to dress in a. casual attire, b. business attire c. business casual d. formal attire.

Around the house, I would prefer a man to dress in a. shorts and a t-shirt, b. jeans and a polo c. a smoking jacket or robe.

What level of public displays of affection is acceptable to you? a. holding hands b. walking arm-in-arm c. a kiss on the cheek d. a casual kiss on the lips e. passionate kiss.

Elina couldn't wait to share with Larry the humor in this well-intentioned, but highly impractical birthday gift. And, truth be told, perhaps use it as a bit of leverage.

Which she did later that evening as she lay on his couch, her feet propped in his lap while he gave her a foot and leg massage.

"What's the deal?" Lawrence said, raising her foot to kiss her ankle, while he kneaded at her calf. "I thought your father liked me."

"He seems to think you and I won't see forever together."

"Forever?"

"Yes, that's why he's hired me a millionaire matchmaker."

"Are you intrigued by the unknown, my darling?" His finger tips drifted up past her knee and ran softly over her thigh. "Or do you have everything you need right here?"

She closed her eyes and sighed.

"Don't worry about me, Babe," he said. "I'm not threatened. A little competition doesn't bother me in the least. If that's what you want. It might be kind of fun."

"I don't think fun is my father's objective. I think he sees that we have that covered, you and I. I get the feeling he is hoping for something different."

"Hmmm."

"What about you?"

"Me?"

"Are you amenable to something different?"

"I like things the way they are, Babe." He moved his body up, so he was lying next to her, face to face now.

"Oh."

"I'm too old and set in my ways." He made swirls with his fingers on her upper arm.

"So, you don't want children?" she asked.

"Children? My life is just not set up for it, Babe." He kissed her lightly on the neck.

"That could be said of all people who don't yet have children. Lives have to be re-equipped, don't they?"

"I wouldn't want to do that. I like my life the way it is." The kisses resumed. "I have no desire to re-equip."

"So, my father was right. You are unchangeable."

"I'm afraid that I am." He gave her a deep kiss on the mouth and then returned to her neck. "But why mess with a good thing?"

"Then, we have nothing to look forward to."

"Do you call this nothing?" He grabbed her into him and pressed his lips on hers.

She pushed on his muscular chest and grabbed his wrist. "No more of this, Larry."

"But why? Why can't we continue like we have always been?"

"Because my husband will not like our passion-filled trysts." She sat up, smoothed out her clothing and raked at her hair.

"Your husband? You sure have a lot of faith in this dating service."

"Hardly. I just know that I'm not wasting any more time. I am quite certain that one day, I will be a mother. And you do not want to be the husband of a mother."

She stood and he grabbed her hand. "Why the sudden interest in breeding, Babe?"

"I'm not exactly sure, but I've heard it's a pretty common obsession for us pregnant women."

"Pregnant?" His eyes went wide with horror and he shot up off that aniline leather couch as if something had burned his behind. "Well, are you going to take care of it?"

"Yes. I have an appointment. But I'm not going to let this happen again between us. I'm afraid we will not see each other again after today."

"Oh, I see," he said, putting his arms around her. "You've just had a little scare. Don't worry. We'll figure out what went wrong and get a more reliable method. But as for tonight, we are surely safe, my love. There is no such thing as double jeopardy in pregnancy. " He slid his hands down below her waste.

She pushed him away, looked into his eyes and shook her head. "I've got to go, Larry."

"Here, wait" he said, reaching into his pocket and pulling out his wallet. He pinched out three crisp $100 bills. "At least let me pay for your appointment."

She collected her purse, straightened the waistline on her flaring skirt and bolted out the door, leaving him standing there, the cash drooping over his hand like a limp noodle.

"Elina," he yelled after her in the driveway as she unlocked her snow-shadow gray Aston Martin Vanquish. "I'll call you tomorrow."

True to his word, Larry did phone the next day, but Elina didn't return his call.

She had it somewhere in the back of her mind that she would give him some time to stew and that maybe he would miss her and want to commit to something deeper. There were moments when she still loved him. And even in the moments when she was, for all intents and purposes, over him, if he had called her and asked her to marry him, she would not have hesitated. But it was getting easier each day to consider a life without him. And she knew there was nothing for her to do but go forward. So she went, headlong into a quest for a new romance, funded by her father, fueled by her desire to recreate for herself what her mother and father possessed before death forged a cruel chasm between them and sent the lonely widower into the arms of a woman incapable of sharing true joy with another human being.

But after the disastrous mixer, Elina decided finding love was more trouble than it was worth at the moment. Besides, she had found something to distract her for the time being. Something big.

5

Mr. Jangles

Crenshaw's ringing phone sliced through the intense curiosity that had formed between him and Father Dante's story.

"I'm sorry, Father," he said. "Just one moment."

He grabbed the phone and spoke in abrupt, cryptic answers. Something related to something that had gone wrong in upper management. "I'll need to deal with it later." He barked into the phone and returned it to its cradle. "Sorry about the interruption, Father. Please. Continue."

"Well, the morning after the mixer, Elina found something on her front lawn."

She theorized that the limo driver must have changed into his running shoes after seeing her to her door and accidentally left one of his dress shoes behind. Actually, it was more than a theory. She had watched him out the window, from the dark cover of her library, as he paid the taxi driver, put the remainder of the money in his pocket, returned to her front porch step, sat down, changed his shoes and ran off down the street into the silvery moonlight. She wondered why he didn't take the taxi home. Then she realized he wanted to save all the money he could for his daughter. She should have given him more, she thought. That was the regret that haunted her all night long. She was not an insomniac, but sleep eluded her that night. The next morning, when she went out to get the newspaper, she noticed the toe of a shoe sticking out from under a bird of paradise bush. She brought it in and put it on the Italian marble table in the foyer next to the five-foot-tall arrangement of fresh flowers, delivered weekly. She passed by the shoe twice a day, once on her way out and once on her way in. Usually, she paused to look at it. Sometimes she would pick it up. Finally, a week later, she decided to return it to the driver, along with a donation to help defray the cost of his daughter's medical care. But that pursuit was put on hold when something requiring her full attention arose. Two of her employees brought suit against a manager for sexual harassment. A number of sleepless nights ensued. But she was not losing sleep over the lawsuit. Every time she passed by the shoe, and every time her head hit her pillow, she thought of a little girl dying with cancer. Finally, the day came when she could put it off no longer. The shoe had to be returned, if only for the sake of her own REM sleep.

"I need to find one of your limo drivers." Her words sounded sluggish within her own head.

A middle aged woman looked up from her paperwork, taking her glasses down over her nose. "One of our limo drivers?"

"Yes. He left something behind, and I wanted to return it to him. Mackey and Associates said they contract through you."

"Left something behind? What do you mean? How does a driver leave something behind?" The woman had a heavily-teased and tenaciously sprayed spherical matrix of artificially red hair. And lipstick to match, painted glossy and ample onto her large lips.

"It's kind of a long story. I just need to find him. So I can return something to him."

"What's his name?" The woman used her most skeptical voice.

"I don't remember."

"Well, we have quite a few drivers. Why don't you just leave the item here and we'll find the rightful owner. What is the item?" She peered over the counter to get a glimpse of the bag Elina was holding.

"He was a Hispanic fellow, dark hair, dark eyes, on the thin side, maybe average height."

"Hmm. I don't know all the drivers, Miss –"

"Peltier."

"Miss Peltier. I'm sorry. But I'll be sure to do some checking if you want to leave the bag."

The woman was far too casual. Elina wanted to tell her it was a matter of life and death. That she must find the man whose foot fits inside this shoe. "Oh, I know. I'll tell you what day he gave me a ride. You must have a schedule."

"When was it?"

"Two weeks ago Saturday."

"I'm sorry. I wouldn't have a schedule that old in the system."

"What? That can't be true. You've got to know who drove your cars when. That's a liability thing."

"Look, I'm not at liberty to give out any information about our limo drivers. If you want to leave the item…"

"You can't just give me his name?"

"I'm sorry. No, I can't."

"Why on earth not? We're talking a limo driver here, not a CIA agent."

"I've been instructed not to give out any information. I'm sorry."

"So, I can't know the name of the driver that was entrusted with my safety? What kind of an outfit is this anyway?"

"You don't watch the local news, do you?"

"What?"

"I'm sorry, Ma'am. I'm not going to be able to help you."

There was no sense in pursuing this any further. Receptionists never relent. Despite their title, which is derived from a root word that indicates that they are to receive visitors, their true purpose is to keep people away from whomever they need to talk to.

When Elina got home, she called one of her friends at the news station, who filled her in on a story about a limousine company that had been found to be employing more than a dozen illegal immigrants. Thus the tight-lipped receptionist.

Elina tossed the shoe onto a shelf in her garage. She had tried her hardest to find its owner, but had hit a brick wall. She should be satisfied with her efforts. There was just nothing that could be done to find the ill little girl.

"Listen, Father, I hate to cut you short," said Lawrence Crenshaw, shifting his lean from the left arm of his chair to the right, "but I have to leave for a tee time in ten minutes. Are we getting close to a conclusion?"

"I'm sorry, Mr. Crenshaw. It's a complicated story."

"Yes."

"I'm sorry to say it's quite long and I don't know what I might do to shorten it, since it is so very important. I don't see how I can finish it before your tee time."

"Give it a shot, won't you, Father?"

"OK. Of course. I will fast forward."

Elina's false fingernail wedged into the doorbell and snapped off. The precision of her aim had been hindered by her interest in the paint-chipped brown door, which bore the light-colored cheap under-wood in two places near the knob, where someone had wedged a screw driver in an attempt to break in. In another neighborhood, you might assume someone had forgotten their key one day. But not in this one. Elina wiggled her severed nail out of the doorbell and turned to descend the stairs, right into the path of three youths with bandana-wrapped heads and muscle shirts.

"Hey, Mamacita, you look like you're a little lost." One of the three men put his body too close to hers.

"No, I'm not lost." she said, trying to step around him. "I'm just looking for someone."

"Who you looking for, Muchacha?" another one asked.

"Oh, please let it be me," said the third.

"No, me, please. I am in great need of being found by a beautiful lady."

"Like someone like her would have anything to do with a couple of fools like you," said the first. "Who are you trying to find, Senorita? *I* will help you. I will be your personal tour guide." He made a crude gesture as breath smelling of onions wafted at her through his crooked teeth.

"Oh, that's very impressive," Elina said. "A difficult offer to refuse. Really."

"Yeah, Goochy," said the one thug to the other, batting him on the side of the head. "You're all class, man."

"Look," she said, trying to squeeze by again. "I'm supposed to be meeting my boyfriend here after he gets done teaching his firearms class, so if you don't mind. I don't want him to see me talking with any other men. He's extremely jealous."

"I can understand that, having to keep an eye on a Mamacita like you."

An elderly black man with a cane hobbled up the sidewalk, stopping at the thuggish assembly and placing his boney hand on Elina's forearm.

The short youth with the snake tattoo put his arm around the old man.

"Is this your boyfriend, Mamacita?"

"Hey, why don't you choir boys go work on your three-part harmony," the man replied. "My good friend here is obviously not interested in the deep and meaningful relationship which you upstanding individuals seek."

"Aw, Pops, don't insult this nice young lady. Just because she is a fox does not mean she is not also smart. Smart enough to recognize all that she has in common with a man like myself who is filled with desire and passion." He leaned into Elina's space, bowed slightly, picked up her hand and kissed it.

The other two young men snickered as Elina briskly pulled her hand away. She wanted to remember not to touch that hand to anything else she owned, until she could wash and sanitize it.

"Ah, get lost, you losers," the old man advised, "or I'll tell the cops what you been doing with your spare time and your ski masks."

"What are you talking about, Gramps? We ain't ripped nobody off."

"Maybe. Maybe not. But the cops are going to think you did after I get through providing details on the goods I found in that old abandoned warehouse."

The three of them grumbled amongst themselves in Spanish and then the first one bowed slightly and said, "Goodnight, Senorita. We will leave you and your boyfriend to your business. Very interesting business that would be very interesting to watch." They all chuckled, flashing their absences of various teeth, as they shuffled away.

The old man shook his head and muttered something under his breath and then converted his unintelligible protest into an audible question, though his gaze was still on some distant point down the street and he may not have expected an actual answer. "What in Heaven's name is someone like you doing in this part of town?"

"I am looking for a Jose Rodriguez."

"Rodriguez."

"Do you know him?"

"What do you want with him?"

"It's a long story. But, in a nutshell, I'm trying to return this shoe to its rightful owner."

The old man, for the first time, looked into Elina's eyes, trying to read her story. "So, you looking for his place of residence?"

"No. He lives right over there. But there's no one home."

"Well, I can take the shoe, Miss, uh, Miss Prince Charming, and give it to him when I see him. I'm his next-door neighbor."

"Well, I'm not sure it's his."

"Oh," the man tried to make his voice sound informed.

"Like I said," Elina explained. "It's kind of complicated. But I really need to find him."

"Look, I don't think Jose is going to be around for a while. I think he's been deported."

"Does he have a daughter?"

"Yes. He got several." He raised one eyebrow. "But what does that have to do with a shoe? This conversation is getting stranger and stranger. Mind telling me what you're up to, Miss?"

"The man I'm looking for is a limo driver who has a daughter who is dying of cancer."

"Oh, that wouldn't be Jose."

"No?"

"No, ma'am. All three of the Rodriguez girls are just fine. None of them are dying." He took off his plaid scally cap and scratched the top of his head, shaved close in tight grey curls. Then he suddenly paused his scratching and looked deep into Elina's face. "Hey, wait a minute. You're not with immigration, are you?"

"Me? No."

"Well, if this is about a shoe, I think you don't need to waste your time. Like I said –"

"OK. Thanks for your help, Mr.—"

"Everybody calls me Bo." He resumed his scratching.

"Bo."

"For Bo Jangles." He put his cap back on.

"Thank you, Mr. Bo Jangles. Have a nice day."

"A nice day to you too. I'll tell Jose you stopped by. When I see him." He flashed her a large smile and tipped his cap.

He waved his long boney hand as she drove off, keeping his eye on her Aston Marten until it left his sight.

She wondered as she drove, *How do people stuck inside these dirty, monochrome lives force their feet out of bed and onto the floor every morning? Every morning, waking to the same misery: exhaust and soot and tipped over garbage cans spilling out hypodermic needles and used condoms, cheap party food forced up through the esophagus by one too many beers.* Elina was certain that the people who lived these awful lives did not party in deference to the ideals of revelry and pleasure, but

63

for the want of anything fulfilling or inspirational to do. There never would be any fulfillment in the slums, of course, except for the fulfillment of prophetic gloom, and Elina could not consider it a fate superior to death.

That evening, *Mr. Bojangles* played in Elina's head as she pictured the leathery old man on Wilmington Avenue tossing his cane onto his front porch stoop and dancing from the waist down, in his thread-bare, baggy pants, scooting his holey soles across the sullied sidewalk. She thought her Bo Jangles as something of a hybrid between the wide-smiling black Bojangles who tapped with Shirley Temple and the honky tonk drunk white Bojangles who spent the night in the county jail with inebriated singer/songwriter Jerry Jeff Walker and shortly thereafter found his life story set to melody on Billboard's Top 40.

A strange realization overtook Elina as the song replayed for the fifteenth or sixteenth time. She had never before this day talked to anyone like Mr. Bo Jangles. Not in her entire life. Not anyone anything like him. At all.

That night, she dreamed of wolves tearing her hair out, follicles and all. After the vicious attack, she ran in frantic slow motion through her childhood home, searching for the wigs her mother wore after her chemo. She never found one and had to drive to work with a completely bald, shiny head. The guard at the parking garage denied her access, pointing out that she looked nothing like the photo on her corporate I.D. badge. So she left and went to the county fair instead, where she decided to ride the ferris wheel, climbing on board next to a young Hispanic girl, who was also bald. As they rose higher on the wheel, Elina noticed there was not a single soul anywhere in sight. The rides were all operating empty. The ferris wheel continued around and around, for what seemed like hours. The little girl looked at Elina with questions in her eyes. It was clear to Elina that this ride would have no end. She felt sad for the little girl, who would surely be missing her mother. She thought of ways to console her, positive things she might say about being on an eternal carnival ride. And then she awoke. She ran her fingers through her silky blonde hair and was grateful for it, even though she had always resented its fineness and had tried every high-end volume booster on the market to no avail. It didn't matter to the men. One of them had once confided in her that, although women think that men like Farrah Fawcett hair, they really prefer Cheryl Ladd's.

Elina felt a little dizzy from the all-night ride on the ferris wheel, but she was better after a cup of decaf and a cinnamon raisin bagel. She got one leg of her pantyhose on and then stopped. She rolled it down over her leg and tossed it back into the still-opened dresser drawer. She grabbed a pair of jeans, picked up the phone and dialed work. "Nicole, I'm not coming in today. I've got some personal business to attend to."

"What about the meeting? The board of dir-"

"I know. I didn't forget. Tell them something very urgent came up."

"Do you want me to tell them you're sick."

"No. I'm not sick. I just have to attend to something very important. It's a matter of life and death, actually."

"Are you OK?"

"Not really. But I'll be much better after I get this all taken care of."

Father Dante's phone vibrated and he fished it out of his cassock pocket and read the number on the display. He pressed a button and put it away. "Nothing I can't take care of later."

"Please, Father, I'm afraid we don't have much time. Can you get to the important part?"

"I'm trying, Mr. Crenshaw, but it's all important."

Just as Elina arrived at South Central, her car phone rang. It was Larry.

"Babe, how are you?"

"I can't talk right now, Lawrence," Elina said, looking for a building that bore some kind of address. "I'm out in a really creepy part of town." She told him why and asked if he wanted to join her.

"Aw, I can't, Babe. My schedule is completely booked today. I just had a minute between meetings and thought I'd call to see how you are. I miss you."

"Oh. You do?"

"Of course. You're the best thing that ever happened to me."

"I am?"

"A rare find. Beautiful. Intelligent. Apparently very compassionate. That's a side of you I hadn't fully appreciated until this moment."

"All the qualities of a good wife, I would suppose."

"There you go again, Babe. Getting all heavy."

"Listen, I've got to go. I'd like to get through at least four or five of these names today."

"Good luck finding the owner of that shoe, Princess Charming."

A man wearing a dingy white sleeveless, tight-fitting T-shirt and a multitude of gold hanging from his neck ceased his shuffling, stood and glared into her car.

"Lawrence," she said, eyes glued to the menacing face, a lump forming in her throat as she put the car in drive and readied her foot for full throttle, "would you do me a favor?"

"What?"

"Do you have your address book handy?"

"Sure, I can get it. Why, what do you need?"

"Go to the letter 'P.'"

"Uh-huh."

"And rip out my number."

"Oh, Babe. That's harsh."

"And I will be updating my book too. The C's need some editing."

She slammed the phone down, still staring at the man, who, noticing she was finished with her call, began to speak through the window, with his large upper teeth bulging out of his mouth.

"Nice ride, Ma'am. Very nice indeed. Have a nice day." He saluted and shuffled on.

He walked about fifteen paces and then collided shoulders with a young man wearing a red bandana around his greasy head. The two of them yelled something into each other's faces, not that Elina could hear any of the sound effects through the closed windows. Of that, she was glad. She didn't want to know what nasty things they had pent up inside their sorry skulls, just waiting for the slightest excuse to release them into a city that already reeked of enmity and loathing.

"If I had a lifetime to waste, maybe." she muttered, eyes glued to the two men. "But I don't."

She watched them exchange a series of rubbery-armed shoves and then each went his own way.

"No. I most definitely do not." She grabbed the wing tip off the front seat and opened her car door. "Thanks for the memories, Larry Crenshaw."

ॐ❊ॐ

6

Cheap Metal Spoons

"Yes, what can I do for you?" The woman's eyes swept up and down over Elina's diamond-studded Gucci jeans and Haute Couture pure cotton purple blouse and then returned to her flawless super-model face.

"I'm looking for Mateo." It was day four of her search.

"He's not here. May I help you with something?"

"He is a limo driver, right? I mean *was* a limo driver."

"Who are you?"

"My name is Elina Peltier," she said, wiping the straggles of hairs stuck to her sweaty forehead. She felt her face flush hot and then clammy. "A limo driver took me home recently. He lost his shoe and I wanted to return it to him. Can you tell me if this is Mateo's shoe?"

The woman glanced at the shoe, puzzled. "I don't know. He didn't mention anything about missing a shoe."

Elina's knees suddenly felt as if they would come unhinged. She took a step back from the woman's door as her heart pounded within her. A thin veil of purple washed over her eyes.

"Are you OK, Mrs. Peltier?"

"I'm OK. I just feel a little weak."

"Here, let me get you a drink of water."

"Thank you."

68

"Do you want to come in and sit down for a little while. I am afraid you will pass out."

"No, it's OK. I'll be fine."

The woman left the door open and returned with an amber-colored glass with dimples pressed around its middle. The ice water went down well, but the purple veil had not receded.

A bolt of pain hit her head. "Uh, maybe I will sit down."

The woman took her by the arm and led her to a green velvet chair, its once plush fibers worn flat on the seat and arms. The door still hung open.

"You don't live around here, do you?"

"No. I live in Holmby Hills."

"Holmby Hills? And you came all this way, just to return a shoe?"

"Well, not exactly." She stared at the black wingtip in her lap. "The driver has a very ill daughter. I thought maybe I could help."

"You a doctor?"

"Oh, no. Nothing like that." Elina looked around and the room began to spin. She closed her eyes and leaned her head on the chair back.

"You are lacking in iron. I can see it in your face. You are a beautiful girl, but very pale. Let me fix you some beans."

"No, don't go to any trouble. I will just rest for a minute, then I need to be running along. I have to keep searching."

"It will only take a minute. I already have beans on the stove. Just rest and I will bring you a bowl."

Elina smiled. "OK. Thank you."

The woman was still in Elina's sight as she stepped into the kitchen. The family room was about half the size of Elina's closet and the kitchen would have easily fit at least three times into her smallest bathroom. The woman returned with a cobalt blue bowl of pinto beans placed atop a white plate, which held a folded flour tortilla. The bowl was chipped white three times along the edge and the plate was stained with a streak of rust, probably from prolonged contact with a cheap metal spoon.

"Thank you, uh. I'm sorry, is it Senora De Luz?"

"Lucy."

The spoon was scratched dull and slightly bent and its rough edge scraped at the inside of Elina's mouth.

"I hope they are not too spicy for you. When I was pregnant with Mateo, I ate this for breakfast, lunch and dinner. I'm surprised his first word wasn't 'frijole.'"

"What was his first word?"

"Tato. That's what we called his grandfather. For Mateo, Tato was the ground below and the sky above and everything in between."

"Mateo is a very nice name. It means Matthew in English, doesn't it?"

"Yes. Matthew. I named him for his grandfather."

"I hate to further impose on your hospitality, but may I use your restroom?"

The woman took her by the arm and led her down the hall. On the hallway wall hung a large portrait of a group of children. Elina stopped and studied it. "Are these your grandchildren?"

"Yes. There are eleven of them."

"They are beautiful. This little girl. How old is she?"

"Nine."

"What's her name?"

"Raquel."

"Beautiful name."

After she was finished in the restroom, Elina made it back to the little velvet side chair and picked up her beans from the rattan coffee table where she had left them. She tried to ignore the spring poking her in the behind through a threadbare cushion, which had a large, permanent imprint of someone's rear. Lucy had dipped herself some beans as well and was holding the bowl in her hand. It was a white china bowl with pink flowers. The only similarity it bore to the one Lucy gave Elina was that it, too, was chipped in several places.

"Are you feeling OK now?"

"Yes, much better. Thank you. These beans are delicious."

The women both raised their spoons to their mouths at the same time.

"Are your grandchildren all in good health?" Elina inquired.

Lucy swallowed hard. "Why do you ask?"

"It's just that the limo driver I am searching for, his daughter is the age of your Raquel. And, I hope I am not being too blunt, but she has his eyes."

The woman stared down the hallway where the picture hung.

"And so do you." Elina hoped a smile would ease the tension. "The same beautiful eyes."

The woman blinked rapidly and looked down at her hands.

"Mrs. De Luz, I know I am a complete stranger to you, and I understand why you are apprehensive, but I promise you, I am not with the authorities. I just want to help. I know this little girl needs help. And I know her father was arrested for lack of documentation. I have the police report and everything. That's how I found this address. I have been turning Los Angeles upside down trying to find him."

Lucy stared at Elina, calculating some kind of risk. "Well, he never mentioned missing a shoe…"

"I know it's a hard story to believe. But it's not a trick. I want to help."

The woman's forehead wrinkled and her eyes filled with tears.

"I have been searching for weeks, Mrs. De Luz. Please." She picked up the shoe from the floor near her chair. "Tell me if this is your son's shoe."

"Just a minute, please. Excuse me." The woman silently walked down the hall and returned in a few minutes, plodding each step, mesmerized by what she was holding in her hand. It was a left wing tip shoe.

Elina smiled and stood and then sat back down as a wave of purple threatened to overtake her again. She took a sip of water and closed her eyes. When she opened them, Lucy was crouching beside her, worried, looking into her face.

"The whole night after the ride in that limo, I couldn't sleep," Elina said, recovering her breath. "I thought of a little girl, lying in the hospital with no chance of survival unless she gets to Memphis." Elina pulled an envelope from her Louis Vuitton Monogram Petit Noe handbag, which sat at her feet. "I brought this for her." She handed the envelope to Lucy, who opened it tentatively and pulled out an American Airlines gift card and a stack of $100 bills.

"That's the traveling money," Elina said, "but I can also help with medical bills."

Lucy De Luz stood, put her hand over her mouth and burst into tears. Elina's tears followed. Elina struggled to her feet and fell into Lucy's arms. They embraced as if each had found her old friend.

"This is so generous of you." Lucy forced the words out through her tears.

"No, it's not generosity. I have a lot of money. I have so much that it means very little to me. And I can't let a little girl die if there's something my otherwise worthless money can do to save her."

"Mateo will be so happy."

"Where is he?" Elina said wiping the tears off her cheeks with her palms.

"He is trying to get back. I don't know if he's crossed the border yet."

"I can't believe they deported him, even though he has a daughter in the hospital." The women returned to their chairs.

"We didn't want to mention anything about his daughter because we were afraid she might be deported too. And she would surely not survive."

"What about Raquel's mother?"

"Oh, she died four years ago. Mateo and Raquel – they have only each other."

"Oh, I'm sorry. And how is Raquel holding up without her father?"

"She is not well. I am very afraid she will lose her desire to live."

"No, she can't do that." Elina grabbed Lucy's hand, as if pleading with her. "She has hope now. Maybe I could go see her."

"Mrs. Peltier, I am very grateful for your help. You don't know what it means to us."

"I do, Mrs. De Luz. Unfortunately, I do. I have a loved one who died of cancer."

"Oh, I am sorry."

"No, I'm sorry. I shouldn't have said that. I'm very sorry."

"No, it is OK. Who was it? Someone in your family?"

"My mother."

"Was it very long ago?"

"I was eleven."

"Oh, I am sorry. That's too young to lose a mama."

"It changed everything for me. My father remarried less than two years later and we never had the same life again. I always dreaded the day that they would announce a cure for cancer because it didn't come soon enough to save the one person I loved most. I never wanted her to be a near miss. Isn't that selfish? My mother would have really scolded me for that. I never thought about all those other people out there dying. But I haven't been able to get Raquel out of my mind since the day I heard about her. And I think my mother would be proud of what I am doing. She would have done the same thing. She had such a big heart. She helped so many people. I will never understand why someone like that had to die."

"It's too hard to ask why, Miss. Peltier. And the best answer will never be good enough anyway.

"You should call me Elina."

"Are you a woman of faith, Elina?"

"Not much, I'm afraid."

"You probably do not know, then, that you are doing the Virgin's work."

"The virgin?"

"The Virgin of Guadalupe." She pointed past Elina's head to the wall behind her on which hung a cheaply-framed print of a woman standing before a sunburst with her hands folded and an angel at her feet. "We have been begging her for help. And she has sent you to us. We have always been poor, and we have never minded until Raquel got sick. Then, we learned the value of money."

"And sometimes it is completely worthless." Elina stared at Our Lady of Guadalupe. "It couldn't save my mother's life." She returned her gaze to Lucy's face, which was plump and dewy, unlined and soft. Not the face of a woman who wastes any time or energy wishing impossible wishes, like those that aim to change what's already passed. "For all the riches we had, none of it could help her," Elina said, straightening the alignment of Mateo's shoes, sitting next to hers. "But maybe now. Maybe now it can do some good. "

⁖✧’✧⁖✧’✧⁖✧’✧⁖✧’

"Excuse me, Father," Crenshaw said, clicking a button on his phone. "Roberta, cancel my tee time. Tell them something important came up."

"I'm sorry, Mr. Crenshaw," Father Dante said. "I'm being as brief as I can be. It's just a complicated story."

"It's OK. It won't be the first golf game I've ever missed, and I'm certain it won't be the last. But please, you have me in a great deal of suspense."

"Well, I'm glad at least now we're not on such a time constraint. Thank you for putting off your game."

"Please, continue. I'd like not to have to cancel my lunch appointment."

"OK. Well, my mother was about to meet someone who would change her life."

Elina and Lucy made their way down the long hospital corridor. Elina floated and Lucy waddled. Elina's hand was tucked into the bend of the older woman's arm, as if the younger

74

woman needed steadying. Maybe she did. Elina was dreading the meeting. She was thinking of it as a meeting with cancer rather than a meeting with a person. But when she got to the room and peeked in the half-open door, she saw, not cancer, but a little girl lying in a bed, watching television.

"Mija, I want you to meet a new friend," her grandmother said, kissing her on the forehead.

Elina stepped closer to the bed and bent slightly toward the girl. "Raquel, my name is Elina. I'm a friend of your father's. I'm going to help make sure you get all the best doctors so they can help you get better."

"But they told me I wouldn't get better."

"Your grandmother got a letter that said you might get to go to a very special hospital in Tennessee, where they have the best cancer doctors in the world."

"St. Peregrine's? Daddy told me about that. Am I going to St. Peregrine's?"

"Yes, if your doctors say you can."

"Will my Papa be there?"

"I don't know." She squeezed the girl's hand.

"Have you been to Mexico?" Raquel asked.

"When I was a little girl like you."

"Where did you come from?"

"I come from a beautiful place called Holmby Hills. It's not far from here. Maybe I can take you there someday."

"Does it have a big grassy yard?"

"Enormous."

"And a big house?"

"With many, many rooms."

"It sounds like Heaven. Are you a guardian angel?"

"No. I'm just a filthy rich girl who is going to make sure you have every material thing you need and ever wanted."

"Are you going with me?"

"Where to?"

"To St. Peregrine's?"

Elina looked at her grandmother, who was smiling and nodding, and then back at the girl. "Would you like me to?"

"Oh, yes."

"OK, then. Maybe I will."

"Where did you get all your money?"

"My Daddy is rich."

"My Papa's not."

"I know. But he's a good Papa, isn't he?"

"The best in the world. I wish he was here."

"So, what do you want to be when you grow up?"

"Well, *if* I grow up, I want to be a marine biologist."

"Wow. Really? What does a marine biologist do?"

"They study dolphins and whales and sharks. Sharks are my favorite. Well actually seals are my favorite. Well seals are my favorite mammals. Sharks are my favorite fish."

"Really? Why?"

"Well, seals are so adorable. And sharks are just cool."

"Don't sharks eat seals?"

"Yeah, Great Whites do. They will eat pretty much anything. Even other sharks. But they don't do it to be mean. They are just hungry."

"Speaking of which, what's your favorite food?"

"Silly Vanilly ice cream with gummy bears."

"Silly Vanilly? Where do you get that?"

"Moo Town. My Abuelita took me there for my birthday. It's sooooo good."

A nurse came through the door with a tray of hypodermic needles. "Time for your shots, Sweetie. Then I'll get you some of that strawberry yogurt that you like."

"Vanilla," Raquel said, rolling up her sleeve. "I like vanilla."

"OK," said the nurse. "We got that too."

"I'll see you a little later, OK, Raquel?" Elina squeezed the girl's hand. "It was very nice to meet you."

Raquel smiled.

"I will talk to the doctors about St. Peregrine's," Elina told her.

"Tell them I have a special reason why I want to live. Tell them I have to see my Papa again."

Father Dante's phone vibrated in short pulses. "Excuse me, Mr. Crenshaw." He flipped the phone open. "Hello, Marie."

There was a short pause. "Oh, no. What are the doctors saying?" Larry Crenshaw swiveled his chair around and began writing something on the computer atop his credenza.

"Oh dear Lord, have mercy." Father Dante's words came out as a woeful sigh. "O.K. I'm leaving right now." The priest closed the phone. "I'm sorry, Mr. Crenshaw. One of our parishioners is in need of Last Rites."

"What?" The CEO swung his chair around. "You have to leave? You can't just leave me hanging."

"I'm sorry, Mr. Crenshaw. I'll be back. But I really have to go. Right now." His hand was already on the doorknob. "Please, if you pray at all, please pray. A father of four young children is about to pass from this world after a terrible car accident. Please, pray for the children and his wife. And for that poor man's soul."

Father Dante wanted to cry as he got into his car. His hands were shaking as he put one on the steering wheel and shifted into reverse. He had never gotten used to this. As many times as he has been at the bedside of death and tried to provide some word of comfort to a grieving family. He never had gotten used to it.

Jim Pollack played guitar at the 10 a.m. Mass every Sunday. His wife always sat in the front pew with their four girls, dressed in bows and shiny black Mary Janes, their mouths opened wide in song, even the youngest little one, who is only two, maybe three. What will Father Dante say to that little girl today? Or her older sister, who is at that age of asking why. Father Dante knew she was going to look up at him with her crystal blue eyes and ask, "Why did God take my Daddy away?" And what will be his answer? Dear God, what will be his answer? He would never admit this to anyone, except for his confessor. But in moments like this, a thought sometimes flitted across his brain, a devastating, nauseating thought that maybe there is no God. The thought was gone in less than a second, but the memory of it haunted him, as it had plumbed such dark depths. He would combat it by recounting all the many reasons why the theory of a Godless universe commands no credibility, not the least of which was his own familiarity with the workings of the Divine. He worked side by side with God, shoulder to shoulder, in the trenches together. He knew Him so well sometimes he could even anticipate His next move. Sometimes. There was no way to deny the existence of someone as close as your next breath.

Once, as his congregation sang, Father Dante had done an odd thing, for what reason, no one could tell, and it started some parishioners, (particularly those who were already annoyed with his unswerving allegiance to Rome), to begin to question the soundness of his mind. As he stood at his usual place behind the altar that morning, the *Holy, Holy, Holy* rang out throughout the sanctuary at its appointed time in the divine liturgy, except on this particular morning, the most lovely, sublime, ethereal voices, as Father De Luz has never heard before, winged up from behind him, where no one ever stood, leaving him with no choice but to turn and see from where the musical splendor came. He had hesitated to turn around, knowing how awkward it would appear, and telling himself it was only his imagination. But he could not resist. There, where the walls of the church once stood, was a choir of angels, too many to count and too large to fathom. *Heaven and Earth are full of your glory.* Their voices rang in sublime harmony. *Hosanna in the highest. Hosanna in the highest.* And then they fell to their knees, holding their wings in perfect stillness.

Every time after that, every time he heard those voices – and that was every time he said Mass – he somehow resisted the urge to turn and behold the splendor of Heaven. The deprivation of the vision did such violence to his soul, that he offered it as a portion of his purgatory. For, to know Heaven is at your very back, and be able to take not even a glimpse of it, is a kind of spiritual torture. This must be, he surmised, what Purgatory is.

ೞ❌ೲ❌ೲ❌ೲ❌ೲ❌ೲ❌ೲ

After Jim Pollack's funeral Mass, Father Dante stood outside the church to offer his condolences as people left.

When a small-framed woman in her late-30s shook his hand, a jolt like an electrical current travelled up his arm, past his shoulder and spread out in a warm wave of pain across the right side of his chest.

"Nice homily, Father," she said.

"Thank you," he smiled. "Where are you from?"

"Burbank. I went to college with Mary Elizabeth. I was a bride's maid in her and Jim's wedding."

"So glad you came."

He kept an eye on the woman as he shook hands with the rest of his congregation. He saw her take a seat on a bench overlooking a large fountain set before a lush expanse of grass that stretched down a slope to the side parking lot.

He hated to interrupt her thoughts, and possibly prayers, but he had to speak to her.

"Beautiful Mass, wasn't it?"

"Yes," she said, glancing up at him and then back at the view. "It was nice."

She seemed surprised when the priest sat next to her. She moved over a couple of inches, even though there was already plenty of room for him to sit.

"Are you OK?" he asked. "I get the feeling not everything in your life is perfect."

"Good intuition, Father. There are many other places I'd rather be than the funeral of a good friend's husband."

"But something else was not right, even before you got that devastating call that Jim had passed. Something inside you is less than perfect."

She looked down at her belly, which had only subtle signs of bulging under her loose-fitting dress. "How did you know that?"

"The Holy Spirit is here."

"Is He? That's good because I have a few questions for Him."

"Really? What are they?"

"The baby I am carrying is not healthy. My doctor gave me a referral for an abortion. He told me it would be inhumane to let the child live. My sister has, in so many words, told me the same thing. And so has my best friend and several of my co-workers."

"So, basically, everyone."

"Yes."

"What about the baby's father?"

"Well, not him. But he's not going to be in the picture anyway, I don't think."

"Not in the picture?"

"We're not getting married."

"He is still a father."

"If I have the baby."

"And if you kill the baby."

She stared into his face.

"Killing the baby doesn't negate motherhood or fatherhood. You will still be parents. Either to a live baby or a dead one."

"I would never abort a healthy baby, Father. Many couples are waiting for babies. I know that. I myself want a baby. But not at the expense of the baby's well being. I mean, if it is going to suffer..."

"What is wrong with the baby?"

"Down Syndrome. And probably a heart condition."

"So, you're thinking an abortion might be merciful. A way of fixing what has gone genetically wrong."

"Yes."

"Who made the baby that you carry?"

She looked questioningly at him. He knew she didn't want to answer.

"Did you and your boyfriend make the baby?"

"No. God made the baby," she conceded.

"Did God make a mistake? Are you going to fix God's mistake?"

A look like something close to fear came upon her.

"Do you see how ludicrous that is? Oh my goodness. I didn't even ask your name. I'm sorry."

"Jen."

"Jen. Who are we, Jen, to try to thwart the plans of God? I am absolutely certain He knows what He is doing. In your life. In the life of that baby."

She nodded and watched the fountain, which was surrounded by an assortment of pink and white lilies.

"And in the lives of all those who will be touched by that baby," Father added. "I'll show you a picture." He reached into the side of his cassock and pulled out his phone. "This is my friend, Jerry."

A smile came immediately to the woman's face as she saw the man in his early 20s, sporting a large, toothless smile, holding a feather duster over his head, making himself into a rooster or a prince.

"Jerry is the custodian here. He keeps God's house clean. And do you know how that started?"

"How?" She was still smiling at the picture.

"One day, about fifteen years ago, Jerry's mother came to Father Francis angry. She told him Jerry was enrolled in classes to make his First Communion and Confirmation, just like all the other kids his age, and all the kids are required to do service projects, but all the agencies she checked into didn't have any need for the talents of an 8-year-old boy with Down Syndrome. She was mad at the director of religious education for not having come to her and asked if it were even possible for Jerry to complete his service hours. Father Francis asked her if she had made an effort to voice her concerns to the R.E. director and she said, 'It wouldn't do any good anyway.' I'm sure you've known people with a chip on their shoulders."

Jen nodded.

"This woman was among their ranks. But the core of her heart was pure. Father Francis could see that. And she really only desired the best for her child. She assumed her child was denied the best – first by God and then by the rest of the world.

So she was angry. Father Francis told her to bring Jerry by the next day and he would see to it that the boy had all his service hours fulfilled. She left in a skeptical sort of huff, but she did come back. Father Francis took Jerry by the hand and led him into the church. He told him, 'God's house is in need of a little cleaning, you've probably already noticed.' 'Yeah,' he said. So Father Francis showed him the broom closet in the deacon's office and gave him a feather duster. He told him he would be dusting for God. That God needed him. That dusting the pews and the statues and the candle sticks would be his service project. But only part of it. Then Father Francis got down, right on his level and looked into that boy's eyes, into his soul, and told him the rest."

Jen's smile hadn't faded, but her eyes moved from Jerry's photo and were now locked on Father Dante's face. "What was the rest?"

"The Church and the world are in great need of prayer and the prayers of a pure and loving soul are the most priceless treasures of our day. Jerry agreed, with a very big smile. To this day, Jerry spends an hour a day before the Blessed Sacrament, after he finishes cleaning, interceding for the needs of this parish, for Father Francis' intentions, for my intentions and for the conversion of the world. And for his family. His mother, particularly, needed prayers. In the beginning."

"Why?"

"His mother had looked at Jerry's disability as a punishment. Subconsciously, that's how she saw it."

Jen looked at Jerry's picture and shook her head.

"Is God trying to punish you?" Father Dante asked.

"What do you mean?"

"You did something you weren't supposed to do, so God is punishing you with a disabled child. So you should get rid of it. And you will have dodged the wrath of God."

She only stared at him.

"You will have beat God at His own game, and He will see how clever you are and give up on trying to punish you."

"No, no, Father. This baby is not a punishment. I want this baby. I always have. But I am alone in this."

"No. You are not alone. You have a person growing inside you. How much closer can you get to another human being? Don't you see the great gift in that?"

"Yes, a baby would be a great gift. But what about all the suffering? Of the child?"

"None of us knows what is in the future, but life is precious. In all its forms, life is precious – with or without suffering. Although I don't think I've ever seen a life without it. All that baby wants is to be with you. That's what will bring her happiness."

"Her?"

"You know, about a year ago, I celebrated a nuptial Mass. The couple had dated for three years and had been engaged for eighteen months. Six weeks before the wedding, the groom was diagnosed with terminal brain cancer. Everyone told them they should call off the wedding. He was given only three months to live. But his bride insisted on marrying him. She said she'd marry him if she only had three minutes to be his wife. Any amount of time was better than none. So standing by his hospital bed, where he would likely die in a matter of weeks, they exchanged wedding vows. It was one of the most beautiful weddings I've ever been to. It was an example of total gift of self, a complete outpouring of the one for the other. All they wanted was to be together."

"Look at this." He gently took his phone back from Jen, pressed the button several times and handed the phone back to her. "This is Jerry and his mom. Look how they glow together. Apart, who knows what they would be. But look how they glow together."

Jen smiled at the photos.

"Do you have a minute?" asked Father Dante. "Come with me. I want to show you something."

They walked in silence as the priest led the woman around the side of the main church and punched a number into a keypad on a large glass door. The small chapel smelled of a mix of fresh paint, new upholstery and a faint whisper of some sort of flower. Not roses. Not any kind of bulb flower. Not lilacs. Something altogether unfamiliar and pleasantly unidentifiable.

Father Dante got down on his knees before the monstrance and bowed until his forehead touched the red plush carpet. Then he took a seat in the second pew and gestured for Jen, who was still standing at the door. She genuflected and sat next to him.

"Whose seat is that empty one, Jen?" Father Dante whispered, pointing to the icon of the last supper on the side wall. There were twelve disciples and an empty seat.

"Judas, I guess?"

"That's what everyone thinks. They always say it's Judas' seat. He was supposed to be there, but he left to betray Jesus, right? But look closely. There are twelve disciples at the table. Judas is the one dipping his hand into the bitter herbs. This is before he left. So who is that extra seat for?"

Jen was silent.

"Adults are always at a loss," Father Dante whispered. "But children know. They will say, 'Me! It's for me!' Children will say that. And one adult has gotten that right."

"Jerry."

"Yep."

Father Dante didn't know what Jen would do, when she shook his hand to say good-bye. But he knew she wanted her baby. Father Dante resolved to pray fervently every day until the baby's due date, which Jen told him was June 14. When he got back to the rectory, he looked on the saints' calendar and saw that June 14 is the feast day of St. Basil the Great, a bishop in the 300s who founded an enormous hospital, which he visited often to help the suffering "make good use of their pain."

Few people knew this, but Father Dante lived on the outskirts of depression. He had a sweeping view of its skyline, but rarely ever entered the city. On the rare occasions that he did, he would be lost for quite a long time in its oppressive grip.

Suburban dwellers are simply not equipped for the one-way streets and traffic circles in the big city. And then there are the interminable tunnels.

Nobody would have guessed this because Dante was, at heart, an optimist. Anyone who knew him would have him pegged as a man of great hope and unshakeable faith. But optimists are subject, like anyone else, to drops in serotonin. And that drop took him underground to the inbound subway.

If anyone had known him well enough or observed him for long enough, they would have been able to tell you that the one tell-tale sign that he might be boarding the train was his decision to turn on the TV. The night after Jim Pollack's funeral, Father Dante flipped it on, hoping for a distraction from an intense sadness that, on most days, he knew could only be cured by time with God, but on a day of plummeting serotonin made him reach for the remote.

There was a documentary airing on unwanted animals. There are just so many dogs -- thousands each day -- killed because there is an over abundance of them. The animal shelter people were saying it's all because people don't spay and neuter. It's a tragedy that all of these puppies are coming into the world, they were saying. Better that they should not exist at all. But Father Dante's first thought was "a tragedy for whom?" They admitted that the dogs are put down in a humane way. They are given a shot, very quickly go unconscious and then die. There is no suffering in that. So would the dog that is put down too early have preferred not to live at all? Father Dante would argue that life is better, even a short life. The desire for survival is so strong, he doubted any animal would ever wish itself out of existence. Father Dante would probably not admit this out loud because people might think he was drawing overly-close parallels between a canine and human life. They showed a litter of adorable puppies cozied together, nursing, no care in the world, just happy to be with their Mama, and he believed at that moment, with all his heart, that those creatures would cherish life, no matter how short. It's hard for the humans who have to put them down, but for the dogs themselves, even if they could just live for that one moment of being nourished and nurtured and loved, isn't that better than no life at all?

Father Dante flipped off the TV, made his way across the dark courtyard, unlocked the chapel and knelt before the large gold sunburst that held, in the form of bread, the Body of Jesus. He offered a prayer for Jen and her baby and the Pollack family and for all those who live in the somber city always on his horizon – that they might make good use of their pain.

He glanced at the Last Supper icon and saw that Larry Crenshaw was sitting in the empty seat– as plain as if the artist had painted him in. Father Dante blinked and the seat was empty again. He tried blinking again to make the man return. And again. But the seat remained empty for the remainder of the night.

7

Chocolate Rewards

"Roberta. Are you named for someone?"

"My father, Robert."

"What's your confirmation name?"

"Father, there you go again. I'm not Catholic anymore."

"Well, your Confirmation saint still is. Who is she?"

"I don't remember."

"No?"

"Father, could I offer you a cup of coffee?"

"No, thank you. I'm fine. You know, they say if you ask to know your guardian angel's name as you are drifting off to sleep, the name will come to you upon waking in the morning. Maybe it will work for your Confirmation saint as well."

"It might. If I cared to know. But to be honest, I don't."

"Well, she's got her work cut out for her then, doesn't she? I'd like to speak with her sometime. Can't you just remember the first letter of her name?"

She shook her head and displayed a tense smile. "Oh, Father."

"You think I am perseverant, you should see how the Lord operates. He will never quit pursuing you."

"God is a stalker? Sounds sweet."

"No, he is a Lover. He pursues you because He wants to give you something, not take anything away from you."

"Seems to me you're forgetting what the Bible says, Father. The Lord giveth and the Lord taketh away."

"What did He take away from you, Roberta?"

She only stared.

"Why are you angry with Him?"

"He didn't take anything away from me. I begged Him to. Day after day. I begged Him. But He ignored me."

"What was it, Roberta? How did He fail you?"

The woman closed her eyes as if she were trying to remember. Then she opened them and fixed them right on Father Dante's. Her phone buzzed, and she picked it up. "OK, Mr. Crenshaw. Thank you." She put the phone down and glanced up at Father Dante. "Mr. Crenshaw will see you now."

"To be continued, then."

Father Dante and Lawrence Crenshaw shook hands and took the same position in the same chairs as the first day they met.

"Thank you for making more time for me, Mr. Crenshaw. I'm sorry I had to cut our meeting short the other day."

"Well, I had no choice but to make more time. I've got quite a bit of time invested and still haven't heard the point of your story."

"Well, let me get to it, then. We'll pick up where we left off."

"Please."

"My mother was not what you would call a morning person. But on one particular morning, dawn robbed her of sleep."

Elina awoke at 6:30 to the melodic chirps of birds outside her window. Her alarm was set for 7:15, but she knew she wouldn't return to sleep now. She had to decide what to wear. She usually prepared and accessorized in advance, but she could not settle on an outfit the night before. What does one wear to a thing like this?

Her white cat stretched out on the window sill, casually twitching his tail against the rich amber muga silk ceiling-to-floor curtains, eyes fixed on whatever it is about a new dawn that fascinates a supposedly nocturnal creature. He looked small against the expansive window, which was both wide and tall and yet was only one of six in the massive third-story bedroom that looked out on an English garden, aburst with orchids, peonies, lisianthus, gloriosa flowers and boxwoods sculpted into animals from just about every link of the food chain and certainly representative of all seven continents. There was a snail, an elephant, a kangaroo, a lion, a red deer, a giant panda, a penguin, a toucan and a llama.

Elina thought about going to the window and looking down at them, but she couldn't bring her feet to the floor. Bed seemed the only safe place. Once she was out of it, the day would begin to unfold, and it would be better if this day should stay folded. Nevertheless, she found her feet scuffing her to her closet, which was actually an adjoining room, 13 by 13 feet, lined with shelves of purses and shelves of matching shoes on one wall, belts, scarves and hats on another and hanging clothes on the other two. In the middle of the closet was an ornate antique mirror standing next to an ecru linen chaise lounge, draped with clothes Elina had worn in the past three days and several outfits that she had tried on and decided against. Her closet was the only room in the house that she took care of herself. The housekeepers never entered, instead leaving her laundered and dry cleaned clothing on a hook on the back side of her bedroom door. The closet was something Elina enjoyed taking care of, organizing, even beautifying. Her hangers were all made of padded raw umber silk, which matched the throw pillows on her chaise. Her hat boxes were covered with the same fabric and the smallest was topped with large silk magnolias. There was a nice amount of natural light from a skylight plus a small window amidst the shelves of shoes, equipped with an awning to block out any rays that might do harm to fabrics and leather goods. Sometimes, Elina would just go sit in there on the chaise, sip a cup of coffee and read. Then, she would close her mystery novel and just sit. These were the times when she felt close to her mother. She and her mother spent large amounts of time in the closet. They would try on shoes and hats and long flowing dresses together and use their fake British accents.

How she wished her mother was here today. She was alone, with no one to give her advice. What does one wear on an occasion such as this? Something comfortable and loose, for sure. Nothing flowery. Black came to mind, but she decided against it because it might be construed, if by no one else but her own subconscious, that there was a reason to grieve. Grief was something she was not willing to concede. This was, after all, a simple procedure, meant to restore all things to the way they were meant to be. How break-through ovulation occurred and why the contraceptive manufacturer's promise of a hostile womb was not fulfilled that month would always remain a mystery. She was certain that she took the pill faithfully, every day, at the exact same time. It was not user error. And yet, here she was, having to take care of all of this the hard way. That is what she regretted -- the pain and suffering involved with undoing the effects of faulty contraception. Unlike many woman, Elina entertained no doubts about what she was to do. This pregnancy was never supposed to have happened in the first place. So the life she carried inside her was never meant to be. She viewed the unpleasant task before her as a sort of time machine remedy. If she could have gone back in time and chosen a more reliable contraceptive -- whatever that might be -- she would have done so, and this pregnancy would never have happened. The abortion clinic provided the next best thing to time travel.

She pulled a red Kenzo Zakada *joie de vivre* dress off the hanger and held it up to her, peering into the mirror. No. Red was wrong. Pictures of fetuses in utero always seem to have a red-orange tone. She needed something less reminiscent of the womb and its contents.

Blue. Blue would be good. Soothing and calm. Peaceful. She had a Sonia Rykiel sweater dress in azure, which she unhooked from the rack and looked at with a fast up and down glance. But no. It fit too tight and it would do nothing to minimize her tummy, which was already verging on pouchy. It was a strange look for her. She never had any excess around the middle. Sometimes she'd even hit the gym twice a day, and gym or no gym, she did three rounds of stomach crunches daily as a matter of habit. She hated doing them, but she denied herself her sweets after meals until they were done. She wasn't, after all, fanatical about exercise, like she was about chocolate.

Ah, there was the answer. She would reward herself after the procedure. She would stop by Vosges Haut Chocolat on her way to the appointment and after it was all over, indulge in her favorite candy bar, the one Larry always called "vile" and refused to buy her. Even though he would frequently stop by Vosges Haut, he insisted on bringing her raspberry truffles instead. Yes. Today called for a deep milk chocolate with hickory smoked bacon + Alderwood smoked salt. She would eat merrily, with great, glad loathing for Larry.

She had a fleeting thought that she should probably treat herself to a full meal before the chocolate. But she certainly wouldn't feel like stopping by a restaurant and she didn't care to talk to the help about what meal to make. She could throw something together herself, but she knew not the first thing about preparing food. It was a hereditary disorder.

Sandwiches were the only food Elina ever saw her mother prepare. Hundreds of sandwiches at a time. A couple of times a year, her family would vacation at their beachfront home in Cabo. Elina's mother would lay out fifty slices of bread at a time in their very large kitchen and top them with a slice of American cheese and two slices of ham. Elina would come along and top the meat with another slice of bread. Then they would do it all again four or five times. The housekeeper they had brought with them from home would wrap them all in Saran and put them in several large baskets. Then the three would go up into the mountains and hand them out to children living in cardboard shacks. Elina remembers once complaining about the drudgery of the work involved. Elina's mother seized the teaching moment.

"You could have very well been born on this side of the border, Elina. And you would be hungry. You've done nothing to earn the great amount of luxury that you enjoy. Nor have I. It's been handed to us and we will never forget that we are no better than the millions of people who go hungry and die." Elina never uttered another complaint.

After Elina's mother died and her father remarried, the family resumed its trips to Cabo. She often thought of those children living under cardboard and how hungry they must be. There was nothing she could do about it, since Phoebe could not be convinced of the merit in continuing the sandwich tradition. She told Elina it would be cruel since they wouldn't be able to do it but a few times a year and the hungry children would come to expect and rely on the occasional food. Americans are warned, she said, not to give food to the children that come begging at the door, their bread bags open, asking for slices to be dropped in. It only creates and reinforces a culture of beggars. Similar to why you don't feed a dog from the table, she had said. If you do, you will have to consume your every meal amid constant whines and tail wagging.

Phoebe, unfortunately, did not feel the need to apply the same philosophy to her three Chinese Crested powder puff, snappish little dogs whom she had so spoiled, they would scream like Tasmanian devils until she invited them onto the table to eat off her plate.

Meanwhile, she would scold Elina if she even accidentally let a crumb fall from the table into Letti's grateful jowls. Letti was an old hairless Peruvian Inca Orchid, whom Phoebe despised. She would hurl insults at the animal, call her ugly and demand that she be put out. Elina's father had bought the dog for her mother, who was always cold. The dog is a perfect heat radiator because it lacks fur. Its bald black skin would keep Elina's mother warm and provide comfort to her as she was battling her cancer toward the end. Inca Orchids are difficult to beat in the world's ugliest dog contests, but Elina thought Letti was beautiful.

"You know, Elina," Phoebe would say, a bulge of filet medallion in her cheek, "that dog should not be competing with us for food. She thinks she's the alpha, or she wouldn't be jumping up like that on your chair while you eat." The woman would say this while her three chubby, over-indulged, sweethearts, Flopsy, Mopsy and Cottontail, lounged on the table top lapping au jus from Phoebe's Royal Copenhagen Flora Danica.

"You shouldn't be so mean to him just because he's hairless," Elina told Phoebe one day. "Your dogs could have been born hairless too."

"No, they could not have."

"Yes, Chinese Cresteds are often born hairless. Just as often as they are born with fur."

"Well, *my* dogs could not have been born hairless or they wouldn't be *my* dogs. I wouldn't have chosen them. I chose the Powderpuff variety for a reason."

Elina didn't know how to argue with that kind of logic. It was very, well, logical. But it seemed, at its core, wrong and false, for reasons she could not even form into a thought.

One day, Phoebe announced that her Powderpuffs were, from that day forward, on a strict diet of dog food only, per orders of the vet, who said that continuing to feed them food fit only for wealthy, over-indulged humans would shorten their life spans.

Phoebe then commenced the practice of putting her dogs outside during mealtime and scraping all her leftovers into Letti's bowl, while assuring the animal how much she would enjoy the delicacies in store for her throughout her remaining years.

"There you go, girl. Now don't breathe a word of this to Flopsy, Mopsy and Cottontail. They will be so jealous, you'll have to sleep with one eye open the rest of your life."

ဆ)❳❲ဆ)❳❲ဆ)❳❲ဆ)❳❲ဆ)❳❲ဆ

"Raquel, how are you feeling?" Elina laid her hand on the girl's forehead.

"Good," she smiled, a bit groggy. Raquel grabbed her hand. "You sure have a lot of rings," the girl observed.

"Oh, yeah," Elina smiled – a bit shyly. "They have been gifts. I don't buy rings for myself. Except this one." She wriggled a ring off her right index finger and placed it on Raquel's. "And now, this one is a gift too. To you."

Raquel smiled at her own hand, pleased with the large pink sapphire rose that now graced her pointer finger.

"Here, I brought you something else." Elina reached into her white lambskin Ossie Clark handbag. "Do you like chocolate?"

"Oh, yes."

"Here. It's a bacon and chocolate candy bar. My favorite thing in the world."

"Oh, um, well, I, um, am not really hungry right now. Maybe I'll try it later." The girl accepted the purple and gold wrapped candy bar and put it on the night stand by her bed.

"I had a feeling you might say that," Elina grinned. She reached into her purse again. "That's why I brought these too."

"What are these?" she asked tentatively.

"Chocolate covered gummy bears."

"Chocolate covered gummy bears! I've never had these before. I love gummy bears. And I love chocolate." She untied the purple string, reached in and popped one in her mouth.

"Do you like bacon?"

"Yes."

"Why don't you try the bacon and chocolate?"

"Well, I like bacon with eggs. Not with chocolate."

"Have you ever tried it?"

"No." She smiled sheepishly. "Maybe I will later."

"OK." Elina smiled. "I've got to go meet with your doctors now. We've got to talk about how we're going to get you better."

Unfortunately, the doctor could not talk about that.

94

"Your offer to help is very generous, Ms. Peltier, but I'm afraid there's no medical help we can offer this little girl."

"But her father and grandmother were told she might be a candidate for an experimental treatment."

"There was a window of time when that might have been the case, Ms. Peltier, but that window has past. Her time is very limited. I'm sorry to say she won't even make it long enough to complete all the paperwork."

"Paperwork? What does paperwork have to do with anything? We have to at least try. We can't just let this little girl die."

"There just is no treatment for the stage she is in – experimental or otherwise. This little girl is going to die, and unfortunately there's not a damn thing anyone can do about it. Believe me, I wish there were. Dear God, how I wish there were."

"How long does she have?"

"Maybe a month. Two at the most. Things are going to progress very rapidly from here on out."

"Does she have to stay in the hospital? If there's nothing you can do for her, why does she have to stay here?"

"We can send her home on hospice."

"Can she travel? A short distance, I mean. I want to take her to the beach. And maybe to Sea World. Wherever she wants to go."

The doctor smiled and removed his dark rimmed glasses. His eyes softened and reminded Elina of her father's in his younger days. "Yes, Ms. Peltier. That would be the way to help. Help her make the most of the time she has."

That afternoon, Raquel was interviewed about all her favorite things, and an interior designer was charged with orchestrating a seven-day makeover of one of the nine bedrooms in Elina's home. The room was transformed into a marine paradise, complete with coral bedside tables, a king-sized bed surrounded on two sides by Tahitian beach sand, stocked with exotic shells and a ceiling-to-floor headboard aquarium to hold a half dozen dwarf lantern sharks, two dozen sting rays and fifty starfish.

The room design was inspired by the rooms at Hotel H2O in Manila, where Elina and Larry had once vacationed. Raquel's room would have been a lot more elaborate if Raquel had more time. Elina would have liked to have even put in a glass ceiling and floor, so that you would be surrounded by sea creatures on all sides and from above and below. There were parts of the Hotel H2O that made you feel strange for staying dry. Elina would have hired the very designer and crew that the hotel hired if time had permitted. But time had become a cruel dictator.

Elina told Raquel that she and her Abuelita could stay at her house whenever they wanted, for any length of time. The live-in chef would see to it that their every culinary desire was fulfilled. Lucy was offered the room next door to Raquel's, but she asked if she could just have a bed in Raquel's room instead.

"Wow," Raquel gasped, when they wheeled her in. "I wonder if this is what Heaven looks like."

"Oh, I'm sure it's much more beautiful than this," Elina said.

Elina told HR she would be taking a six-week leave from her position in the family corporation. She would not be missed. Elina went to the finest schools, not because she was a scholar, but because her father financed stadiums and auditoriums and they could not deny his daughter's admission. While enrolled as a communications major, Elina was able to maintain passing grades while maintaining her social life. She didn't feel the need for real learning since she was already promised a lifelong position in her father's conglomerate. And a very good one at that – vice president of communications. She had a full staff of twenty-two under her, managed by the director of communications, who did the actual work

When Elina and Lucy told Raquel one morning that they were going on a surprise adventure, a look of complete joy overtook the child.

"It's Papa, isn't it? You're taking me to see Papa!"

All the happiness that the two women felt in planning the trip dissipated as they realized they couldn't give Raquel the one thing she really wanted. And needed.

But joy soon returned when they reached their destination and realized that, though Raquel had suffered in her short life as much or more than many souls do in their long life spans, she was still child enough to live in the present moment. And so, the girl pressed her palms against the massive blue and watched the dolphins swim past her behind two stories of plexi-glass, soft flute music wafting in from overhead speakers, a backdrop to the graceful choreography of the mysterious other-world that seized her every thought and emotion and pressed them deep into the azure waters. Tears streamed down her face as the dolphins made their rounds before her.

"They're so beautiful," she wept.

Elina had positioned Raquel's wheelchair sideways, so its one wheel was flush against the plexi-glass, allowing the girl to be as close as possible to the creatures she loved.

A full forty-five minutes later, Raquel turned to the two women to see if they were still there. They were sitting on a bench just behind her. "Will you help me stand up, Abuelita," she asked. "I want to see them better."

Elina and Lucy stood one on each side of her, holding her under the arms, as she craned her neck to see to the top of the tank. A mother and its calf swam right past her face. Raquel gasped and smiled.

A few moments later, she asked for her wheelchair. "Bye, guys," she told the dolphins. "I'm glad I got to meet you."

Lucy decided Raquel had a maximum of another hour's worth of energy left for the day.

Raquel's estimates were higher. She wanted to see everything. Lucy told her to pick one more thing. She resisted the temptation to promise the girl they would return some day to see the rest.

"Can we see the killer whale show?"

Without question, at least ninety-nine percent of the audience found the pre-show video, projected on the screens behind the whale pool, sappy and contrived. Elina and Lucy were in tears. It started with footage of a girl and her father climbing a mountain. As the dad grabs his daughter's hand and pulls her to the top, a broad smile spreads across her face. Her father points out at the sea below to a family of dolphins leaping across the waves as the girl looks on with awe. And then the next scene shows her all grown up on a boat, pointing out leaping whales to a group of kids in life Jackets. Next is a boy helping an injured dolphin, in a shallow lagoon off an island paradise, then him as an adult working with a team of environmentalists to save a beached whale. Finally, there's a clip of a girl mesmerized by a whale behind the plexi-glass at Sea World. The whale mimics her every move, turning as she turns, waving when she waves. Then, she's all grown up training whales and entertaining crowds with Broadway smiles and unbridled enthusiasm for the choreographed stunts of highly-intelligent sea creatures.

Raquel was entranced by the video. Lucy and Elina did their best to hide their mourning for the loss of Raquel's future.

After the show, Elina told Raquel she could choose anything she wanted from the gift shop. The place was expansive as an ocean. It was a nautical nightmare for most parents, who at the end of the day were exhausted and just wanted to go home, but had to watch their children meander through the aisles of enticing and over-priced taudries and narrow it down to just one thing. But Elina was glad to be able to offer Raquel such a large variety of the things she loved -- dolphin sweatshirts, gigantic plush killer whales, amateur scuba diving sets, marine biologist Barbies, ocean life pop-up books, starfish backpacks and shark coloring books. Elina reminded Raquel several times that she could have whatever she chose and as much of it as she wanted. Raquel picked up many items, inspected them, smiled and returned them to the shelf.

"Don't you want that?" Elina said about a pink sweatshirt with a splashing cartoonized Shamu. Raquel had held it up to herself and then folded and put it back.

"That's OK," the girl said shyly, looking at her grandmother.

"Please choose some things, Raquel," Elina said. "I want you to have whatever you like. Don't you worry about what your grandmother said about not being extravagant. This time, it is OK. Be extravagant." Elina only assumed Lucy had told Raquel to be conservative in her choices so as not give into greed.

"It's OK, Mija," Lucy told the girl. "Miss Elina wants you to have something you like. Go ahead, Gorda."

After a considerable amount of prodding, Raquel made a choice -- a small bottle shaped like the ones they put model ships in, small enough to fit in the palm of your hand, filled with about a dozen sharks' teeth, marked with a shark decal and the Sea World name and logo. It was $7.99.

"It's OK. It's OK," Lucy kept telling Elina. "She loves it. It's all she needs."

After buying the souvenir and while Lucy took Raquel to the restroom, Elina went back in and toured the store, trying to remember everything that had brought a smile to the girl's face. She took one of each of those things to the register, along with something for Lucy as well -- a set of eight gold-rimmed lowball glasses emblazoned with gold seahorses.

That evening, as Raquel drifted off to sleep, holding her bottle of shark teeth, Elina collapsed crosswise onto the king size bed adjacent to hers. Lucy sat on the edge of the bed, wriggling her toes and twirling her ankles, trying to reward her tired feet for a day of faithful service.

"We will never forget this day, Elina."

"We never will. It was beautiful. I wish Raquel hadn't been so shy about getting what she wanted."

"It is just the way she is, Elina."

"Yes. You can't say that for most kids these days."

"She's always been that way, our Raquel. One day, at church, she heard them announce they would be collecting donations for a clothing drive outside after Mass. So Raquel looked at me, all worried, and whispered 'I forgot to bring all the clothes that don't fit me.' So when we got outside, she took off her favorite jacket – the one with all the Winnie the Pooh characters I had gotten her for Christmas -- and she put it in the bin full of donated clothes. I said, 'Raquel, are you sure you want to give away your favorite jacket?' She said she had other ways to stay warm, but some kids had no clothes at all and no place to live."

"That's beautiful. I wish I could feel that way about my stuff."

"You are very generous, Elina. Is there anything I can do for you? I know I can never repay you, but is there even one small thing I can do?"

"Yes, actually. There is."

Lucy's eyes brightened. "Tell me. I'll do anything."

"That one day I came to your house looking for Mateo, you served me some beans," Elina said, rubbing her eyes.

"Yes."

"Will you make those again?" She propped herself on an elbow and looked at Lucy. "Those were the best beans I have ever had."

"No. Really?"

"Oh, yes." She lay back down. "I love Mexican food, and I eat it quite often, but I've never tasted beans so good in my life."

"Well, thank you. Of course, I would be so happy to make you some," she said rising from the bed.

"Where are you going?"

"I'm going to go get them started. They take quite a while to cook."

"Oh no, Lucy, not tonight. We need to get some rest. It's been a long day." Elina stood up and took Lucy by the shoulders, pointing her toward the bed. "I'm going to hit the sack myself. I'll see you two in the morning." She kissed Raquel on the forehead and positioned the sheets around her shoulders. "Sleep tight, Angel," she whispered.

Lucy followed her through the door, down the hall and to the expansive staircase.

"I'm just going to get the beans started to soak. It won't take but a minute."

"But tonight, Lucy? It's so late."

"You have a craving. And they are so good for you. Raquel loves my beans too. Maybe she'll take a little when she wakes up."

ဆာ❧ℭ❧ℭ❧ℭ❧ℭ❧ℭ

Daybreak found a large pot of pintos simmering atop a cobalt-enameled La Cornue stove, custom made in an atelier near Paris. Lucy had spent the night traversing the stairs, first up and then down, then up again, sitting alternately with her restlessly sleeping granddaughter and the boiling beans. Raquel had murmured Elina's name several times in her sleep.

Elina sat in front of a steaming bowl of beans and a stack of homemade tortillas. "Why did you stay up cooking all night?"

"I was up anyway," said Lucy. "And I wanted you to have beans when you woke up. They are good for breakfast. The protein is good to start your day."

"They're just plain good," Elina said, sipping at the broth. "I could eat them for breakfast, lunch and dinner. And these tortillas. They are wonderful."

"Thank you, Mija." She stood at the pot, stirring. "I'm going to give a little to Raquel." She plunged the ladle into the soup and stirred and then poured them into an Arte Italica with half daisies embossed in antique brown. "I'll let them cool down for a minute."

"You need to eat too," Elina said. "Why don't you join me?"

"Maybe I will. You know, Mija, I can teach you to make these beans you love so much. There's really nothing to it."

"Oh, I don't cook," Elina said. "I don't know the first thing about it."

"Then I should teach your cook how to make them."

"He would never be able to pull it off. Only you can work this magic."

Sadness suddenly clouded the old woman's eyes.

"What's the matter Lucy?" Elina gently grabbed her wrist.

"Mateo used to call them magic beans. His father told him the story of Juanillo y la Planta de Frijoles. You have that story here, I think. The one about the boy who climbs the big plant and finds the duck that lays the gold eggs."

"The goose, yes. Jack in the Beanstalk."

"Yes, Jack in the Beanstalk," she smiled and nodded and then the smile slowly faded. "I wish Mateo was here. I hope he is not hungry."

Elina put her hand on Lucy's. "What is his favorite food?"

"Half an orange with Tajin fruit seasoning sprinkled on it. He would eat that like candy. He also loves my carnitas. I taught his wife to make it just the way he liked it. En paz descanse."

Elina smiled to hide the twinge of irrational jealousy that grabbed at her insides. "What was she like?"

"She was beautiful, like Raquel. Loved life. Loved people. The best thing about her -- she loved my Mateo. She was good to him. And she was a wonderful mother."

"How did they meet?"

"Well, she worked in an ice cream store and he loves ice cream. He and his friends would go as often as they could. One day they noticed that his ice cream was much bigger than the rest of his friends'. They all joked with him that the girl who scoops ice cream must like him. The next time they went, it happened again. And the next time, same thing. So, you see, it wasn't a joke. She really did like him best. So--" she tipped her head to one side and smiled, "he married her."

Lucy looked out somewhere into her past, far away. "Mateo being the baby – and the only boy – I had always wondered how I would feel about a girl snatching him away. I wondered how he could ever find anyone good enough."

"But he did."

"Oh, yes. She fit right in with our family. Like one of my own daughters. It was like I raised her myself, she was so much like us."

"Must have been terrible to lose her."

"Yes. I still miss her."

"I'm sure Mateo does too."

"Oh yes. He was so good to her. You know, so many of his friends get married and still have girlfriends on the side, you know. Not Mateo. He wouldn't think of it. Never. She was his best friend."

Elina thought about what it would be like to be Mateo's best friend. It wasn't too hard to imagine. The limo ride had kind of been that way, at least for her. She wished she was back in the limo with him again. It was so easy, being with him. It had never been that easy before, with anyone else.

℠❳❲❳❲❳❲❳❲❳❲❳❲❲

Lucy placed a smashed bean into Raquel's mouth, but the girl seemed unable or unwilling to chew and swallow it.

"Do you want something else, sweetheart?" asked the day nurse, who had arrived at dawn.

Raquel shook her head and closed her eyes.

"Do you like your Abuelita's beans as much as I do, Raquel?" Elina asked, stroking the girl's forehead.

"Swallow the bean, Gorda," Lucy told her. "You don't want to choke."

"How about a tortilla?" Elina asked.

"No," Raquel said, her eyes still shut.

The two women looked at each other. They were reading each other's minds. Failure to eat. They each silently forbid the other to think it. The end could not be here already.

Lucy wiped the stray hairs off Raquel's forehead, smoothing it down and behind her ears. "You've never been much of a breakfast person, have you Gorda?"

"I like Pop Tarts."

"Oh, yes," Lucy said. "You would always eat those."

"Well, then, we'll get some Pop Tarts," Elina said, jumping out of her seat. She walked down the massive hallway to her bedroom intercom and requested her housekeeper arrange with one of the house employees a quick run to the grocery store.

"What flavor?" the housekeeper wanted to know.

"Flavor? I don't know. Get them all."

Raquel refused each in turn as Lucy wiped at her eyes with the back of her finger.

"What do you want to do today, Raquel?" Elina asked.

"I want to see Papa."

"I wish I could bring him back to you, Raquel," Lucy said. "I would give anything."

"Why isn't he here?"

"I know he's trying his hardest to get here as fast as he can. It won't be long now. I'm sure it won't." Elina lay at the bottom of Raquel's bed, her chin propped on a pillow. She rolled over on her back and stared at the ceiling. "I'll tell you what would be fun, Raquel. Let's get your Abuelita to tell us some stories about when your Papa was a kid."

Raquel nodded and managed a soft smile.

Lucy tipped her head back and sniffed. "Well, let's see. My Mateo as a little boy. He was such a joy. Most of the time." She pointed her finger in the air to punctuate that last remark. "I'll tell you what. Tomorrow, I will go get the big picture album and we will look through it and talk about Papa. Would you like that Mija?"

"Uh-huh."

But there was no waiting until tomorrow. Elina arranged to have the chauffer drive Lucy to her apartment right away to collect the memories.

There was Mateo posing for the camera with a boy his exact height, arms hanging over each other's shoulders, both smiling wide. The shot next to it was of the boys' feet. They were wearing mismatched shoes.

"Kids used to spend their free time swapping shoes with each other," Lucy said. "They didn't have TV or video arcades. Simple things had to be enough."

"That doesn't sound very fun," said Raquel. "I'd rather play Pacman."

"I think most kids would, but your Papa never had anything like that." She turned the page of the worn album, covered with dingy blue denim and trimmed around the edges in crochet lace that used to be white. "Here he is picking tomatoes."

"How old is he there?" Elina asked.

"Maybe about nine or ten. He worked a lot. We all did." She turned another page. "Here. This is him on his first soccer team. He was so proud to be on an official team. He usually just played with neighborhood kids. You can see he took the game very seriously."

Lucy handed the picture to Elina, who drew it close to her face so she could see the detail in the little boy's expression. The eyebrows were torqued together and his eyes squinted an unflinching determination into the afternoon sun.

"And he likes to play basketball," Elina said.

"Oh, yes, basketball!" said Raquel, her spark returning. "He loves basketball. How did you know?"

"He told me. During our limo ride. He told me all about playing with you."

"Yeah, it's my favorite sport."

Elina flipped the pages, growing an inexplicable attachment for the little boy. Toward the end of the book, he was growing up, but he still had his boyish smile. Even in his wedding photo. Elina imagined what it would have been like standing at the altar with him. A twinge of longing seized her stomach. It was unpredictable and unfamiliar. Never before had she imagined such a thing. Out of all the men she had known, she had never envisioned herself dressed in white, standing next to any one of them.

ஐ✄ை

8

The Color of Love

The nurse came and went, each day giving a report that Raquel was slipping closer to death. It was not a matter of weeks now.

For the most part, Raquel ceased talking, except to ask in feeble, one-word requests for the most simple things. Water. Blanket. Medicine. Shark teeth.

And then, there was this moment, when she awoke from a nap and said, with a weak smile, "I saw Mommy. She is waiting for me."

"But your Daddy wants to see you too," Elina said. "He will be here soon."

"She has to wait until Mateo comes," Lucy told Elina after Raquel drifted back into sleep. "She just has to. I've been praying and praying, asking the Virgin's help."

"There's no news from Mateo?"

"I got a letter. He was in San Luis Rio Colorado. But that was several days ago and it is a very dangerous place. I hate to even think what could happen there."

"He'll be OK," Elina assured her. "He seems very resourceful."

"That he is. He once saved a man's life. He was 85 years old and drove into the river. Mateo jumped in and pulled him out of the sun roof just as the water was filling up to the poor old man's chin."

"Wow. Was this back in Mexico?"

"No. Here. Mateo would not think twice about risking his life, even for a stranger. Such a good man." Tears filled her eyes. "So much like his father. En paz descanse."

"How did his father die?"

"Heart attack."

"I'm sorry. How old was he?

"Sixty-seven. We had 49 years together. But it wasn't enough. It could never be enough."

"Forty-nine? You got married young."

"It's what you did back then, you know? In the place we are from. Girls did not go to college or get jobs like you, Elina. We got married. I was lucky. I got a good man. In Mexico, it is not always so."

"In America, it is not always so."

"Or in any other place on earth."

೫✄ಐ✄೫✄ಐ✄೫✄ಐ✄೫✄ಐ✄೫✄ಐ

Elina was able to keep Raquel with her for another week, but called 911 when she had some kind of a seizure. They admitted her to the hospital, where they expected her to die within days. She did nothing but sleep until she heard his voice.

"Raquel, Raquel. It's me. It's Papa. I'm back. I'm here now. I'm not going to ever leave you again."

"Papa. Oh, Papa. I can't. I can't believe it."

"I missed you, Mija," he hugged her tight. "Everything's going to be OK now."

"Elina told me you'd come." Her words were labored and faint, but it was the most she had spoken in days.

"Elina?"

"Yes, she let me stay in her big beautiful house. And my room had dolphins."

107

"Really?" He looked up at Lucy and whispered. "Is she delirious?"

"No. It is true."

"She's my fairy godmother," Raquel clarified.

Mateo looked at his mother for an explanation.

"It is all true, Mijo. Raquel really does have a fairy godmother."

"She's so beautiful, Papa," Raquel whispered. "And there she is."

Elina was smiling in the doorway.

Mateo smiled back. "I'm not sure what exactly you're trying to tell me, Mija," he told his daughter, "but you are right. She is beautiful."

"Mateo," Lucy said, grabbing Elina's hand and leading her to Mateo. "This is the woman you drove home once, Mijo. She remembered you telling her you have a daughter with cancer and she tracked us down so she could help."

"So she could help? With what?"

"She wanted to pay for Raquel to go to St. Peregrine's. But when the doctors here said she is not a candidate, she decided to do everything she could to make sure Raquel is happy."

"Not a candidate? So, they're not going to treat her?"

"I tried to be happy at Sea World, Papa, but all I really wanted was you."

"Well, now I'm here, Mija. And I'm never going to leave you."

"They say – everyone says – they all tell me I'm going to Heaven soon. You don't mind do you? I will be with Mama."

Mateo's eyes and nose filled with tears and the muscles in his face twitched as they held back sobs that would have been violent and profuse if they had their way. "I don't mind, Mija. If that's the way God wants it. But I will miss you terribly. To tell you the truth, I'm not sure I will ever be able to smile without you."

"Elina will keep you happy. She helped me smile when you were gone."

Mateo looked up at Elina. His eyes locked on hers and neither could contain their tears any longer.

"Thank you," Mateo said, grasping her hand. "Thank you for taking care of my Raquel."

In the long dark hours of night, sitting in a dimly-lit hospital room, each holding one of Raquel's hands, Elina and Mateo talked of the kinds of things casual friends don't.

"I have this recurring dream. Do you have any recurring dreams?"

"No, I don't dream," Mateo said. "Not any more. Not since I was a kid."

"Well, I rarely do. But when I do it's always weird. I wake up with my heart pounding and I'm short of breath and I can never get back to sleep. I've had this one dream maybe a half dozen times."

She walks through a vast forest, sticks cracking and leaves rustling behind her. She strides faster and faster and the brush behind her swishes at ever quicker intervals. Whatever is following her is quickening its pace. She runs into a cave and hunches down, trying to quiet her breath. But her inhaling and exhaling are still so noisy – like the wheezing of an asthmatic – she decides to hold her breath. And then, as if deprivation of oxygen hastens the delivery of young and functions as an epidural, she goes into labor and effortlessly gives birth to a baby boy. She presses him to her breast, lost in the joy of new love, temporarily forgetting about the unknown beast that pursues her. Then, she hears the hoarse breath of something massive and powerful beside her – looming at her left ear. Sheltering the baby in her bosom, she turns halfway toward the eerie sound and sees a large, friendly floppy-eared animal, like a Burnese Mountain Dog, with lush fur marked with black, white and caramel-colored patches. In his ample jowls, he carries a flaming torch, which he places at Elina's feet. She feels the heat from the fire on her left foot, drawing her attention to the fact that she is wearing only one shoe – a high heeled magenta pump.

109

"What do you think it means?" Mateo asked.

"Too many anchovies on my antipasto, too close to bedtime," Elina said.

It would be a number of years before she would discover the true meaning of the dog and the torch. But for now, it was one of many details about herself that she would choose to reveal to Mateo and that would consequently bind the two together. Perhaps, she began to believe, even permanently.

Meanwhile, Elina's father grew increasingly perturbed at her absence from her high-backed full-grain buttery leather executive chair.

"Oh, come on, Dad. I have a B.S. job anyway. I never actually do anything all day."

"You are the face of the company, Sweetheart. You might think power lunches are unimportant, but there's a reason why they're called that."

"I'm not interested in power, Daddy."

"What are you interested in these days?"

"Life. And death. And that's about it."

෨❳෬❳෨❳෬❳෨❳෬❳෨❳෬❳෨❳෬

Over the next several days, Raquel was awake only for a total of about an hour a day. She spoke only of things eternal.

"Daddy, what is Heaven like?"

"Well, I'm sure it's beautiful. It probably has all sorts of wonderful food. Beautiful flowers. And best of all, people who love you."

"Mommy."

"She'll be very happy to see you."

Elina hadn't thought much about Heaven since she was a kid and her mother sat her down one day after school and told her she was going there. Elina begged to go with her.

"Not yet, Baby," her mother said. "It's not your time yet. You still have such wonderful things to do in your life. Heaven is not ready for you yet."

110

Elina wondered how she could go on to do wonderful things in her life without her mother. Nearly twenty years later, she still had not quite figured that out. Although, in the last several weeks, she had begun to develop an inkling.

"You are a strong and remarkable woman, Elina," Mateo said over a plate of virtually untouched pressed turkey and instant mashed potatoes smothered in canned brown gravy. "I don't know if I could have done what you have done."

"What do you mean?" The two were having dinner on rolling, portable trays in Raquel's hospital room.

"You chose to love someone you know you will have to part with."

Elina smiled slightly as she poked at the iceberg lettuce in her cobb salad. She didn't have an answer for Mateo on that one because she herself was surprised at what she had done. "Remember that feeling when you were a kid, going on vacation and all the way there, you were depressed because you knew in just seven days, you'd be coming back and it would all be over? And then, the whole time you're there, you're increasingly more depressed with every moment of fun that passes because it puts you just that much closer to the end? It was like the more fun you had, the more depressing it became because it was all going to end far too soon? I've lived my life thinking that way, knowing it will all end far too soon. Dreading the end instead of enjoying the middle."

"In reality, Elina, there is no such thing as what you speak of. When vacation is over we have an even better thing waiting for us."

"Daddy?" Raquel had awoken.

Mateo put his fork down, pushed his tray away with a little too much force so it rolled halfway across the room and moved quickly to Raquel, grabbing her hand and kissing it tenderly. "Yes, Mija. I am here."

"Do you think I'll be able to fly?"

"I don't know. Do you want to fly?

She smiled faintly and nodded.

"Then, you will fly like an angel. No wish goes ungranted in Heaven."

"Horseback riding? Are there horses in Heaven?"

"Don't know for sure about all that. But I do know there is pure happiness in Heaven."

"How will I be happy without you?"

"You won't be without me. You'll be as close as my next breath. Closer even than you are now."

Raquel reached for her father and he moved in close, so she could wrap her arms around his neck. "I don't want you to be sad, Papa. Please don't cry too much when I—when I go. To Heaven."

"I promise," he said, wiping his eyes behind her back. "I will be happy for you, that you are with Jesus and Mary and all the saints. And your mother."

"And I will be happy for you that you are with Elina." She closed her eyes, and the already loose embrace dissolved.

More tears came, and Elina handed Mateo a box of tissues.

Raquel opened her eyes again. "Are you going to marry her?"

Mateo looked up at Elina and smiled through his tears. "Wouldn't that be a fine day, Mija?" He wiped his eyes and nose with the tissue.

"I will be your flower girl from Heaven." The girl's eyelids were growing heavy again and the words came out increasingly slower. "I will drop flowers down on you."

"A *very* fine day," Elina agreed.

"Red," said Raquel, drifting into sleep. "Red is the color of love."

Those were the child's last words.

Elina notified H.R. that she was taking another week – this time for bereavement.

"I can't believe she's gone," Mateo said, sitting on his front porch stoop on the evening after the funeral. "I am grateful I made it back in time to kiss her good-bye. I just wish I'd had more time with her. But there could never be enough time. There's never enough time to spend with an angel. Raquel, she was an angel."

Elina decided Raquel's room would remain exactly is it was. She invited Mateo and Lucy to stay as long as they wanted. At first, they declined, saying it would be too hard without Raquel. But after the funeral, Mateo needed to be near something that had been near to her, so he took Elina up on her offer and slept in his daughter's bed. Lucy slept in her usual spot, in the neighboring bed.

"I told housekeeping not to launder Raquel's sheets," Elina told them. "Is that OK?"

"Thank you, yes." Mateo said.

"When my mother died, I slept in her bed for a long time, just to be near the smell of her. My father didn't mind. I think it helped him to have a piece of her next to him. I was the closest thing he had to her. And I didn't mind. I wanted her to live on through me -- through my genes, or the blood coursing through my veins, or the laugh that everyone said was a carbon copy of hers."

"I know the feeling," Mateo said.

"Yes, of course you do. I'm sorry. I hope I haven't made you sadder."

"I couldn't get any sadder."

"I bet you miss your wife all over again."

"In all new ways, now that Raquel is gone. Having Raquel was like holding onto a piece of her, something amazing we did together. Raquel was our masterpiece."

Elina squeezed his shoulder.

"I felt her with me yesterday, at Raquel's funeral. I know she was there. It was as if I placed Raquel's hand in hers. That's what I saw in my mind's eye. And I saw that Raquel was happy to be with her mother. A thought passed between us -- me and Raquel. She knew I was not happy, but she told me I would be someday. That's what she said, without words, in the thought that we shared." Mateo's first instinct was to argue. No, he would never be happy again. But there was no arguing with her. She possessed a kind of gentle sovereignty, as if someone had given her the authority to guarantee hope. It is at the height of arrogance and in the absence of wisdom that one would argue with an angel. So, he bit his lip.

"I know she's right, Mateo. I know you'll find happiness again."

"Out of obedience to an angel, I'll have to try. I don't even want to, but I'll have to try."

"If I can be of any help in that endeavor–" Elina didn't continue because it sounded as if she were making a pass at him. An ill-timed pass which would make light of the gravity of what had transpired. "I know there's probably nothing any human being can do, but if you need anything at all, please ask. Take as long as you'd like and stay here. You don't need to worry about money or a job or place to stay. Just rest."

He and Lucy stayed for two more days. Then, they stood on the pillared porch, taxi waiting in the circular drive. "It's time for us to get home," Mateo said, overnight bags on each side of him. "We need to get back."

Elina wondered "to what?" She thought of their small, rundown apartment with its chipped bowls and rough spoons and mismatched thread-bare furniture. Then she realized he meant that they needed to get back to the way things were before they had suffered immeasurable loss. Everyone standing there knew that would never happen.

"I will call you tomorrow," Elina said, embracing Lucy and then Mateo, pushing the tears back behind her eyes, what few were left to cry.

"Thank you." Mateo was not as effective in containing his tears. Elina's embrace provided a safe place for them to land.

Elina did call the following day and for eight days after that, and then weeks went by when the two did not speak. Elina began to feel funny about being the one to make the call. A woman shouldn't be in that position. Mateo didn't want to make the call because, after all the selfless things Elina had done, he did not want to continue her burden. And so, because the two were of the opposite sex, the telephone remained on the hook. That's not to say that both of them were not thinking about the other. Incessantly. The way lovers do.

Elina returned to work, watching the clock all day, through power lunches and executive board meetings designed to accomplish little but justify the salaries of those who do next to nothing but write yearly reviews of those who keep the place running. When 5 p.m. came, she'd hit the company gym dressing room, change into her designer jeans and a cable-knit sweater and head to the cancer ward of Children's Hospital, where she volunteered to read stories and play board games with the patients whose parents could not be with them at the moment. One day, she decided to cut out of work early to avoid rush hour traffic. It was two in the afternoon when she put the top down on her Espresso-colored Mercedes, turned the stereo volume up to forty-four and abandoned her long blonde hair to the swirling and riotous wind of the highway.

Just as she was thinking about how much she'd like to see Mateo again, John Cohen's new song came on the radio:

Baby, I know life with me
Is not exactly what you might see
On the pages of Modern Bride
Who could predict that you and I
Would find a love to deepen any sea
Would find a love to make demons flee
Some days fly like ravens
Some days fly like doves
Everyday I'm flying
Deeper into your love
Maybe it hasn't always been this way
But it will surely always be
No force in this world
Could come between you and me

Elina imagined Mateo singing those words to her. Nothing she could think of made her happier than that thought. She picked up the car phone as she drifted to a stop at a red light.

"Hello, Mateo." She put the top up on her convertible to drown out the whizzing traffic. "How are you?"

"Fine, Elina, fine. It's good to hear your voice."

"Good to hear yours." A short pause. "Would be great to have the visuals to go along with it."

"The visuals?"

"Yeah. What are you doing right now?"

"Well, right now I'm on break. But I won't be for long. Then I work until eight. I would love to see you, Elina. Is that too late?"

"No. That's great."

The hours, which usually flew when Elina was with the children, crept like apathetic snails. She wondered what it would be like when she and Mateo first saw each other. She was sure they would embrace. But what kind of embrace would it be? Would there be distance or would time have stood still as it does between old friends?

For some reason, no embrace took place when Mateo opened the door, smiling and telling her how good it was to see her. The two sat in adjacent chairs, sensing something large had grown between them, something that could be dissolved in a single instant at the moment that either one of them decided they'd had enough.

"How's work?" Mateo asked.

"Unfulfilling. How's yours?"

"Even worse than that. I'm going back to Mexico."

"Mexico? Why?"

"I can't find steady work, and the feds know where I live. There's nothing for me here."

Nothing? Elina knew she was not entitled to the pain, but it socked her in the gut nonetheless. "Are you sure you want to go back? You risked so much to get here."

"For Raquel. Now I have no reason to stay."

With that, the distance between them was set. Elina knew her umbrage was unwarranted. She and Mateo hadn't seen each other in weeks.

"What will you do in Mexico?"

"I will try to return to my life's work."

"Which is?"

"Do you remember I told you that I am sort of an expert in ancient Aztec language and culture?"

"Yes. The code. What is it called Na-." She struggled to remember.

"The Nahuatl codex. Yes."

"You can't pursue your work here?"

"There's not much of a need for Nahuatl experts in the United States. Not that much in Mexico either. I probably cannot make any money at it. But it is a passion of mine. Someday, I plan to write a book about the Virgin of Guadalupe. Some kind of historical fiction."

"Our Lady of Guadalupe?"

"Yes. There is a team – anthropologists, theologians, scientists – studying the miraculous image. I was working on the codex that is written on her tunic and what it says about the theological truths revealed when she appeared to Juan Diego some 500 years ago. We had just started when Raquel became sick and I had to bring her here for treatment."

"Your work sounds fascinating. Is your mother coming with you?"

"Probably not. She has a life here. She didn't have one in Mexico."

"You're going to miss her."

"Yes. Very much." His eyes rested in hers. "And I will miss you." He took her hands in his. "You have done so much for us, Elina."

"In the end, I'm so sorry that it wasn't enough."

"It means everything to us."

Elina put her arms around his middle and rested her head on his flannel shirt. It had a sweet smoky smell – like a far-off barbeque – that made her feel connected to the entire universe.

"When will you leave?" she asked.

"I don't know. Soon."

"Keep in touch, Mateo." She held his hands in hers. "Please. I don't want to lose track of you."

"No chance of that, Elina. You mean too much to us."

On the way home, she thought about his use of the first person plural whenever he expressed feelings of affection. She knew this was his way of keeping the relationship out of the realm of the romantic. And that's what troubled her. That was the very realm she wanted to enter. Not with anyone else. Just with him.

ဆၜသ၌ဆၜသ၌ဆၜသ၌ဆၜသ၌

The next day, Elina decided a lunchtime shopping spree might lift her spirits, but the trip proved uninspiring. So after two hours of frequenting her favorite boutiques on Rodeo Drive, she found only a $442 Luxe suede jumper. She dropped the shopping bag in the back seat of her Mercedes just as her car phone rang.

"Hello. Elina here."

"Well, if it isn't the ever elusive Elina Peltier. Where have you been, my love? I've had a heck of a time getting in touch with you."

"I'm sorry, Mavis. I've been kind of busy. It's nothing personal. I haven't had time to return anyone's calls."

"Well, I have urgent business to speak to you about, Love. I have several gentlemen who just won't rest if they don't get a date with you. They have been driving me up a tree. They all claim they haven't stopped thinking about you since the mixer, which apparently wasn't such a disaster after all."

"No, I don't think I'm up for a date right now, Mavis. I'm sorry. I'm just not in the state of mind."

"Oh, Lovey, these are some really nice men. Look, I'll tell you what. I don't usually do this, but I'm going to take all the work out of it for you and just tell you that you need to be focusing on this one particular gentleman. Just one date with him, Elina, and you'll see what I mean. He's really into you and he's a real sweetheart. His name is Rodney Sweet, as a matter of fact."

Elina knew a date might get her mind off of Mateo's leaving. But she hated the idea just the same.

"OK, Mavis. One date."

ೞ⧳ೞ⧳ೞ⧳ೞ⧳ೞ⧳ೞ⧳ೞ

Elina sat in front of Mateo's apartment for several minutes, trying to determine exactly what she was going to say. A frightening thought harassed her, but she successfully beat it down. He couldn't possibly have gone back to Mexico yet. She had just seen him last week. He wouldn't have had time to get out of the country that fast. So another thought tried its hand at unnerving her. This one she was not able to defeat. *What if he were not pleased to see her?*

She gave him a shy smile when he opened the door. She thought she saw a light in his eyes, but wondered if it was wishful thinking. The warm wide smile, though, could not be mistaken.

"Elina! Come in! What a nice surprise! Mama, look who's here!"

"Oh, Elina!" Lucy got up from the dinner table, set with a couple bowls of pintos and a short stack of flour tortillas. "Ai, it's so good to see you, Mija. You look beautiful! You are beautiful!" The women embraced and Lucy kissed Elina on the cheek. "Sit and have something to eat. We are just having a late snack."

"No, no, I can't stay. As much as I love your beans. I only have a few minutes."

"Please, please!" Lucy said scurrying to the stove. And before Elina knew it, she was sitting at the table with food in front of her. But she couldn't eat.

"What is it, Elina? Are you not feeling well?""

119

"Just a bit tired lately."

"Ai, me too. Maybe there is something going around."

Lucy excused herself after finishing her food, saying she had to go check on the neighbor's dog – let him out for the night since his owners were out of town. Mateo got up to kiss his mother on the cheek and walk her to the door. He returned to the table and placed his hand on the back of Elina's chair. "Come sit in here, Elina," he said, motioning to the olive velour sofa, worn nearly to threads on all three cushions. She sat on the far left and the he took a seat on the far right.

"Mateo," Elina inhaled. "I just discovered something tonight, and I don't know what it means. I thought maybe you could help me figure it out."

"I'll try."

"I just came from a date with this very wealthy, very important man. Upstanding, charming, interesting. It was a good date."

"Oh, how nice," he said politely.

"We were out on the harbor in a boat. Good conversation. Good food. Nice ambience. Gorgeous sunset. And then, right when our lobsters arrived, and I caught mine staring me right in the eye, my date asked me this really intriguing question."

"Really? What was that?"

"He asked me, 'If this were your last day on Earth, what would you want to do?'"

"Hmmm. Interesting question. Maybe not so easy to answer."

"For me, it was easy."

Elina moved toward Mateo and, resting her head on his flannel shirt, wrapped her arms around his waist, staying quiet there, taking peaceful breaths. And then, without looking at him, and still in that same position, she said, "This is what I would do."

Mateo put his cheek to the top of her head and squeezed her close.

"So, what do you think it means?" she asked, still not looking at him.

"I'm not sure," he said, stroking her hair. "What do you think it means?"

"I think–" She cleared her throat. "It means–" She cleared it again. "I think it means that I'm going to be very unhappy when you leave."

"That's what it means?" A smile stretched broad across the majority of his face.

"Why are you going back to Mexico? Is your research that important?"

"It's what my heart second most desires."

"Second most?"

"Yes. I dare not ask for what my heart desires most."

"Why?"

"A man like me does not ask a woman like you for his heart's desire."

"Mateo," she said, taking his face between her hands and looking into his eyes. "What is your heart's desire?"

He kissed her lightly on the lips and pressed her head into his chest. She waited for the answer.

"Elina, Elina, Elina," he stroked her hair in rhythm with the utterance of her name. "Such a beautiful name. What does it mean?"

"It's a Greek name. My mother was Greek. It means "bright light" or "torch."

"Then I am certain. We are meant to be together."

"Why do you say that?" Her smile was wide as she looked into his large brown eyes.

"Do you know what Luz means?" He smiled down at her.

"No."

"It means "light." If you marry me, your name will be 'light of light.'"

⚛

9

Starched

"You'll be happy to know, Daddy," Elina said, twirling the phone cord around her finger, "that I am in love."

"I had a feeling." Elina imagined her father with a broad smile, one that said two things at once: *I told you so* and *Money well spent*. "Mavis told me she had convinced you to go out with a really fine catch. Aren't you glad you did now, Sweetheart?"

"Yes, Daddy. I'm very glad. It really clarified things for me. I can't wait for you to meet the man I'm going to marry."

"Marry? Well that went quickly."

"He's so wonderful. When can we all get together for lunch?"

"I don't have my calendar in front of me, Darling. Just call Allison, and she'll get you on the agenda."

"I can't wait for you to meet him, Daddy. Do you think you might be available tomorrow?"

"No, Phoebe is out of town."

"Daddy, could we just make it us for the first meeting? I'll set something up after for Phoebe to meet him."

"OK, Honey. That's fine. Just call Allison. Looking forward to it, Sweetheart."

Elina had never seen Mateo nervous before. Not only had she not seen it, she never could have even pictured it. But she figured he must be because, as he sat drumming his thumbs on the steering wheel of her Aston Martin, he couldn't even find the lever for the parking brake.

"Don't worry Mateo," Elina said, grabbing his hand and squeezing it tight. "Daddy is going to love you. I know I haven't painted the most complimentary picture of my parents, but they really aren't bad people. Well, not my father anyway. Do you want me to drive?"

"No, it's OK. I'm a professional." He winked at her as he put the car in reverse and backed out of the alley behind his place. The tires crunched over something that sounded like a soda can. Or maybe beer.

"What's he really like?" Mateo asked, returning his hand to Elina's after shifting the car into drive.

"Kind. And somewhat starched."

"Starched?"

"You know, like a dress shirt. Not flannel like you."

"Do you like flannel?"

"Flannel, fleece, all the Saturday morning fabrics. I like a good, crisp Luigi Borrelli on occasion too. On a Saturday night or a work day."

"A what?"

"A nice dress shirt. Done the way only Italians can do them."

"What was your father like when you were little?"

"I don't have that many memories of early childhood. Not enough."

"What do you remember?"

"I remember dinner parties. My mother used to have a dress made for me that was identical to hers. She would spend hours doing my hair. Usually an up-do with golden spiral curls cascading down, sprinkled with hair glitter. She would do it herself because I never let a stylist touch my hair. She would mimic whatever the stylist did to hers. Then, I remember feeling very special serving hors d'oeuvres off of silver trays. And the guests would be so complimentary, whispering to me that the ones I was serving tasted so much better than the ones offered by hired help."

Elina glanced at Mateo's soft smile.

"Then, after my mother passed away and my Dad remarried, my stepmother never let me serve our guests again. She said it was beneath the members of our family, since we had the means to hire help to do such menial tasks. So I spent evenings in my room, sprawled out on my bed, listening to the far-off laughter of reveling adults between rounds of my own sobbing."

"Did you tell your father?"

"He told me just to let her make a few decisions, so she would feel like part of the family, so she would feel welcome. That's pretty much how she was permitted to systematically take over every aspect of our lives. And so dawned a tyranny that has endured until this day."

"So you have been oppressed."

"In a strange sort of over-privileged way, yes." She turned the knob, searching the radio for classical music. "You know, though, it's funny. Do you know what my first childhood memory is? I mean the very first thing I remember about being on this earth?"

"What?"

"You'd think it would be something to do with my mother, right? She was, to me, the all-important one. But, my first memory is of my father's ears."

"Really? Does he have unusual ears?"

"Not really, no. I just have this very vague memory of playing with them. I don't know how old I was. But I vaguely remember being in his arms -- like at a ballgame or some outdoor event -- just fascinated by the springy-ness of his ears -- you know pulling on the ear lobe and kind of flicking them and folding them and watching them return to their original shape. And he was engaged in conversation or something, so it was as if he didn't notice. He had a very high tolerance -- can't remember him ever being annoyed or short-tempered."

"Did you have a nanny?"

"I did when I was very small. And then again later after my mother died."

"Did it ever bother you having no brothers or sisters?"

"I had an imaginary sister. She was very nice. She was only a year younger than me and we did everything together."

"What was her name?"

"Cosette. I named her for the Les Mis character after my mother took me to the musical. Cosette and I became very close when my mother died. I knew she understood everything I was going through. Her mother died too."

Mateo and Elina were silent after entering the massive wrought iron gates of Green Haven, until the mansion came into view.

"This is where you grew up, Elina? So beautiful."

A man with a polite and dignified smile answered the door. Gerard was in his late fifties and wore a white coat, black bow tie and a rather large blue star sapphire on his pinky, which looked particularly weighty because he himself was no bigger than Sammy Davis Jr.

Charles Peltier greeted Elina and Mateo with apologies that he couldn't have arranged to have lunch with them that day because of his tight schedule, but would they please join him in an afternoon sherry and selection of imported cheeses Gerard would be serving momentarily.

The three of them sat in leather wingback chairs in a very large study that seemed to be constructed almost entirely of warm-toned exotic woods and black leather.

"So, you two met at Mackey and Associates," Charles Peltier said, pouring wine into three petite, stemmed glasses.

"Yes," Elina confirmed.

"Oh, very good," Elina's father said. "Didn't I tell you Mavis can work magic, Honey? What line of work are you in, Mateo?"

"Well, my passion has been the study of the Codex Escalada as it relates to the image of Our Lady of Guadalupe."

Charles Peltier looked confused and glanced at his daughter for an interpretation.

"He's an anthropologist, Daddy, with an emphasis in religion and linguistics."

"Oh." He still looked confused. "So, uh, what exciting discoveries have you made?"

"None yet. But God willing, I will be able to resume my work."

Elina knew her father was, no doubt, trying to figure out how Mateo made it onto Mavis' list. She was not at all unhappy that the conversation had led to the impression that she and Mateo had met through the agency, but she knew her father's questioning would eventually uncover the truth. Still, she hoped to stave off the whole truth long enough for her father to grow in appreciation for the rare person Mateo is. Surely he would see it, just as she had. She and her father were not that far apart in how they viewed people. They had even once been kindred spirits before her mother died. The father she remembered was still inside there somewhere, she theorized. Maybe the depth of true devotion that Elina and Mateo felt for each other could remind him again.

"Mateo had to take a brief sabbatical from his work to deal with a family tragedy," Elina said.

"Yes," Mateo said. "I lost my daughter to cancer."

"Oh, I'm sorry. Do you have other children?"

"No, my wife died of influenza when my daughter was fairly young. I'm certain we would have had more children."

"Your wife died from the flu?"

"Yes."

"She was otherwise healthy?"

"Well, she struggled with asthma. But she had always lived a normal life."

"How tragic." Charles Peltier took a sip of his wine. "I lost my first wife to cancer."

"I am sorry for your loss. It is unbearable, the pain. But, you know, life doesn't end for the living. We go on. We even find happiness again. That is the task."

"And my daughter has brought you happiness?"

He looked at Elina and smiled. "Oh, yes."

Mr. Peltier's phone rang, and he had a terse conversation with someone delivering a unwelcome news. He hung up and shook his head in disgust. "I'm afraid we're going to have to cut this short. But I'm sure I'll be seeing a lot more of you, Mateo. I suspect I'm going to have to have one of my tuxes dry cleaned in the not-so-distant future." He put his hand on Mateo's shoulder as the two walked out of the study together behind Elina. "Mrs. Peltier will be anxious to meet you. She gets in from Lake Tahoe tomorrow. She's had a few days up there with a few of her girlfriends. I'm sure they spent the majority of their time drinking white Russians and bashing husbands. I doubt you'll ever know what that's like, Mateo. I don't think I've ever heard Elina utter an unkind word about a single soul. She is a rare and lovely gem, Mateo. The man who marries her will have won a great treasure."

☙❦☙❦☙❦☙❦☙❦☙❦

A sudden round of coughing overtook Father Dante and Lawrence Crenshaw buzzed Roberta for a glass of water, which arrived within seconds in a crystal glass rimmed in gold, etched with a Crenshaw Enterprises logo. The water was about as cold as water can get without turning into ice, which made the thinness of the crystal seem even more luxurious against his lower lip.

"She was, you know.' Father Dante said as his throat cleared of its momentary affliction. "My mother was a great treasure. And my father always treated her that way. It's not always that way between married couples."

"That's for sure," Lawrence Crenshaw said.

"I get profoundly sad sometimes when I go to Wal-mart and see husbands with their heads cocked and a disgusted look on their faces and their wives or live-in girlfriends trailing ten paces behind with stories of misery or vacancy or resignation inscribed on their faces. It is so devoid of the beauty I remember marriage to be. My father would push the grocery cart with my mother's hands wrapped around his bicep – like they were going to the ball. They would let go of each other only to retrieve something from the shelf, then back together they'd go. My parents never forgot how much their love cost. They did not take it for granted."

"How much it cost?"

"That marriage came at a very high price."

Soon after the shared bottle of sherry and before a date could be chosen for Mateo to meet Phoebe, Elina's father called her with a bit of a problem.

"Sweetheart, there's something strange going on with you and your Mateo. I can't quite figure it out. Maybe you can help me."

"What do you mean?"

"I spoke with Mavis about Mateo. She had never heard of him."

"Why is that so strange?"

"You said you met him through the agency."

"I did?"

"Yes."

"Well, I did. I mean I did meet him at the agency. At the curb, actually."

"Honey, what's going on? Just give it to me straight, would you? Because I am an old and busy man, which makes time very precious to me, which means I don't want to spend it on guessing games."

"OK," she said, drawing a long breath. "I will tell you the whole story. But first tell me – did you like Mateo?"

"Yes, I liked him alright. He seemed like a well-intentioned fellow."

"Would you still think so if he were not rich?"

"Yes, I would still think so if he were not rich. There are well intentioned poor people in the world and well intentioned rich people. And middle class people too. Now, can I hear the story, please? I have a meeting in five minutes."

"He was the limo driver who took me home from that ridiculous mixer you made me attend."

And this is where Charles Peltier's brain completely clouded over. "A limo driver? What does that mean?"

"What do you mean, what does it mean? You know what a limo driver is, Daddy. All rich people know what a limo driver is. The person who drives the limo. You know, the one with the steering wheel in his hand?"

"You don't need to get sarcastic, Sweetheart. I'm just trying to understand. You want to marry a driver?"

"Well, he's not a driver anymore, actually. But yes, I want to marry him."

"And what does he do now?"

"You remember. He told you he is an anthropologist."

"Oh, yes, of course. Honey, did you go out with any of the men Mavis found for you?"

"Yes."

"And you didn't like any of them?"

"Yes, I liked one."

"Well, then…"

"I didn't love him. I love Mateo."

"How do you know this Mateo isn't just after your money? He, of course, had to know you have money when he asked you to marry him."

"He didn't ask me to marry him. I asked him."

"So he chased you until you caught him. Very sly fellow."

"He's not sly. He was going to go back to Mexico. I practically had to beg him to marry me, Daddy."

"Back to Mexico? Why?"

"For his research."

"If he's such a great anthropologist, why was he driving a limo?"

"It's not always easy to find work in that field, especially in the U.S. and especially when the topics you are studying are in

Mexico."

"So why was he here in the first place if his work is in Mexico?"

"He came here to get cancer treatment for his daughter."

"Oh."

"Daddy, don't worry so much. Be happy for me. I'm finally in love."

"There's just something fishy about his story, Honey. Something doesn't add up. I don't want to see you get hurt."

"Daddy, he completely checks out. I'm not naïve and stupid, you know. I'm approaching thirty here."

"Why don't you two come over to the house this weekend. I'm sure Phoebe would like to meet your Mateo."

"Sure, Daddy. We'd love to." Actually, the thought was dreadful. It was going to be a cruel inquisition, executed over truffles and petit fours. To calm herself, Elina tried to convince herself it wouldn't be as bad as all that.

As it turned out, it was even worse.

ဆၢ❦ભ❦ဆၢ❦ભ❦ဆၢ❦ભ❦ဆၢ❦ભ

"Mateo, I just can't get over it," Phoebe said shaking her head. "You look just like a gardener that we had for many years. Charles, doesn't he look just like Eduardo?"

"Phoebe, Darling, would you like to tell Mateo and Elina about whipping the pants off me on the golf course this morning?"

"Oh, there you go exaggerating again. You were quite the formidable opponent, my Darling." She placed her hand on her husband's thigh. "Do you play golf, Mateo?"

"No, ma'am," he smiled, shyly. "I don't. Basketball is my sport."

"Did you play a lot back in Mexico?" Phoebe asked.

"No, actually. I've played more here."

"Where in Mexico are you from?"

"Teotihuacan."

"My goodness, that's a mouthful," she said. "Where is that?"

"Not too far from Mexico City."

"Oh, I see. We have vacationed in the Riviera Maya and occasionally in Cabo. But other than that, we haven't seen too much of Mexico."

"It's a beautiful place," Charles said.

"Yes, the beach was quite lovely," Phoebe agreed. "So what brought you to the states, Mateo?"

"I came for my daughter's treatment. She had cancer."

"Oh, did they grant you a special visa for that?" Phoebe asked.

"This is a very humanitarian nation," Mateo said. "America has been very good to us. Sadly, in the end, it was not enough to save my daughter."

"I'm so sorry," Phoebe said. She took a sip of her cocktail. "Are they allowing you to stay indefinitely?"

"Actually, no."

"No?"

"They are not allowing me to stay at all."

"So you will have to return to Mexico?"

"At some point, yes. Unless I get citizenship."

"Well, wouldn't getting married give you automatic citizenship?" Charles asked.

"Oh," Phoebe said. "Isn't it just amazing how things have a way of working themselves out?"

"So tell us about Teotihuacan, Mateo," Charles said. "What was it like growing up there?"

"It was a hard life. Often there was not enough clean water. Always there was never enough food. I was fortunate enough to have a second cousin who was a professor. He paid for me and my brothers to go to school. We were able to give our children a better life than we had. A little better."

"Charles, Honey," Phoebe said. "Have you forgotten about our tennis match with the Nelsons? We will have to be running along soon."

"Yes, Darling, I remember."

"Well," Mateo said, swiftly getting to his feet and holding his hand out to Elina's father, "it was a pleasure. Thank you for your hospitality." He shook hands with Phoebe on the way to the door. "It was very nice to meet you, Mrs. Peltier."

Phoebe bowed her head slightly and smiled with tight lips.

"I'm sorry we have to rush off," Charles said. "We've had this game planned for a while."

"That's OK, Daddy," Elina said, pausing in the massive three-story marble foyer.

He gave her a kiss on the forehead. "We'll talk soon, Honey."

Elina and Phoebe maneuvered into a short, stiff embrace. "Oh, Phoebe," Elina said, "I forgot to ask. How was your Tahoe trip?"

"It was fine, but Tahoe has gotten so commercial. Next time, we're going to find a cozy little villa in Italy."

"Oh, a long trip."

"Just a weekend."

"Fly that far for a weekend?" Elina said. "I hate flying these days. Last time I flew, there was a security breach and we all had to sit at the terminal for two hours while they scanned everyone and the luggage. That was on the way back from Paris, remember Daddy, I told you about that?"

"Well, just make sure all your flights are domestic from now on," Charles Peltier advised, "and you can use the private jet."

The massive Peltier mansion receded into the distance in Elina's rearview mirror.

"Well, that went quite as expected," she said.

"That Phoebe is exactly as you described her," Mateo smiled and shook his head. "You were not exaggerating."

"Now you see, I was actually going easy on her."

"Charitable even."

"Thank you."

"So what do we do about Phoebe?"

"Nothing. Until she does something about us. And she will."

"She will?"

"Oh, yes. Believe me. She already has something cooked up."

They drove in silence for several minutes. At a red light, Elina grabbed Mateo's hand and smiled at him. "Phoebe gives rich people a bad name. They're not all like that, believe me. Actually, not even the majority are like that. I wish you could have met my mother."

"I wish so too, my love. But I feel I already know her." He kissed her hand. "I've seen the best of her in you."

"No you haven't. She was a much better person than I am. I don't understand why someone as good as my mother had to die. I needed her. What good could have possibly come from that? My life fell apart after she died.

"So you are angry with God."

"If there is a God, yes. I am angry with Him. Aren't you? He took your daughter."

"He didn't take my daughter. He gave me a daughter. For all her days on earth, He let me have her. He didn't give anyone like her to anyone else. And she was a great gift. *Is* a great gift. No, God did not take her from me. Death took her."

"But why? Why did God let death take her?"

"Should God give every person the exact same number of years to live? How many years should that be? 72? 84? 100? What kind of creatures would we be with that kind of guarantee? No, there will always be people who die young. The question is, which one of us is He going to give those people to? If it was possible, would I have traded my daughter for one who would have outlived me? Would you have traded your mother for a different one – one who was cancer free and would have lived to see her grandchildren?"

"No. Of course not."

"Don't you think God knew when He sent you to your mother that she would die and leave you? Should He have not given her a child? If He had not, the child would not have suffered the loss of her. Should she have missed out on all that love? Or should He have sent her a different child, who now would be asking the same questions you are?"

"Of course, I would not have wanted any other mother. The time I had with her was the best of my life."

"Well, then, you are happy with God's choice. The mother He chose for you was the perfect mother for you. It just so happened that that particular woman had a shorter life span than some other people. Longer than some too."

Elina wiped tears from her eyes and placed her hand back on the steering wheel.

"He sends the crosses He must send to the people He must send them to," Mateo said, looking out the passenger window at the passing wealth. "We will not figure out why. It's all interwoven with a much larger plan, which we don't have eyes to see and which can only be for the good of all mankind."

"Only for the good? How do you know that?"

"I know God."

"Then, I guess that's my problem. I don't."

"And you don't want to?"

"No. I guess I don't."

"That, I don't believe. Every human heart has a longing. At the very core of everything we are, everything He made us, is the desire for perfect love."

She drove in silence.

"Do you not desire perfect love?" he asked her.

"I found perfect love. In you."

"No. One day, you will see. One day when I have done something all too human, you will see there is only one perfect love."

"Only one?"

"He died for you."

"You would die for me."

"Yes, but that doesn't mean I won't disappoint you in the meantime. We knew a couple back in Mexico. The wife, she was always complaining about her husband. And there were lots of reasons to complain, let me tell you. She used to talk to my wife about her plans to leave him. My wife would try to talk her out of it. One day, a tornado came through San Fernando. This couple, they made it to the bathroom, into the bathtub. He laid his body over hers. The tornado came and ripped everything up. Everything in its path. The debris -- it crushed everything. This woman, she survived. But her husband didn't. He gave his life for her. If she had left him, who would have been there to save her? And who could have known that? How could anyone have known he would die for her? And at his funeral, all she could do was weep and tell everyone what a perfect and loving husband he was. All of those grievances she voiced while he was alive were like specs of dust. In the end, all his many imperfections were consumed by that horrific act of nature, leaving behind only one thing."

"Love."

"Si, Mi Vida. And I'll bet she never voices another complaint about him as long as she lives."

"And I will never voice one about you. You are my perfect love."

They drove in silence for several minutes, holding hands and watching the miles peel back layers of opulent wealth, until all that was left was concrete drab. She parked the car in front of his apartment, took the keys from the ignition and sat looking at him. He kissed her softly on the lips. One, long, lingering kiss. Then he looked deep into her eyes. "You are a stubborn woman, Elina Peltier. But I will tell you this. If I have perfect love in me, it doesn't come from me. Human love is incapable of perfection. If, in the end, I lay my body over yours and die for you, then you better start believing in God. No other love can do that." He kissed her on the forehead. "And you know I would. Happily."

"I wish my parents would believe that."

"They did not like that I was illegal."

"Not at all. I've never wished this about a man before, but at that moment, I wished you were not so bloody honest."

"They see me as a criminal."

"No, nothing that harsh."

"Sometimes I see myself that way. I didn't like doing what I had to do. I broke laws. I falsified documents. Is it wrong to do those things? Probably."

"There are people going about it the right way. Waiting for their number to come up. Doing it illegally is not fair to them."

"We came here for my daughter." Mateo's voice cracked. "I did everything I did for her." He could scarcely get the words out through his tears. "Wouldn't you have done the same for your child?"

Elina put her hand on the back of his head and guided his forehead to hers. Their faces were inches apart. Elina wanted nothing more than to cast herself into the depths of his soul – with all the love and agony that lie within.

"Without a moment's hesitation," she whispered. "I would have done the same."

10

Treasure

"I'm sorry, Honey, but we can't approve of your marriage to Mateo." Charles Peltier sipped on his Pina Colada, served poolside in a shapely, frosted glass. "You will be risking all we have ever worked for. You have worked hard in your life. We have worked hard. We can't throw all that away."

"You're assuming he's marrying me for my money. So, in your view, is that the only thing I've got going for me?" Elina stood to adjust the massive umbrella, casting shade on herself and her father. "I'm so hideous, he has hatched a plan to marry and divorce me and rob me of my money."

"You are far from hideous, Sweetheart." He etched an abstract design with his thumbnail in the frost of his glass. "That's why any man would gladly marry you. But not all will have pure intentions."

"Well, there's always the trusty pre-nup," Elina said taking a drink of her iced tea. "That ought to keep everyone honest, if that's what you're worried about."

"Not completely," Phoebe chimed in from her sunny perch on the side of the pool, where she skimmed her toes over the sparkling blue. "He can go on a spending spree the day after you get married, and you won't be able to say one thing about it."

"Is that what you did?" Elina asked her.

"Of course not." Phoebe kicked drops of water up and watched them arc into the sun. "You know I did not do that."

"How did we know that you weren't going to?"

"Upbringing, partially. I had money of my own. I didn't need your father's."

"You didn't have nearly as much money as my father. Will you pass the tray, Daddy?" She took one of the lemon wedges impaled by a small red plastic sword and stirred her tea with it. The ice made a pleasant tinkling sound against the crystal. "That I know because few people do. How do we know you didn't marry him to get more?"

"Elina," her father scolded.

"Well, fortunately we don't live in the middle ages," Elina said. "Mateo and I do not need your blessing to get married. It is a luxury, not a necessity."

"Ah yes. When you're young, all you need is love," Charles Peltier said with a smirk.

"You remember what love was like, don't you, Daddy? You must remember."

Charles glanced at Phoebe. "Well, it's not like he has to remember back very far," said Phoebe, indignant. "Your father and I are not exactly dried up old prunes."

"Though we do occasionally *eat* dried up old prunes," Charles said.

"Oh Charles, why must you always make light of serious matters. We're talking about your daughter's future. Elina, Darling, we only want the best for you. That is why we have come to this very difficult decision. We just can't let you go through with this marriage. Now, we know you are an adult, and you are free to do what you please. But we are hoping you will make the right choice. Because the wrong one will inevitably ensure that there will be a very high price to pay."

ဆရဲချရဲချဆရဲချရဲချဆရဲချရဲ

The next day, Mateo convinced Elina to go to Mass with him. It didn't take much convincing, really. Elina wanted to be anywhere Mateo was.

Again, the kingdom of heaven is like a merchant searching for fine pearls," the priest read at the pulpit. *When he finds a pearl of great price, he goes and sells all that he has and buys it.*

Elina looked at Mateo, who had one arm around her. His eyes were closed and his head was slightly bowed. She knew he was somewhere alone with those words. He looked precious and vulnerable, and she knew at that moment she had found her pearl. She was willing to give up everything to be with him.

"My family will never understand," Elina told him on the drive back to his house. "They will always see you as someone who has deceived their daughter in order to siphon off millions of dollars from the family fortune."

"They have a hard time trusting me because they don't know me. Give them time."

"Time won't make any difference, Mateo. They calculate everything according to losses and gains. They see it as a no-lose proposition for you, which makes them highly suspicious."

"And what about you? What will you lose by marrying someone who loves you to the depths of his heart?"

"Thanks to them, I will lose a great deal: my family and my inheritance."

"What do you mean?"

"My father and stepmother have decided to write me out of the will and terminate my position."

"Oh, I see." Mateo looked stunned and nauseous.

"But I don't care, Mateo."

"Elina, we can't get married under those conditions."

"Look, Mateo. I didn't tell you that to make you feel bad. If it's between you and my meaningless fortune, I choose you."

"Your fortune is not the important thing, Elina. You will be giving up something far greater than money if you marry me. I cannot come between you and your family. It wouldn't be right.

I wouldn't have wanted someone to take my daughter away from me."

"You're not taking me away, Mateo. They are taking themselves away from me. They are the ones who have set it up as a choice that I have to make."

"They are not really setting up a choice. They are fully counting on you to choose them."

"And my money."

"Yes. They don't know how else to stop you from marrying me."

"There is nothing that can stop me from marrying you."

"Except me."

"Why would you do that?"

"I don't want to tear a family apart, Elina. I already know what it feels like to have a family ripped apart. You can find someone in your class. In your circle. Your parents will embrace him and you will be fully happy. Complete."

"So, you are saying that it is no longer a choice to marry you."

"That is what I am saying."

"No money. No marriage."

"That is *not* what I am saying. I am saying no family blessing, no marriage."

"So my step-mother gets to decide the fate of the rest of my life."

"Is it just your step-mother?"

"And her puppet husband. Otherwise known as my father. *My* father, who decided to choose her over me. And now, you would have me choose him over you? My allegiance to him should have ended the day he stood in front of the altar and promised his life to a woman who despised me."

"How could she despise you? I think you were probably imagining things and you both have suffered through years of misunderstandings."

"You met her. You know what I'm talking about."

"Look, Elina, I don't want you to choose between me and your family. You'll have to give up everything you love, everything you know. That's just a recipe for disaster, Elina. You will expect me to make up for all the things you are missing and I won't be able to do it and you will grow to resent me."

"No, I won't. Mateo, you're saying there's no way I can be happy with you, and I know there is no way I can be happy without you. So basically, I'm just up a creek then. There's no hope for me to find happiness."

"There's always hope to find happiness. But the person you marry, Elina, plays a big part in determining that. Don't you see the hurdles we would have to overcome? Don't you think you could find happiness with someone more suited for you?"

"Maybe I'm just a romantic, Mateo, but I don't happen to believe a person can love just anyone. I happen to love you. I didn't plan it. I didn't seek it out. But here it is, and there's not a damn thing I can do about it. And I'm not giving you up. I won't. Unless you tell me you don't love me."

He stared at her, trying to think of something to say.

"And if you do," she said, "I will call you a liar."

He hugged her into him and pressed her head into his chest. "Elina," he whispered. "You are such a beautiful lover. You love like a person with their whole life ahead of them. Me, Elina, I love like someone who has left things behind. You know, babies, they feel pain so much more than adults do. As you grow your nervous system dulls and you don't feel things so deeply, and you've had all kinds of experience with pain, so you know a little bit more about how to handle it. Adults don't cry when they skin their knees." He tipped her chin up so he could look into her eyes. "I have a feeling you still might."

"I'm tougher than most people give me credit for, Mateo. And many people have also underestimated my tenacity." She wanted to scream at him that she has indeed had experience with pain. Hadn't he been listening to the accounts of her childhood? But then she realized her losses did not come close to his.

"I don't want to underestimate you, Elina. Or offend you. It's the last thing I want to do. I just know, and I'm sure you would agree with me, that someone looking in on this from the outside would–"

"Blah, blah, blah, Mateo. I don't care about onlookers. The bottom line is I don't want to live without you. And I know you don't want to live without me. Tell me you do and I'll call you a liar."

"You are a fiercely stubborn young woman."

"Tell me you don't like that and I'll call you a liar."

"I will not tell you that. I am not a stubborn man. And I am not a liar."

"Which means?"

"You have left me with no choice."

୭୭⧓୧୨⧓୧୨⧓୧୨⧓୧୨⧓୧

Putting the wedding party together was a bit of a struggle. Elina's best friend was not supportive of the marriage because it would mean the loss of the family fortune, all for the sake of a frivolous, impetuous move that she would surely regret when reality set in. Most of her other friends were of the same mind. She did have a few friends who were not opposed to the marriage, but they were in her outer circle, and Elina felt it would have seemed strange to them to be asked to be her maid of honor. So, she chose the one person who shed tears of joy when she learned of the impending union. Raquel's hospice nurse, Samantha. Elina did not, of course, have to choose a flower girl. Raquel had made a promise, and an angel's word is good as gold.

Just before she walked down the aisle, Elina had to use the restroom. On her way, she passed by a side chapel, and there on the window sill she found a pile of red rose petals. She smiled and surmised that someone must have left a bouquet of roses there in honor of the Blessed Mother for whom the shrine was named. They must have begun to wilt and drop their petals, prompting someone in charge of maintenance to remove the vase but absentmindedly leave the petals behind. But then Elina noticed the petals were a moist velvet, vivid red as if someone had just pulled them from a freshly-blooming rose. Elina imagined, as she walked along the white runner toward her beloved Mateo, that she was walking on those red rose petals.

Although Mateo was able to convince Elina it was only right to invite her parents to the small and modest wedding, Charles and Phoebe decided to be on a private jet to Aspen. Five minutes from its estimated time of arrival, the jet crashed into a mountain. There were no survivors. Mateo and Elina received the horrifying news less than an hour after they were wed.

They postponed their honeymoon and the newlywed couple leaned hard into each other at the funeral, as the prophetic words of Mateo's pastor echoed in their heads.

"Throughout your lives together, there will be joy and comforts and there will be hardships and even tragedies that will break your hearts in two," Father O'Neil had said in his homily at the nuptial Mass. "Through all these, you must cling to each other and cling to the Lord."

Elina mourned her father's memory, more than she mourned him. She had lost him long ago to Phoebe. But she had never grieved over that loss. When she was a little girl, he was a different man. While not a perfect father, he was accessible and funny, playful and empathetic, even to a little girl's whims and heartbreaks.

When Elina was small, she loved to make beautiful things – bangly jewelry, colorful hair adornments and glittery pictures, ornamentals for her room or for her friends' rooms. One of her favorite passtimes required the careful placement of a multitude of plastic beads on spindles to create a design. The beads would then be pressed with an iron, slightly melting the plastic and fusing the beads together, so the design could be hung by a string or sewn onto a purse or backpack or canvas cap. One day, while her mother was having lunch with a friend, Elina spent over two hours on one of her creations. It was in the shape of a rose. She used red beads because she knew red was the color of love, and she very much loved her mother – more than anyone else in the world, actually. Many times more than she loved her father, though she loved him also. But she always knew her mother was the one person she could not live without. She could picture life without her father, but the picture of life without her mother was unbearable to look at. She worked hard on that rose, meticulously placing the variant shades of red beads exactly the way the directions required. So it might as well have been the end of the world when, before her father could help her fuse the design with an iron, she bumped against the table, sending a thousand beads rolling in a thousand directions. She burst into tears, sobbing at the loss of her mother's birthday present.

"Don't worry, Elina," her father told her. "I'll take you to the store to get Mommy a present. You can pick anything you want for her."

"No, this was going to be special," the girl mourned.

"We'll find something special for Mommy. Come on, let's get Annie to clean up this mess."

"No, Daddy, you don't understand. Mommy always says she likes the things I make for her best. Because they have all my love in them."

Elina refused to be consoled with the thought of picking something off the shelf -- even something costly and rare. So Elina's father got down on his hands and knees and picked up beads, collecting them in his clubby hands. Then he knelt by Elina at her child-sized table and helped her put them all back into the mold again -- one by one, whistling Classical tunes, like Julius Fucik's *Entry of the Gladiators* and Handel's *The Arrival of the Queen of Sheba*.

Elina had told Mateo this story three weeks before their wedding as they were on their way to pick out rings. She looked over at him and suddenly realized he was crying.

"You miss Raquel," she said squeezing his hand. "I'm sorry."

He wiped his face on his sleeve. He watched the road for several minutes and then said, "I don't know how I will ever feel complete again."

It was then that Elina realized that she and Mateo did not feel the same thing for each other. She felt completely complete because they were together. He did not.

ಬ⦂⦂⦂⦂⦂⦂⦂⦂⦂⦂⦂⦂⦂⦂⦂⦂⦂⦂⦂

The day Lawrence and Phoebe were laid to rest, Elina learned from the family attorney that her parents had apparently not had time to complete all the paperwork required to write her out of their will prior to their untimely deaths. The newlyweds, who had decided to use Elina's personal savings to pay off Mateo's sizable medical debts and purchase a $200,000 four-bedroom home, were now the rightful owners of a $13 billion estate.

So, they made these plans: sell the mansions in Holmby Hills, Windsor Square and Beverly Hills Flats, the Victorian on Nob Hill, the chalet in France, the villa in Spain and the summer estate in the Hamptons and move into the 7,000-square-foot "cabin" in Aspen. Buy a neighboring home for Lucy. Start a substantial college fund for their kids' future, keep a number of lucrative stocks that would support them in a typical upper middle class fashion for the rest of their lives. Give everything else away. Donate a great deal to cancer research and paying families' expenses while seeking medical care for their critically ill children, especially in impoverished nations. Donate a large percentage to alleviating hunger and financing education in the poorest countries. Elina would volunteer for various causes and enter fully into the joy of motherhood. Mateo would write books and screen plays and continue his work on the Virgin of Guadalupe from their family home in Aspen.

A few days after the De Luzes had hatched these plans, the attorney called again.

"Elina, this is David. I have some bad news."

Elina's heart skipped as her mind, for a split millisecond, in the shortest of all time spans, concluded the bad news must mean something had happened to her father. Then, she remembered it already had. There was apparently still a small measure of denial about her father's passing.

"What is it, David?"

"I'm so sorry to have to tell you this, Elina. My assistant, Jill, just informed me that she located a document that I did not know had been completed by your parents."

"What is it, David? What's going on?"

"Your inheritance, Elina. Charles and Phoebe completed the paperwork to change their will. So you will not be receiving your inheritance. I'm so sorry. I didn't know that Jill had gotten the document signed already. I should have checked with her before talking to you, Elina. I'm so sorry. I would be happy to pay you an appropriate sum of money for any emotional hardships this error might have caused."

"No, it's OK." Her hands were shaking. "It's OK, David."

"It's a shame, really, because I know your parents were just trying to protect you. They expected these remedies to be temporary and fully intended to write you back into the will after your marriage, you know, I hate to put it this way, Elina, but you know, after your marriage failed."

"So where is the estate going?"

"Various charities mostly."

"Well, that's pretty much where it would have ended up anyway," Elina said, trying to infuse a lilt into her voice. "Might as well skip the middle man."

"I must say, Elina, I was not expecting this gracious response. I've been chewed out over a hundred bucks before. But we're talking billions here. I hope Mateo handles it as well as you are."

"Mateo will handle it fine. He's had losses much greater than this." Without warning, tears flooded her eyes and she could not stop herself from breaking into a sob.

"Elina, I'm so sorry. Really. I can't tell you how much I wish all of this would never have happened. I'll check in on you in a few days. If you need anything, just call, OK kid? Just call."

She managed to croak an "OK" out of her tightened throat and hung up.

Even though Elina had lived a life luxurious beyond imagining, she had never accumulated much wealth. She didn't have to. There was always an endless supply of money available through her family. Not much was in her name. Not even the cars she drove, which she chose anew every month or so by entering her father's two story garage and picking one of the three dozen sets of keys out of the safe.

Elina remembered her large collection of ridiculously high-priced belongings, sitting in the tudor revival. That stuff would fetch a fortune at auction. Her perfume collection alone might support her family for a year. Then she remembered that all of those belongings were lost to her as well. Elina had tried to return to the house shortly after her parents' funeral and found the locks had been changed. Phoebe was highly efficient and had thought of every last detail.

She gave the rest of her tears permission to flow into a teal sateen throw pillow, hoping to have cried them all out by the time Mateo returned from Mass. He had gone to daily Mass for seventeen years, employment schedule permitting. Elina had promised Mateo she would occasionally go with him. They talked of it that first night after the funerals as they lay together watching the leaf shadows dance on the ceiling. Naked and entwined under a blanket after having made love for the very first time, they planned their newly revised future, which at that moment in their understanding of reality, included complete financial security. What that meant to them was that, unlike most couples who have to go their separate ways each morning and spend their day in toil and strain, Mateo and Elina would always have the luxury of being together. Now, Elina wondered as she wept, how she would tell Mateo that their future had been revised once more.

Mateo took it as Elina expected.

"Well," he said, "it was never ours to keep. We come into this world with nothing, not even a pair of pants. And the great many of us die in a hospital -- again without any pants."

The news was easier on Mateo because he had not lost anything. He'd only lost the idea of it. Elina knew exactly what she was losing, though she could not know what its absence would mean.

৪৩৵৻৫৵৻৪৩৵৻৫৵৻৪৩৵৻৫৵৻৪৩৵৻৫৵৻৪৩৵৻৫৵৻৪৩

Mateo and Elina had postponed their honeymoon -- a road trip to San Francisco -- until their three-month anniversary. But when the time arrived, a honeymoon just didn't seem practical with a baby in the house. And they couldn't have cared less. They were completely consumed with love for that precious gift, whom they named Dante, which means "everlasting and enduring."

Love was their only treasure.

In lieu of a honeymoon, Lucy watched the baby, while Mateo drove Elina to the top of a cliff overlooking the ocean. He turned off the ignition, rolled down the windows, cued up the John Cohen and invited his bride outside for a slow dance under the overcast sky. Their feet shifted in the dirt as the dark sea yawned wide in the distance. And aside from these few details, they were unaware of everything but the warmth of the other's breath on their necks and the unbridled, unstoppable, nonnegotiable force of a familiar love song.

Baby, I know life with me
Is not exactly what you might see
On the pages of Modern Bride
Who could predict that you and I
Would find a love to deepen any sea
Would find a love to make demons flee
Some days fly like ravens
Some days fly like doves
Everyday I'm flying
Deeper into your love
Maybe it hasn't always been this way

148

But it will surely always be
No force in this world
Could come between you and me

80⅗℃⅗80⅗℃⅗80⅗℃⅗80⅗℃⅗80⅗℃⅗

"Whoa, whoa, wait a minute," Larry Crenshaw said. "A baby? What baby?"

"The baby she spoke of to you. Your baby, Mr. Crenshaw."

"What? You said she took care of that."

"Well, she fully intended to have an abortion. But something came up."

"Something came up?"

"Well, she first rescheduled the appointment to find the owner of that shoe. Then, she was on her way to the abortionist when she got a call from Lucy, telling her that Raquel was asking for her." The girl was headed for emergency surgery and wanted to see Elina before she went under. So, Elina made a U-turn."

"And never rescheduled?"

"Rescheduled twice."

Crenshaw drew his eyebrows together.

"When it was clear that Raquel was going to pull through after the surgery, Elina made another appointment."

On the morning of the procedure, before she could get out the door, one of the workers who was soldering something in the room being designed for Raquel started a small house fire. When the firefighters left, Elina rescheduled the appointment for the following week. On that morning, Lucy called to tell her the doctor approved Raquel's discharge, so she would be able to come stay with Elina any time Elina could arrange it. She told Lucy she had to take care of a small health issue and that Raquel and Lucy could come stay with her in a few days. She stopped by to look at Raquel's new room before leaving the house. She marveled at what a great job the designer had done. She couldn't wait for Raquel to see it. She had an uneasy feeling about putting off Raquel's discharge. She wanted so badly for Raquel to see

149

the beautiful room that had been designed for her and to begin fulfilling whatever desires she could squeeze in before death claimed her. A few days' delay may be nothing for someone with a life span of 82 years. But Raquel had only an eye's blink left. One day may be twenty percent of her remaining life. Or fifty. But Elina had to keep her appointment. Taking care of this problem was not going to get any easier with another delay. Besides, there would be no uncomplicated way to have it done once Raquel and Lucy moved in. So, zipping along the freeway in her father's Lamborghini, Elina found herself torn between helping a dying child and causing the death of another. Not that she would have put it in those terms.

"So, she turned the car around," Crenshaw guessed.

"No. She kept driving."

She checked in at the abortionist, put on the gown and prepped. The ultrasound technician came in to verify how far along the pregnancy was. Elina asked to see the ultrasound. The tech told her there wasn't a lot of time before the doctor was coming in and they needed to move things along, but Elina sensed the resistance was meant more to hide something than it was to keep an efficient schedule.

"I would really like to see it," Elina said. "I'll pay extra for the time it takes."

"Oh, it's not a matter of money," the technician said. "It's just office policy. We have to stay on schedule for the sake of all our patients."

"Well," Elina said, "I could free up your schedule for you. There are a number of other places that perform the same services."

"True," she said. "But I doubt you could get an appointment today. And you really can't afford to let any more time go by. You have cancelled several times already, haven't you?"

"How do you know that?"

A momentary look of something akin to panic passed over the woman's face and then she glanced at the manila folder next to the ultrasound screen. "It's in your file," she said. "That's all. I didn't mean to offend or pass any judgments."

"Can I see my file?" Elina sat up and stretched out her hand.

"Listen," the woman said, glancing at her watch. "I think we have a little bit of time. Here, if you want to see the ultrasound, just lay back down, I'll just swing the screen towards you."

Elina reclined again and the tech returned the wand to her belly.

Elina was expecting to see a nondescript blob of latent potential, the ingredients for a human person. But it was clearly something else. A perfectly shaped profile -- a large eye, the hint of a mouth, big belly, a tiny butt, feet and fingers. All limbs in motion, one or two occasionally springing off the spongy outer contours of this inner world, perhaps subconsciously practicing in frenetic anticipation of something larger awaiting. And then, could that be what Elina thought it was?

"OK, I think we got a good image," the tech said, removing the wand.

"Wait, no," Elina said. "I want to see it again."

"Ms. Peltier, we really do have to proceed in order to keep our schedule." She turned the screen away. "There are other women waiting."

"Just thirty seconds more," Elina said, getting up and pulling the screen back.

The tech sighed. "OK, real quick."

The fetus had settled, thumb in the mouth. A few seconds later, the thumb was released again and the movements resumed. And this time, there was no question. Elina was carrying a boy.

Another tiny, whole human being, living within her.

At that moment, Elina found herself wondering if fetuses ever cry. No, she reasoned. There is no need to cry in the womb. All desires are taken care of ahead of even knowing they exist. Food, warmth, the comfort of closeness to another human being -- delivered automatically by the female body.

The feeling of being with her own mother, a feeling that used to return to her often, but had faded over the years, came to her now. That oneness with another human being who wants nothing else but to press you into her life-sustaining embrace in that still, steady, immovable moment in time. The baby within Elina maybe felt that already, at peace and trusting, completely unaware that something could destroy it, that something wanted to.

"OK," Elina said. "I've seen enough." She got off the table, holding the back of her gown shut.

"Oh, you're fine here," the tech said. "You can just lie back down and relax. The doctor will come to you."

"No, he won't," Elina said grabbing her clothes. "I have somewhere else I need to be."

"You don't want to put this off any longer, Honey. It doesn't get any easier as time goes on."

"Oh, don't worry. I'm not going to make anybody's job any harder. I won't be back."

"Well, if you change your mind, just know you always have a choice–"

"A choice, yes. That's what you offer here, and you do it very well. But it is not the right choice for me." She laid her hand on her belly. "And it is clearly not the best choice for him."

11

Half a Million Tortillas

"So," said Larry Crenshaw. "You want me to tell you that I believe that I'm your father."

"Yes. You are my father."

"You would like me to believe that your mother suffered and let her son suffer through poverty, knowing full well she could have gotten support from me, and never herself decided to inform me that I have a son?"

"We didn't suffer through poverty. We had what we needed. Sometimes we even had a little extra. But yes, that's the kind of woman my mother was. She would not have come after you for your money. I know many people would have, but not my mother, though I will have to tell you, living without excess was not exactly easy for her."

For starters – and this is not an exaggeration – she had never cleaned anything in her life. Not floors, nor toilets, nor clothes, nor cars. Throughout her life, she was responsible for washing only one thing – herself. And that she was responsible for only because it would have been awkward to hire that done. People who have cleaned something at some point in their existence seem to overlook the fact that it is a learned skill. There most certainly is a wrong way of cleaning.

So one day Elina came to Lucy and asked her to teach her how to take care of a home. Lucy had to start with the absolute fundamentals.

"Never mix ammonia with bleach, Mija, or you will pass out."

"Put the toilet bowl cleaner in first and let it soak while you're doing the rest of the bathroom."

"Always check a man's pockets for pens before putting his clothes in the washing machine."

In Lucy's family, the females knew all of this by the time they were nine. Here Elina was close to thirty years old and hearing it all for the first time. Amazingly, she was a pretty quick study. There was one thing, however, she never got right, even until the day she died. Elina was intimidated by few things. But the combination of soap scum and hard water deposits was among them. So Dante and his sister Sylvie grew up with dirty showers.

But they ate well. Elina spent a great deal of time at Lucy's elbow, learning all she could about cooking. Of course, she had to learn how to make those beans. But also, tortillas. When Lucy made tortillas, her hands looked like the dough itself. There were parts of them, around the long outer edges of her fingers, that looked cracked, like the dough looks when there's too much flour and not enough water. Elina only knew this because Lucy had shown her what it looks like when dough needs more water.

"How many do you make for one meal?" Elina asked, propping her elbows on the counter. Lucy pressed a ball of dough into Elina's palm. It felt soft and warm and the smell of flour offered an inexplicable sort of comfort.

"Press it into a circle, Mija. Like this." She put it on the floured counter and pressed with the heel of her hand. "To feed my family, I always made a dozen."

"At each meal?"

"Uh-huh."

"So thirty-six a day?"

"Well, we didn't have tortillas at every meal. Usually not for breakfast. We would have pan dulce and some scrambled eggs."

"So twenty-four a day?"

"Yeah. Probably."

"That's almost 9,000 a year."

"Ah, really?"

"Uh-huh."

"You are good at math, Mija. How did you figure that out so fast?"

"I just happen to know that's how many hours are in a year. And you were married almost fifty years ago, right?"

"Yes."

"So since you were married, you have made something like 450,000 tortillas."

"That's crazy. That can't be true."

"Es la verdad, Lucy."

"Really?"

"Yes."

"No wonder I am exhausted."

"Here, let me help." She took another ball of dough and pressed it like Lucy had shown her. "Why don't you just buy them?"

"Oh, because there is nothing like a homemade flour tortilla. The rich, they have their caviar and whatever other fancy foods. But none of it can even come close to this, Mija." She smashed the small disc of dough onto the floured board, bore down on it a number of times and held the perfect circle up before Elina's eyes. "This here can make you feel rich." She peeked out from behind it with a large, almost mischievous grin, put the circle back on the board and reached past Elina for the rolling pin. "Eat a tortilla out of a plastic bag and you are poor again."

The clicking of the rolling pin returning again and again to the start of the circle made Elina think of one rainy afternoon with her mother in the kitchen, rolling out (separately) the pink, yellow and orange fondant and turning it into gerber daisies with a cookie cutter. Once, Elina asked her mother, what exactly is fondant?

"Edible play dough," she said, licking her long slender fingers. "That's the best way I can describe it, sweet Elina." She plopped a daisy onto a white-iced three-tier cake. "Isn't it wonderful?"

The cake was for Elina's tenth birthday. She and her mother had talked about ordering a cake from the La Patisserie Artistique or having the live-in pastry chef make a three-dimensional, 12-layer juke box. But Elina's mother persuaded her it would be fun to make her own cake. It didn't take much persuading, really. What little girl does not like to mess around with edible play dough?

ಬಃ)€(ಞ)€(ಞ)€(ಞ)€(ಞ)€(ಞ

As much as Elina and Mateo loved each other, there was, on occasion, a disconnect. It always took them by surprise, as much as it shouldn't have. Like the first time they ate watermelon together.

"Remember seeing how far you could grind a watermelon down to the green when you were a kid?" Mateo asked, holding a half circle of well-gnawed rind up like a trophy. There were only hints of pink in three or four small places.

"No. I always thought you weren't supposed to eat the white part." Elina had cut the red flesh of the melon into small cubes and was eating them slowly and individually with a fork.

"Never hurt us." Mateo said, scraping his teeth over the final patches of pink.

"I never liked the part next to the rind. The middle is the best. We used to take watermelons to the beach. We'd each get our own -- my mom and daddy and me. We'd sit there and eat out of them with a spoon. Just the very center, and heave the rest into the ocean to see how far we could throw them and if they would come back. Watermelon always tasted best at the beach. Salty and sweet."

"You put salt on your watermelon?"

"Oh, yes. But only at the beach, for some reason."

"We put Tajin."

"Tajin? What's that?"

"You've never had Tajin? It's a chili seasoning. I'd save up all week to buy something at the fruit stand on Friday's after school – a half of an orange or a wedge of melon. With Tajin."

Mateo had learned to waste not a single crumb or drop or shred or morsel. Elina had, all her life, thrown things away. Even good things. Good things that were just too plentiful. But marrying Mateo would slowly change her and eventually she too learned not to waste. Especially after Mateo died. There was no excess of anything. There was only one thing Dante ever remembers being wasted at his house.

Every morning, Elina brewed a full pot of coffee. She and Mateo would finish it by the time they left for work. After he died, she still brewed a full pot of coffee. She would have a cup or two and then pour out the rest. She could have adjusted the number of scoops and the amount of water and brewed only as much as she would drink. But she refused. For the three decades she lived without him, she brewed a full pot of coffee.

"I should have made less," she would say as she poured the coffee down the drain. "Well, next time."

Occasionally, while she was scooping the coffee into the filter, she would say, "I should probably make a small pot today, but you never know who might drop over."

No one ever did.

"How did your father die?" Larry Crenshaw asked.

"He had finally gotten back to the job he loved -- researching the Codex Escalada in hopes of proving its authenticity as it relates to the history of Our Lady of Guadalupe."

He was on his first trip back to Mexico after receiving new grant money. He had called Elina when he landed in Mexico City to tell her how much he already missed her.

"I am grateful for the opportunity to pursue this work, but it stinks being away from you and the kids."

"I wish you were here, Mateo. You would not believe the kind of day I've had. The shower drain got clogged and I had to go at it myself. You would not believe what I pulled out of there, Mateo. I wasn't sure whether to call haz-mat or animal control. I could swear I saw it breathing. I considered just tying it up in a plastic bag and throwing it in the trash, but then I wondered if the ASPCA would come after me for animal cruelty."

"Oh, Elina," he said, chuckling. "When I get home, I will get those pipes taken care of. We've got some major plumbing issues in that house."

"It's OK, Mateo, your very capable wife fixed it already."

"Well, it's going to take a little more than pulling a clog of hair out of the drain, Elina, my love. Every home's plumbing is like a football team. You've got your quarterback that passes the ball to the receiver. That's the supply line. Then you've got the receiver, who gets the ball and takes it to the end zone. That's the hot and cold water supply pipes. Then, you've got your guard. That's the waste vent pipe. It keeps the other team from tackling the quarterback. Entiendes, mi vida?"

"Mateo?"

"Si, mi vida?"

"Why do men, to explain concepts that women don't understand, always use football, another thing women don't understand?"

"Because men aren't smart enough to come up with any fashion analogies, my love."

"I miss you, Mateo. Hurry home."

Elina was peeling potatoes the next day when the phone rang, causing her to jump and drop one into a bowl of water. The ringing phone didn't usually startle her, but she had been deep in thought about what kind of welcome they would give Mateo on his return. She took a few deep breaths to steady her adrenalin before she picked up the phone. Dante, who had just come in from a game of stickball to pester his mother for a pre-dinner snack, heard her say, "What do you mean? What do you mean?"

from the front hallway as he kicked off his shoes. And then her frantic, "No. No. No!"

She dropped the phone and crumpled to the ground, sobbing.

Dante grabbed the phone and hung it up because he didn't know what other action to take. Then he bent down with his mother and begged her to tell him what was wrong. But he already knew, or believed that he did, and began to sob. "Papa, Papa, Papa, oh, Daddy."

Elina grabbed onto her son and squeezed him so tight, he couldn't breathe. Or was it the grief suffocating him? He couldn't tell, and it didn't matter because he didn't care about breath anyway. The phone rang again and continued to ring as the two wept together.

Mateo was killed when the Cessna, taking his team to a remote area of indigenous peoples who speak the Nahuan language, crashed into a cattle ranch in Central Mexico.

Elina remembered his words to her, that night they danced on the cliff overlooking the sea.

"I don't want a day to go by when you don't feel my love. I mean really feel it. We only have a certain number of days here on Earth together. I don't want to waste any of them."

Father Dante paused to read Larry Crenshaw's face. He saw nothing there.

"My father certainly did not waste a day, Mr. Crenshaw. There were wasted moments, yes, as in any marriage, when two people let their disagreements turn to anger. But never a wasted day. No, a sunset rarely ever saw their ire. Those two were truly made for each other. And for me. And my sister."

"Father De Luz, what is it you want from me?"

"Just for you to know the truth."

"But don't you see that anyone could spin a tale like this? And the motive would not be hard to determine. I am a very wealthy man."

"I am not looking for an inheritance. I have, in the silence of my own soul, taken a vow of poverty. Your money would be worthless to me. So now, what would my motive be?"

"My money would not be worthless to your favorite charity. Think of the good it could do."

"I can assure you. I am no Robin Hood."

"OK, then. What do you want from me?"

"I'm not sure I want anything from you."

"Then why are you here?"

"Maybe I'd like to give you something."

"What would you want to give me?"

"A son."

Crenshaw rubbed his temples.

"It's something money can't buy. And it's free."

"So is a load of crap."

"Can I convince you to take a paternity test?"

"I'm a busy man, Father."

"You are semi-retired. Surely, you could work in a three-second saliva swab. What do you have to lose? If it's negative, you've proven me wrong and you'll never have to deal with me again. If it's positive, you've gained a son."

"You're assuming my life has been unfulfilling before you walked into it. I've been quite happy, actually."

"So you don't want a son."

"Never given it much thought."

"Well, now that you've thought about it, what do you think?"

"I guess it would depend on the type of son."

"What type would you want?"

"I don't know. Maybe one that can tell a condensed version of his family history. One that doesn't take up my time with futile attempts at persuading me to get unnecessary medical tests."

"OK, then. I will find another way. I will find some way to prove it to you. Who I am. And who you are."

"Best of luck to you, Father. Let me know what you come up with."

"Please, Mr. Crenshaw. How else could I have known all of this? All the history of your relationship with my mother? Who else besides her could have written that letter?"

"She could have told many people that story. She could have even told it to a priest on her deathbed. And perhaps even her son who is a priest. But that doesn't make him my son. The two of them could have set up an elaborate scheme before she died. Or she may just suppose that her son is mine. But who knows whose baby it really was. Maybe even someone from that ridiculous dating service. Maybe even a limo driver. Maybe even the garbage collector."

Father Dante felt a rush of blood enter his face and neck. He was not terribly familiar with this emotion as it took a great deal to anger him. He was so much like Mateo in temperament. But he knew anger would do nothing but forge a larger chasm between him and Lawrence Crenshaw. So he swallowed hard and drew a long stream of oxygen into his lungs.

"You can say such hostile things against a woman with which you once shared your bed?"

"I shared my bed with a lot of women. None of them were paragons of virtue, I can assure you. I am quite certain your mother was not either."

Now the blood that had rushed to his face began to boil. Father Dante wanted nothing more than to storm out of that office and never return. Why was he wasting so much time and energy on this one soul? He could save forty others. And at that moment, he came to understand Jesus' directive to shake the dust from your feet.

"I'm sorry, Father. I have offended you. But you know how diabolical people can be. Especially when there are large sums of money involved."

"I am a priest, Mr. Crenshaw. I have a pastor to answer to. And a bishop. And Rome. There is a line of accountability. Just like in your line of work."

"And there haven't been priests who have left the priesthood when something better comes along? I dare say priests are men too, subject to the same desires as the rest of us -- women, money, power."

"There is nothing better, Mr. Crenshaw. I can assure you I am not interested in any other life than the one God has called me to."

"Ah, a noble knight you are."

"Can we meet again next week? Maybe Monday? At the same time and place?"

"And spin our wheels again?"

"God willing, I will have something more to tell you. Something that will convince you."

"Why don't you just call me when you have something for certain."

"It's nearly impossible to get in touch with you. Can't we say Monday at 9:30?"

"You are that sure of yourself?"

"I am sure of the truth. As far as proving it, that will take a miracle. But I have seen quite a few of those in my life."

Crenshaw just stared.

"How about you? Have you seen any miracles?"

"Well, if the Elina I knew raised a son who is a priest, maybe I have. The Elina Peltier I knew was not the least bit interested in matters of faith, unless you consider high fashion a religion."

"Funny what authentic love can do. And a really horrible headache."

"I'm sure there's a story behind that."

"You've come to know me well, Mr. Crenshaw."

"OK. I'll bite."

"O.K. Well, on the eve of my father's 40th birthday, he suffered an excruciatingly intense thunderclap headache that had him writhing in pain on an emergency room gurney."

The doctor's first guess was brain aneurism. Tears rolled down Elina's cheeks as she held Mateo's hand, waiting for the CT results. While on what they both thought was his death bed,

Mateo petitioned Elina to fulfill his role as spiritual mentor to their children. That would require her to learn the Faith in some detail. It wasn't beyond the realm of possibility that such an investigation would change her, maybe even bring her to the Baptismal font. Once one sets one's mind to studying Christian history and theological truth, the ascent to Faith often comes quite naturally. This is what he was asking of her. To explore. To study intently. And in his heart of hearts, if he could have been so bold to ask such a thing, he would have begged her conversion. But he didn't. Only God can ask that of a soul, so Mateo left it to Him.

The suspected aneurism turned out to be a strange brand of migraine. But Elina never forgot her promise. To Mateo, she promised to make sure the children had all their religious training. To herself, she promised to investigate and try to understand the faith that had formed the man she loved, the man she most admired in all her life. So, when he finally did leave this world, for reasons completely unrelated to a headache, she made good on both promises.

"And that's how my mother eventually became Catholic."

"I guess anything can happen," Crenshaw said. "It's nothing I would have predicted."

"People change. Particularly when a child enters their lives."

"Wouldn't know about that."

"Maybe you'll find out some day. Maybe even Monday."

12

Knitting

Whenever anyone asked about her son's vocation, Elina liked to tell stories of the uncommon wisdom he possessed in his youth. One of those stories was about how she found her 10-year-old boy praying one day in the hallway outside his bedroom. His two friends were in his room, having a grand time mocking a boy from school. They claimed to dislike the boy because his hair was always greasy, which means, they surmised, he must rarely take a shower. This was reason enough to find him deserving of scorn, but if there hadn't been that, any other number of victims with any number of "imperfections" would have sufficed – too skinny, too fat, too short, too tall, glasses too thick, hair too short, nose too big, eyes too beady, throat too bulgy, voice too high, freckles too numerous, facial hair too early, elbows too boney, legs too hairy. Those boys needed someone to pick on, and because the boy with the greasy hair was the shy, socially-awkward type, he would be safe. He would not retaliate and neither would his friends because he had none.

When the topic of "Oscar the Greaseball" came up, Dante told the boys he had to go to the bathroom and stepped into the

164

hallway to pray. He prayed for Oscar to be unscathed by the boys' loathing. He prayed for his friends to learn compassion.

Elina found him in the hallway, sat down next to him and put her arm around him.

"You know, when I was a kid, there was this boy that everyone made fun of. He had a long, wide face, droopier on one side than the other. He had leg braces to help him walk, but I still couldn't see how he could do it because his toes were so turned in toward each other, and each step was so unstable and awkward and precarious looking, it always seemed like he was going to go crashing to the ground. And he flailed his arms when he walked. It was like his elbows had an invisible cord between them, holding them back behind him, adding to his imbalance. But he stayed upright. And he just kept walking, even as kids hurled insults at him or ignored him or greeted him without affection with one word – his last name, Scalera. I can't remember ever saying one word to him, but if I had to do it over again, I would have made a point of becoming friends with Jim Scalera. I know my life would have been richer."

"You want me to be Oscar's friend, don't you?"

"You don't want to?"

"All the other kids will start making fun of me if I hang out with him."

"You know, Dante, all you really need in this world is one true friend. Oscar just might be that. I know for certain the boys on the other side of that door are not true friend material. They just don't have it in them. Oscar might not either. But you never know until you get to know him. I think you know all you need to know about Steve and James."

"But I'm praying for them to change."

"And they just might. Meantime, I think Oscar probably needs a friend."

Father Dante sure needed one right now. Father Francis was a wonderful and wise adviser, but he didn't know Dante through and through. They shared only a short history together. Father

Dante picked up the phone.

"Hey, Oscar, whatcha doin'?"

"Father Dante, how are you, my old friend?"

"I've had better days."

"Are you still missing your Mama?"

"Yeah. I will miss her until the day I die."

"She was such a great lady, Dante."

Oscar had no idea, really. There were few things Dante hadn't told Oscar, but he never did tell him why Dante sought his friendship in the fifth grade. Oscar grew out of his greasy hair and lax hygiene and became actually quite handsome in his young adulthood. But he never let it go to his head. He was the sensitive type, who would smile and blush when a girl paid him any attention.

"Oscar, I really need your prayers."

"For what they are worth, my friend, you got 'em. But don't you have a lot of holy people you could ask for prayers?"

"None of them love me quite as much as you do, man."

"Dante, what's up? I can hear something in your voice."

"I'm just a little unsteady right now, Oscar. I'm feeling – like I've never felt before. I'm not sure what's going on."

"Whoa."

"I know. People usually come to me for answers. And I have to say, I ain't got none of those right now."

"Uh-oh. Must be bad. Your grammar is going. Hey, you wanna go have a beer tonight?"

Dante let out a slight chuckle. "No, buddy. That won't help. Just pray. Whenever you think of me, say a prayer. Or better yet, whenever you think of beer, say a prayer for me. And give my love to Elizabeth and the kids."

Father Dante took the keys off the hook and made the short walk across the courtyard, through the silent rose garden and down the driveway to the rectory mailbox. He needed a distraction and a way to unwind. So he was hoping there would be a package from his supplier. Father Dante had only one addiction, but it was a formidable one. He had been without it for almost a week now. His friend from seminary, Father Cecil, who now lives in Rome, promised to send a shipment two weeks ago. He was usually really good about following through. But there was no telling how long the international mail would take. Father Dante inserted the key and turned, bracing himself mentally for an empty mailbox or one stuffed with junk mail. Yes! There it was. A padded envelope. He grabbed it out and felt that there was a box inside. No, two boxes. He ripped into it, leaving the rest of the mail inside the mailbox, which was still hanging open, his keys dangling from the lock. Yes, Father Cecil, God bless him. He had sent two boxes of Pocket Coffee! Only the Italians could have thought of this – a mini-shot of espresso encased in a small dark chocolate vessel, wrapped in a dark brown square of paper with a bright red stripe and gold lettering. Pocket Coffee was Father Dante's daily treat, around 2 or 3 p.m. If he were to be honest, he would tell you it is his favorite food, and on some days he began thinking about it as early as 11 a.m. It is a brilliant marriage of the two most delicious flavors in the world. It requires no preparation, no utensils and not even a napkin, in most cases. It can be consumed while standing, sitting, lying down, walking, jogging, running, skipping or hopping. Whoever invented it ought to receive the Nobel Peace Prize. And that might not be such a stretch ever since Al Gore.

Father Dante sat on a bench in the courtyard, opened a box of Pocket Coffee and slid one out. He was about to unwrap it when Lawrence Crenshaw entered his mind. Not like Lawrence Crenshaw ever really left his mind of late. But at that moment, the obstinate old man took front and center and made it impossible for Father Dante to proceed with his unwrapping. The priest just stared at the sweet morsel of caffeinated confection and thought, "Prayer hasn't been enough. This will require fasting." So he decided to give up Pocket Coffee until Lawrence Crenshaw submits to a paternity test. Immediately, he questioned his own judgment in making such a sacrifice. It was a possibility that Lawrence Crenshaw would die without a sure knowledge that he has a son, and Father Dante would never have Pocket Coffee again.

That afternoon Father Dante e-mailed Father Cecil to thank him for the shipment and ask him to hold off on sending any more, until further notice.

He wrote back instantly. "Why? Did you get a bad batch? Was the coffee crystallized? Maybe it sat too long. Or maybe the weather conditions while in route were not favorable."

"No, no, they are fine," Father Dante replied. "I'm just making a little sacrifice."

"Let me know when I can send more," was the reply. "Praying."

Father Dante sat back in his chair and closed his eyes. Lupita hummed an unintelligible tune as she ran a feather duster along Father Dante's bookshelves.

"Lupita," he said when she had finally gotten to the end of a verse. "Would you offer up prayers for a special intention?"

"Yes, Father." She ceased her dusting for a few seconds, smiled and then resumed.

Father Dante had tried to convince Father Francis that they did not need a housekeeper.

"I am perfectly capable of running a brush around the rim of a toilet," he told the elder priest.

But Father Francis over-ruled Father Dante on the basis of age and wisdom. Plus, he advanced three very solid arguments. First off, the priests were far too busy with their priestly duties to have any spare time left to keep a tidy home and cook for themselves. Second, Lupita needed the income. She was a single mom of seven children, aged 9 through 19. Third, it was beneficial – maybe even necessary – for the well-being of Lupita's soul to be at the rectory. He was not at liberty to elaborate, he told Father Dante, but he would have to be trusted on this. Father Dante had heard Lupita's confessions on a number of occasions and could not guess what Father Francis might be referring to. He never even liked to assign her a penance, since washing Father Francis' socks should have been enough. He never gave her more than three Hail Marys.

Father Dante finally saw it Father Francis's way, even though he had inherited his mother's disdain for the idea of someone else cleaning up your dirt.

One year, Mateo thought he had come up with the perfect Christmas present for Elina. He sold his guitar to buy her maid service, enough for at least one thorough, deep, spring cleaning. Cleaning was never one of her fortes. Learning how to clean must be like a language, best learned at an early age – difficult to master as an adult. Not only was Elina never taught, she never even had a chance to learn it by immersion. No one in her family spoke that language. She never witnessed her mother cleaning a single thing – not even her own plate from the dinner table. Well, there was that one time Joan Peltier stepped in a wad of green apple bubble gum and had to take a tissue and pluck it off the sole of her chocolate brown Gucci crocodile-skin boots, while riding in the back of a limousine. But other than that one solitary instance, Elina's mother never removed, restored, shined, polished, scrubbed, scoured, sponged, swabbed, mopped, cleansed, washed, wiped or rinsed a single thing. So Elina was completely incompetent in the area of basic life skills when she married Mateo. If it wasn't for Lucy taking her under her wing, Elina's life would have been a wreck.

Mateo had no way of knowing how sensitive Elina was about her incompetence because he had never held the ability to remove rust deposits from a grout line in particularly high esteem. Probably because he never even took notice of rust stains. So, after giving her the gift of maid service, it was most surprising to come home early from work one day and find an exhausted wife who had spent the morning on her hands and knees, on ladders, in corners, on ledges, trying to rid her home of years of shameful build-up.

"What are you doing?" he asked, standing over her as she scrubbed the tracks of the arcadia door with an old toothbrush. "I thought we were going to hire someone to do the cleaning this month."

"I had someone come give me an estimate today," Elina said, still scrubbing with one hand and wiping the straggle of hair that had stuck to her forehead with the back of her other rubber glove. "She basically told me our house ought to be condemned."

"What? It's not that bad. What is she talking about?"

"Then why are we getting someone to clean it?"

"Well, so we don't have to do it for once."

She stopped scrubbing and looked up into his face.

"Apparently, we don't do it, Mateo. Ever. The woman was horrified."

"Oh, now, my love, that can't be true."

"I almost had to get smelling salts to revive her, Mateo. She was in shock. She ran her finger over places I've never even thought to clean. And she curled her lip. She said she had no idea the house would be that neglected and in need of such deep cleaning. And that she would have to charge us quite a bit more than she quoted on the phone. All the while, bragging about her ability to clean in a way that all woman should, but most women can't. And you know what I've been doing all day? Besides scrubbing things with toothbrushes? I have been trying to convince myself, that, although I have never cleaned a baseboard in my life, I am still a good person, a loving mother and a devoted wife." Elina went back to work, as if somebody's life depended on the removal of more than two decades of black grime from the door frame.

Mateo grabbed a nearby rag, sat down next to Elina and began to wipe along with her, as if he too now cared that the actual silver-toned track that had served thousands of door openings and shuttings had not been visible, beneath the years of dirt, to any human being since 1967.

"Well, what was she expecting?" Mateo groused. "An already clean house? Why would we be calling a cleaning lady to clean an already clean house? Our dirt should make her happy. It's job security. What is wrong with her? A cleaning lady that doesn't like dirt. Now I've heard everything."

"She's neurotic or something, Mateo. Our dirt is too much for a neurotic housekeeper."

Mateo placed his hand on top of Elina's rubber glove, halting its fanatical scouring. He looked into her eyes and smiled. "What are we doing, Elina? Don't we have better ways to spend our energy?"

She sighed and smiled back at him. "You think?"

He took the rubber glove off her hand and kissed it. Then he got to his feet, staggering a bit, still holding her hand in his. "Come on," he said, pulling her to her feet. He picked her up, like a groom picks up a bride, and carried her down the hall.

She decided, as they lay entwined together under a sheet in the gray hue of a cloudy spring afternoon, that the dust bunnies could wait. Or even multiply for all she cared.

"Lupita," Father Dante said, as the last bookshelf had been dusted. "Do you like coffee? Here, take these home and enjoy them."

৺⅜ⱥ⅜৺⅜ⱥ⅜৺⅜ⱥ⅜৺⅜ⱥ⅜৺⅜ⱥ

Father Dante awoke to a knock on his bedroom door. The yellow brightness of the room was unfamiliar to him. He couldn't remember the last time he had slept this late.

"Father Dante, are you all right?"

"Oh, yes, Father Francis," he hollered, scratching his head with both hands. "I'm getting up."

"Join me for breakfast. Mrs. Jacowitz brought sausage casserole."

"God bless her. Is there coffee?"

"It's brewing."

Father Dante had decided not to set his alarm. It was Saturday and Father Francis was scheduled to say morning Mass. He looked at the clock. "Nine-fifteen," he muttered, as he pulled his sock on. Even though he had slept in, he felt more tired than usual.

He found Father Francis in the kitchen, sitting at the table with a cup of coffee, reading the newspaper.

"How did Mass go?" Father Dante asked, standing at the counter pouring himself a cup.

"Beautiful." He sipped his coffee. "Are you not feeling well?"

"I just needed to catch up on my sleep." He sat down opposite Father Francis and stared into the pan of casserole waiting in the middle of the table. "I've been a bit-. I don't know."

"Troubled?"

"No, not troubled." He cut into the casserole and dished out a piece for each of them.

"Not troubled?"

Father Dante passed Father Francis a plate.

"Thank you."

"You're welcome." Father Dante tasted the casserole, with eyes closed so the sense of sight did not distract from the sense of taste. "Wow that's good. God bless Mrs. Jacowitz."

"God bless Mrs. Jacowitz."

"All my life," the younger priest's words pressed past the casserole, "I was raised with the certain knowledge that my life has some deep purpose. Never have I ever questioned that. And that is what has gotten me out of bed every morning."

"And now, it requires Mrs. Jacowitz's casserole. What has changed?"

Father Dante took another bite. "Now I don't know what that purpose is."

"That letter your mother dictated to me has thrown you for a loop. Why? You don't expect me to believe that a change in your lineage changes your purpose."

"No. It's not that. It's just that I can't reach him."

"Give him time. You are unplanned."

"And unwanted I suppose. But sorely needed."

"A wise man once said: Every man needs a son. If he's the only male in the house, there's no one else to blame for his bad aim in the bathroom."

"Beautiful, Father. Profound."

"Yes, yes, Father."

"I know that's probably why you keep me around."

"Partly, yes. And also because you are a damn good priest."

"Not so sure about that. Lawrence Crenshaw is my own flesh and blood, Father Francis, and I can't reach him. I walk down the street and strangers whose presence would make the hair stand up on the back of your neck will give me a nod of respect because I am wearing this strip of fabric around my neck that represents something that they probably don't even believe in. But they know I believe in it and have given my life for it, and that's a concept they understand. So they will listen to me. But my own flesh and blood, he will not listen."

"The concept of giving his life for something does nothing to move him because he has never loved anything that much."

"That is my fear for him. That he has never loved. Why can't I reach him, Father? What am I doing wrong?"

"You mean as a Father or as a son?"

"Both, I suppose."

"Does a woman stop knitting because her yarn is not an afghan? She keeps working, stitch by stitch. If she changes her method because she thinks herself a failure for not already completing the afghan, she will end up with a sorry mess of mismatched stitches."

"It just seems so futile. I have lost hope that he even has the capacity to hear me."

"Then go and spend your time as you always have. With the ones who will listen. Do not waste your time worrying. Why did Jesus tell the disciples to shake the dust from their feet and move on to the next place if the town they were in was inhospitable to the gospel? Not because God does not hunger for the conversion of every soul. But because our time here is finite. We only have so many days. You cannot afford, with your gift of compassion, to sleep in another day and spend the remainder of the morning in lamentation. Father Dante, you must get up and shake the dust from your feet."

"I am not ready to shake my feet."

"Then keep knitting, Father. As I see it, those are your only two options: shake or knit."

ꙮꙮꙮꙮꙮꙮꙮꙮꙮꙮ

Father Dante sat in the Confessional waiting. The woman who had called to make an appointment was twenty minutes late now. Father let the Rosary beads dangle from his fingers. He had started praying the Sorrowful Mysteries, but had stopped at the Scourging at the Pillar. Larry Crenshaw. Lawrence Crenshaw. Larry Crenshaw. What words will reach him? What could possibly open his mind to the possibility of a son? What's in it for Larry Crenshaw? That's what Father Dante would have to figure out. That would be the way in. Unfortunately, that would be the only way in. Father Dante hated to be a cynic about this. It is against his nature. But it is necessary in this case. So be it.

A woman came through the open door and sat in the chair facing him, without looking at him. She kept her head down.

"Welcome," Father Dante said. "Are you the one who made the appointment?"

"Yes. I'm sorry I am late, Father."

"That's quite alright. Gave me some time to pray.'' He held the rosary up momentarily and then clutched it back into his fist. "And think."

The woman managed an uneasy smile.

"May the Lord bless you and help you make a good confession."

"Bless me, Father, for I have sinned. It's been four months since my last confession. I've missed Mass six times since Leroy died. I've never missed Mass in my life, but I just haven't been able to bring myself to come to Church since the funeral. I don't want to go anywhere. I don't want to see anybody."

"The grieving process takes time. Things will improve. With

God's grace. The Mass will offer your greatest source of healing."

"I know. I just don't want to go. I haven't slept even one night since Leroy died, yet I don't want to get out of bed. I don't think I'm ever going to find any peace."

"Anger robs us of our peace. But if you surrender even a small bit of it to the Lord, give it to Him, cry out to Him with it, one day you will find it has taken a back seat. And then surrender even more, cry out even louder, and you will see it is no longer even a travelling companion."

"Hard to imagine, Father. How can I not be angry? Someone shot my husband through the head and stole him from me. And from my children. No, I don't forgive him. Whoever he is."

"Do you want to forgive?"

"No."

"Do you *want* to want to forgive?"

"I don't know."

"There's been no arrest. It must be difficult not knowing who to be angry with. Are you sure there isn't someone else you're angry with, besides your husband's killer?"

"You mean God?"

"Many people are after losing a loved one."

"Yes, I am angry. With God. I don't want to be."

"It will pass. Just come back to Church."

The woman nodded.

"Anyone else?"

"You mean am I mad at anyone else? For my husband's death?"

"Yes."

"Well, this I really don't want to admit."

"You are safe. If not in the Confessional, then where?"

"OK. I am mad at-" she took a deep breath. "Sounds crazy, but I am mad at my husband."

"For what?"

"For the choice he made that night. He played the hero and destroyed my life." Tears threatened her eyes now. "I mean, was

175

he thinking about me at all? About his children? Why was he so reckless."

"I read about it in the paper. It was beautiful. He saved a woman's life."

"Yeah, but what about my life? Our life? His children? Now they have to grow up without a father. That woman, she was old. She had lived her life. She probably doesn't have too many years left. Maybe not even a year. But my children, they have a whole lifetime of grief ahead of them."

"And they have a father who exhibited perfect love in the last moment of his life, meriting him some eternal reward that you and I cannot even imagine. Would you have preferred something less for him? He died in a state of perfection. He gave his life for someone. There isn't any higher form of love. With one single, split second act, he put aside whatever flaws and imperfections he might have had and catapulted himself right over the gates of Heaven."

"So, I should be happy for him?"

"Exceedingly."

"That he got a bullet through his head and will never see his children grow up?"

"He will see them. Do you think death is stronger than love?"

"My children have not stopped asking me why. What do I say to them?"

"Tell them the truth. That their father is still with them, watching them from Heaven."

"What good will that do? We need him here."

"I lost my father when I was a boy. It changed my life in dramatic ways. I would like to tell you, if you have a few minutes."

On Dante's ordination day, it rained. It was the only time he had seen the little raven-haired girl with wet hair. She spun in the drizzle outside the Cathedral, her face pointed to the sky, the joy of heaven misting her shiny round cheeks. She stayed only for about fifteen seconds.

"I wish your father could be here to see you, Father Dante," Elina said, kissing her son on the cheek.

"He is." Dante smiled and hugged her into his tall frame.

"Yes," she smiled. "I forgot that for a minute." She looked into his deep brown eyes. "Do you ever forget, Dante?"

"It's OK, Mama Dulce. Even if we forget, God remembers."

God's remembering is why Dante became a priest.

The last time Mateo left for Mexico City to continue his work on the codex, Dante begged to come with him. Mateo promised when Dante was older, he would take him to the Basilica of Our Lady of Guadalupe. "It will be our pilgrimage," Mateo told him. "You will see amazing things."

"Please, Daddy, I want to go now. I am old enough. Please." Dante was verging on tears.

"We'll plan it someday, Mijo. I would love to show you all I know about the Blessed Virgin."

Mateo never came home from that trip. Dante assumed all his dreams laid in pieces on the ground with the wreckage. But one day, when he was seventeen, Father Milo announced after Mass that he would be leading a pilgrimage to the Shrine of Our Lady of Guadalupe in Mexico City. Dante's heart leaped. And then it sank, when he picked up the bulletin after Mass and saw that the trip was going to cost $867. There was no way he could come up with that kind of money. Every penny of De Luz savings had already been earmarked for Dante's college expenses, and that wasn't even enough for the first semester. He was certain his mother would not agree to a trip to Mexico. He went home, closed himself in his room, turned on Simon and Garfunkel, leafed through photos of his father and prayed in the form of a complaint (or maybe complained in the form of a prayer) to his father that he never got to go with him to the shrine. Mateo had not kept his promise and quite irrationally, Dante was mad about that. If his father had taken him with him, Dante would have perished in that plane too. He felt cheated, but he wasn't sure by whom. Surely there wasn't some grand plot underway in the universe to deprive him of a father and an encounter with the Mother of God. Dante decided to leave the matter in her hands. If she wanted to see him, if there was a reason for him to kneel inside that great Basilica, staring up at the miraculous image, she and Mateo would have to make a way.

After Mass two weeks later, Father Milo greeted Dante in the narthex with a handshake and a question. "Dante, are you coming on the pilgrimage?"

"Well, I would love to, Father, but I'm going to have to pass this time."

"Why?"

"I'm afraid I don't have the money."

A large smile grew over Father's face. "Yes, you do, Dante."

"I do?"

"A parishioner came to me last week to put down a deposit on the trip. He wrote the check for twice as much. I pointed out his error and he said it was no mistake. 'Someone will be in need of this pilgrimage who doesn't have the money to go,' he told me. Today, when I woke up, I wondered if I was going to find out who it was that was meant to go. And here you are."

"Really? I'm going to the Basilica? Finally? I can't believe it."

"Believe it. See, with God as your travel agent, there's no telling where your path will lead."

Dante was awed by the pilgrims who crawled over stone and dirt to get to the church. He wished he too could reach the Virgin on bloody knees, but for some reason, his knees would not bend.

Standing before the image of Our Lady of Guadalupe, miraculously imprinted by Heaven in 1531 on St. Juan Diego's tilma, Dante thought he heard her call him "little son." He thought he saw her looking at him, just for a second. Her downcast gaze lifted and her eyes met his. Just for a second. Maybe even less.

Dante had inherited a library of books about her from his

father. But at the Basilica gift shop he picked up one he hadn't seen before. It was about the inability of science to explain the tilma. He bought it and devoured it in one night in the hotel room. The next day, this time on his hands and knees, he went to see her one last time before the flight home, Father Milo was standing beside him. "She speaks to you, doesn't she, Dante?"

"Now I understand why my father arranged for me to come here."

About a month later, in the confessional, Dante told Father Milo that he was considering the priesthood. Father Milo smiled and assured him of his daily prayers.

Dante has always been convinced that it was the prayers of Father Milo, Mother Mary and his father that got him through to ordination day and sustain him still in his vocation. And the prayers of other souls in heaven who have remained anonymous. He imagined Our Lady and his father working together to guide and form him. Maybe that wouldn't have been possible if his father had remained alive on earth. They, no doubt, worked on Elina too. Possibly from the moment Mateo left this earth.

The Sunday after Mateo's funeral, Dante begged to go to church. It was the last thing Elina wanted to do. She couldn't figure out how she was even going to find the strength to get dressed. She wanted to stay in bed all day.

"But Mama Dulce, we can go there and be closer to Papa. Please. Please, Mama Dulce. Can we go?"

"OK, Dante," she said. "What time is it? Can I just rest a little longer?"

"We have to go now, Mama, please. We don't want to be late. Remember Papa always hated being late."

"Hated being late? What do you mean? Late was his middle name."

"For Mass. He hated being late for Mass."

"Yes, for Mass he was on time. Always on time." Elina squeezed her eyes shut tight, hoping to pen in the tears. "I just wanted to give it a few weeks before we got back into our full schedule, Dante. We need to take some time. I just can't face a bunch of people right now."

"Please, Mama, we can sit in the back and leave right after the blessing, before the final song. Please, Mama Dulce. I won't ask to go anywhere else."

"OK, Dante. OK."

The two did indeed sit in the back. Elina cried through the entire Mass. She went to the restroom to try and quiet her sobs three times – after the Gloria, during the homily and a third time during the consecration, right after the memorial acclamation. *We proclaim your death, oh Lord and proclaim your resurrection, until you come again.* An elderly woman found her in there, washing her face. She smiled at Elina. "Are you OK, Honey?"

Elina shook her head as she blew her nose. The woman put her arm around her. "I lost my husband too," she said. "I still miss him. But it gets easier, Honey. It really does."

Elina wondered how the woman knew.

"But you're in the right place, Honey. You just keep coming. There's nowhere in the world you can be closer to him than in this place where heaven and earth kiss."

Every week after that, Elina took Dante to Church out of love for her husband and son. But she sat there harboring doubts. They were the same doubts that prompted her to make this promise to Mateo when they were contemplating a life together: "I will go to church with you. I will not interfere with whatever religious beliefs you pass on to our children. But I'm afraid, I will never become Catholic. I would love to tell you I would do anything for you. And I would, but not that, Mateo. Not that."

Then, one day, which happened to be the first anniversary of Mateo's death, Father Milo delivered something powerful in his homily. If you would have asked her what the homily was about, she couldn't have told you. She was lost in thought, as she usually was at church. And pretty much anywhere else too. Lost in the thought of Mateo – the love of Mateo, the absence of Mateo and the possibility of an invisible yet eternal presence of

Mateo. But one sentence from the priest's homily pierced through, and it was this: "Jesus healed many people of their physical ailments, but he came primarily for something else -- to heal our souls."

Elina had lost enough of her loved ones to know that granting people lengthy earthly lives couldn't have been God's primary focus. But there was only one way she would find any healing. And that was through clinging to a grieving human being's only hope – that one day we will all see each other again.

ಬ⊃)ᏦᏓᏒ⊃)ᏦᏓᏒ⊃)ᏦᏓᏒ⊃)ᏦᏓ

Father Dante decided he would spend the night in the chapel praying. He had read of saints who had done the same, with very fruitful results. So he entered the presence of Jesus in the Blessed Sacrament at nine with rosary beads and a bottle of water.

At about one o'clock in the morning, he moved to the St. Joseph statue, hoping to draw wisdom from the man who was chosen to be an earthly father to God himself. As he knelt, with his forehead on the floor, he reached out his hand and touched the statue's feet. He lifted his head slightly until the feet came into view. And that's when he noticed something he had never noticed before. The distance between the first and second toe was quite large, just like his own.

Dante remembered his mother always talking about how Sylvie's feet were an exact replica of Mateo's only smaller and "a bit sweeter in aroma." Dante noticed that his feet looked nothing like his dad's. And he thought it a little odd that they looked nothing like his mom's either. There was excess distance between the large toe and the one next to it. The second toe was slightly longer than the first and the next three toes were virtually all the same length. This observation sparked a lifelong obsession with the study of feet. Had he lived in Nova Scotia, the obsession might have eventually passed. But sunny, flip-flop climes like southern Cal lend themselves quite nicely to the study of feet. And in all the many years of foot observation, he found not one foot like his own.

And so, there in front of the St. Joseph statue, he became convinced that the answer to his question lay at the end of his leg. If he could have tracked Larry Crenshaw down at this hour, he certainly would have. As it was, he would have to wait. Back rested against the wall, Father Dante closed his eyes and drifted off into peaceful sleep, right there on the plush red carpet in front of the foster father of Jesus.

Father Dante awoke with a white knitted sweater draped over him from his shoulders to his waist and a blue windbreaker over his legs. Parishioners who came to the chapel in the middle of the night to pray must have donated their clothing to keep him warm. He smiled at their thoughtfulness, a sense of pride welling up in him, like a father's when he witnesses the charity of his children. The clock read 4 a.m. He folded the sweater and the jacket, placed them on one of the pews and glanced at the only other human in the chapel with him – a man in his 40s, who was kneeling in a pew, eyes closed, deep in prayer. Father Dante said a prayer of thanks to Jesus in the Blessed Sacrament, genuflected and made his way back to the rectory through the chilled pre-dawn air, rolling his head around as he walked to loosen the stiffness in his neck. He went through his morning routine an hour earlier than normal and ended up at the church at 7 a.m., deciding to pray a rosary before the divine office and 8 a.m. Mass.

Mrs. Sommer, the woman who prayed a rosary for Father Dante every day, looked unusually pale when she shook hands with him before Mass. Her hands were cold and clammy.

"Are you feeling alright this morning?" he asked.

"Oh, yes, Father. Thank you. Just a little tired. These old bones. Can't sleep very well anymore."

"Aw, insomnia is the worst."

"It didn't look like you had any trouble sleeping last night."

"So that was *your* sweater." He took her hand and squeezed it. "Thank you, Mrs. Sommer."

The woman sat in her usual third row, on the aisle. She tipped her head back, forehead glistening, and fanned herself with a church bulletin. Even in all his garments -- alb, chasuble, stole and censure -- Father Dante was feeling quite comfortable. He wondered why Mrs. Sommer was not. During the readings, as he sat in the presider's chair, he closed his eyes and bowed his head as usual, listening to the Word proclaimed. But every thirty seconds or so, he felt compelled to glance at Mrs. Sommer to make sure she was OK. Right before the end of the second reading, he saw her swoon left toward the aisle, her mouth gaping open. He jumped from his seat, trotted down the sanctuary steps, his green chasuble furling behind him, and caught her just before she collapsed onto the floor. His microphone still on, he could be heard throughout the church asking for an ambulance and the retrieval of the oil of the sick. The deacon ran into the sacristy and returned with a key to open the ambry. He removed one of the three large glass decanters of oil -- the one bearing the initials O.I., marked for the Latin *Oleum Infirmorum*. As Mrs. Sommer lay dying and Father Dante said the prayers he had said so many times in administering last rites, he thought of how easy it was going to be to tell her loved ones of her passing. She died at the age of 89, in the presence of Jesus in the Tabernacle, during Sacred Liturgy, in the arms of a priest she had prayed for daily and will remember her always in his prayers. A death doesn't get any better than that. He whispered a prayer of thanks to St. Joseph. After emergency personnel came and took the unconscious woman away, he led the congregation in a Hail Mary for her and resumed Mass. Then, he breathed a silent request: "Keep praying for me, Mrs. Sommer."

After Mass, a little boy, about six years old, took a running start and slammed into Father Dante's legs with an exuberant hug.

"Be careful, Mijo," his father warned, "you don't want to knock Father down. I'm sorry Father."

"Oh, I never need an apology for a hug." Father Dante bent down and looked into the boy's face. "Have you been saying your prayers, Alberto? Here, let's say one together. A very important one."

The two said it in unison:

Hail Mary, full of grace, the Lord is with thee
Blessed art thou among women
and blessed is the fruit of thy womb Jesus
Holy Mary, mother of God, pray for us sinners
now and at the hour of our death. Amen.

"Wonderful," said Father Dante. "You have memorized it. Now you have access to the power of heaven."

"Well, I've been praying to receive the body of Christ. When can I receive the body of Christ, Father?"

"The Lord has special plans for the time and place, Alberto."

The boy reminded Father Dante of himself. He remembered pestering his father incessantly for permission to partake in the Holy Banquet.

"Daddy, when can I receive Jesus?" he would ask after every Mass.

"When you are a little older, Mijo. You have to prepare for your First Communion. Then, on that wonderful day, you will receive Him, and the Lord of the universe will live inside you."

"I want that now," Dante insisted.

"It is not your time yet, son," his father would say, gently pulling him onto his lap. "But soon, very soon, it will be."

"When?"

"When you are in third grade."

"How old will I be then?"

"You will be nine."

"Nine? How many years is that from now?"

"Well, you are six now. And the difference between six and nine is just three short years."

"Three years! I can't wait three years, Papa! Can't you break the bread Father gives you and give me half?"

"No, Mijo, I can't do that because you have not yet received your First Communion."

"Why can't I receive my First Communion now?"

"I will talk to Father, Mijo, since you have such a strong desire. But in the meantime, you will just have to be patient."

"I can't be patient. Not about this. I need Jesus in my heart right now."

"Why, Mijo?"

"Why? Doesn't everybody need Jesus?"

His father smiled. "I tell you what. Until that special day when you can receive, each time I come back to my seat after Communion, I will point to the side of my mouth where the Eucharist is and you can give that cheek a kiss. And you won't be just kissing me. You will be kissing Jesus."

And that is the agreement the two of them kept for the next six months until Father Milo could arrange for Dante to have communion two years before the usual age.

On his Communion day, out in the narthex after Mass, grinning up at Father Milo, Dante exclaimed, "For a long time, I have been kissing Jesus. Today, he kissed me back!"

Father Dante made up his mind that if Alberto asked him again about receiving Holy Communion, he would talk to the director of Catechesis about letting him receive early. There's no telling what an extra three years of Communions would do for his soul. There's no telling what it had done for his.

ೞ✖ೞ

13

Juggling Oranges

Lawrence Crenshaw rocked backward, propped his elbows on the arms of his large leather executive's chair and touched each of his fingers on his left hand to each of the corresponding fingers on his right.

"So, I'm assuming, since you are here, that you found a way to prove I am your father."

"I have." Father Dante sat tall, not quite on the edge of his seat, but not letting his back touch the chair's either.

"Well, let's hear it."

"OK. I hope you don't mind," he said using his right foot to wrestle his left black dress shoe off, "but you will need to take off your shoe."

"Oh no, don't tell me the Cinderella storyline is emerging again in this loopy drama."

"No, no. This has nothing to do with shoes," Father Dante said hoisting his sock off. "This is about feet." He put his foot up high enough over Lawrence Crenshaw's desk to illustrate his point. It was an odd spectacle, a barefoot man in a formal, tailored black cassock. It looked good on monks in brown mohair and even long bearded friars in gray habits. But diocesan priests do not, as a general rule, bare their feet. "Would you please? Just indulge me for a moment."

"You know, ever since I met you, I've been waiting for Rod Serling to pop out and offer an explanation for this bizarre twilight zone you've managed to build around me. Really, Father, I don't know what to say. But you've got me so curious, you can damn well bet I won't be able to resist the invitation to take off my shoe."

He used the toe of his left shoe to force off his right, crossed his leg over his knee and removed his sock. "There. What revelation, pray tell, lies in the naked foot?"

"Actually, it's in the toes." Father Dante hoisted his foot up on the desk. "Here put your foot up here."

Crenshaw cocked his head to one side to indicate his reluctance and disgust and put his foot next to Father Dante's. It was perfectly clear. St. Joseph had not been wrong.

"What do you see?" asked Father Dante anxiously.

"Two ugly feet, one of which is in desperate need of a pedicure."

"Our feet are made exactly alike, Mr. Crenshaw. Just look at them."

"Yes. Mine has five toes and yours has five toes. Remarkable."

"But *look* at the toes."

Larry Crenshaw was blank.

"Look. Look at that space between the first two toes and then the length of these three toes. That's very odd. Do you know how odd that is?"

"No."

"Most people have toes that are of varying lengths, Mr. Crenshaw. Nobody has feet like this."

"Well, apparently somebody does. One hundred percent of the people in this room do, as a matter of fact." He stretched his sock back over his foot. "Look, Father, I'm very sorry about the loss of your mother. And your father. But I don't think you're going to be establishing any family ties here. I'm very sorry."

Father Dante took a business card from his cassock pocket, his one foot still bare. "Here's a DNA testing firm. I took the test and they have my DNA on file. Whenever you're ready, you can just call them and make an appointment."

Larry Crenshaw did not reach out his hand to take the card. "I'm sorry, Father."

"I'll just leave it here," Father Dante said, putting the card on the desk and stretching his sock over his foot, mindless of whether the seam was crooked or would bunch up when he got it into his shoe.

"It's been a pleasure, Father. If the collection plate ever runs dry or you need help with your building fund, I'll put in a good word for you in our community outreach department."

"That's a very kind offer," Mr. Crenshaw. "But again, I am not interested in your money. If you don't mind, I'd like to tell you a brief story."

"Whoa, whoa, whoa, Father. I've heard a good number of your stories before, and I can tell you under no uncertain terms, I haven't the time for another one."

"I promise. This one is brief. It's about another man named Lawrence. He was the deacon to Pope Sixtus II. Two hundred years after Christ. When the Roman prefect led the Holy Father away to be martyred, Lawrence tried to follow. He asked him 'Where are you going, Father, without your son?' Pope Sixtus replied, 'My son, I am not abandoning you. Greater strife awaits you. Stop weeping. You will follow me in three days.'

Believing the Church to be wealthy, the Romans demanded that Lawrence turn over to them all the treasures of the Church. St. Lawrence agreed and told the prefect to follow him to find the riches. Leading him to the poor, the saint declared, 'These are the Church's treasures.' And it was true, since the church had distributed its money to the poor. That's where its treasures were. The Church has a long history of treasuring the poor because Christ treasures the poor. So, you see, Mr. Crenshaw. I am not interested in your treasure since I have my own."

"Yes. I've heard it said by those of you who read the Bible that the good book doesn't speak too highly of money – the root of all evil."

"No. That is a common misquote. The *love* of money is the root of all evil. We are not meant to love money. We are made to love God."

"So, you do not resent growing up poor."

"I didn't grow up poor."

"Well, OK. You don't resent growing up un-rich? I mean, you could have had all of this," he swept his hand through the air and made a fast glance around the expansive office. "If you are who you say you are."

"Sometimes, especially when I started into my teenage years, I would wish I were rich. I would think about the many things I wanted that I could not have. Now I can't even remember what they were."

"I'm sure you'd remember some of them if you happened to fall into some money."

"Mr. Crenshaw, I can think of a great number of saints who grew up rich and forfeited the family fortune to follow God. I can't think of even one who went from poor to rich. I'm not interested in family fortunes."

"Thank you, Father Dante. I have a meeting I need to prepare for. But thank you for coming." Larry Crenshaw stood, pulled up his sagging trousers and held out his hand.

"I hope to hear from you soon, Mr. Crenshaw." The two men shook hands.

"As I said, Father, it's been a pleasure."

୬୬ࢲ୧ଽ୬ୗࢲ୧ଽ୬ୗࢲ୧ଽ୬ୗࢲ୧ଽ୬ୗࢲ୧ଽ

A month after Mrs. Sommer's funeral, Dante concelebrated her granddaughter's wedding with the groom's uncle who was an Augustinian priest from the Diocese of Joliet in Illinois.

As Father Dante sat beside the presider's chair looking out at the congregation, his eyes fell on a woman in her late 40s, seated beside her blank husband, whose arms were folded in apathy. As Father Lorenzo talked about the blessedness of Holy Matrimony and the need for radical love in a world bent on seeking what's convenient, Father Dante thought he witnessed the silent swirlings of that woman's mind. "Poor, girl," the woman thought, as she stared expressionless at the bride. "She has no idea what she is in for."

The woman in the next pew back thought, "I remember feeling what that young bride is feeling right now. The joy, the expectation. Little does she know how quickly it fades. Little does she know."

Across the aisle, an elderly woman, sitting all alone, spoke silently to her husband through the heavenly veil. "Jerry, remember when it was you and me up there? It was just a blink of an eye ago, Jerry. Remember? I want to come and be with you soon, Jerry. I miss you so bad. Please tell Jesus. I want to come."

The woman behind her thought, "I wonder why nobody tells this couple what is really ahead -- how difficult marriage really is. Why do they lie to young people? Why are we all pretending?"

The couple behind her sat, arms entwined, smiles on their faces, remembering the moment they took their wedding vows. "How much more I love her today than I did even then," the man thought. And his wife: "May that young woman be as happy as I have been. Even through the trials and heartaches. Even through the pain of drifting apart and being pulled back together a thousand times, I would not trade even a moment of this blessed life with my sweet husband."

"I wish I could do it all again," a man sitting next to them thought. "I'd do it all different. I'd really love her this time. I'd *really* love her."

Father, by your power you have made everything out of nothing, Father Lorenzo prayed. *In the beginning you created the universe and made mankind in your own likeness. You gave man the constant help of woman so that man and woman should no longer be two, but one flesh, and you teach us that what you have united may never be divided.*

Father Dante thought, if he had two lives to live, he would have spent one in the beautiful bonds of Holy Matrimony, though he never knew a girl he would have considered marrying. None of the girls he ever met measured up to the ideal, which Dante had created in his own mind, but which was based on a real person: Elina De Luz. Although he always knew, intuitively, that his mother could not have been as perfect as his biased love had pegged her to be, he had to admit, the new information he had learned about her youth forged greater distance between the person he knew and the one she truly was. Not that she was unauthentic. Just that he had not been privy to the past events that had formed her into the person he loved so much. And once he became enlightened about them, he couldn't help but view her in a different light. She was a much more complicated person than he had thought. There were layers, like onion skin, which he never saw before. He had only seen the onion. This revelation did not spur a crisis because he knew this: that underneath the onion skin, it was not a rutabaga or a squash. It was still an onion.

When Dante got back to the rectory, he found three grocery bags full of oranges on the counter.

"Where'd we get these?" he asked Father Francis.

"Mrs. Trendle. She said just let her know if we need more."

"God bless her."

"God bless her," Father Francis agreed.

Dante picked out an orange, grabbed a steak knife from the drawer and sliced once. As his teeth sunk into it, he was immediately in another place – that indescribable, vague, joy-filled place in the memory triggered by the sense of smell, so acute in childhood.

As a child, the smell of fresh oranges always lingered on his hands after three or four washings, unto the following day, in fact. He liked to, on occasion, say that oranges are somewhat responsible for his vocation. A couple times a year, Father Milo would go around the neighborhood gathering up all the kids he could find and board the metro rail bound for the home of an elderly couple with a sprawling back yard, full of citrus trees.

The priest could juggle seven oranges at a time. He would start with two and all the children would glue their eyes to him and smile. Then he would ask someone to toss him another and a third orange would join the rounds, and the children's smiles would broaden. Then he'd call for a fourth and the children would say "wow, Father" and "cool." By the time he got to seven, there were gasps and thrilled laughter. Some bit their nails as they watched, waiting for something to go awry. But it never did. Dante realized years later that the priest honed his juggling skills for the same reason Father Dante draws. Not for the skill itself but for the fruit it bears.

"Look up into those trees, Dante," Father Milo said one day. "What do you see?"

Dante shrugged in typical 11-year-old boy fashion. "Lots of oranges?"

"That's right, Dante! A great abundance. And why do I have to go rounding people up to pick them?"

Another shrug. "So you can practice your juggling?"

"The harvest is plenty, says our Lord. The laborers are few. Those oranges are like souls, Dante." He stooped down and picked up a hardened, brown orange that had served as a meal for some kind of varmint and had been bombed by a bird dropping. "This is what happens when they are not harvested, Dante. This is what's happening all around us." And then, a look of deep longing came over him, like someone suffering from intense thirst. "Where are all the harvesters, Dante?"

Father Milo and the kids tossed oranges into Mr. Sanchez's pickup until the bed was fully loaded. As Mr. Sanchez drove off, bound for local soup kitchens and food pantries, Father passed out large paper sacks to all the kids and told them to fill them up for their families.

Dante never ate an orange, or even looked at one, without thinking of Father Milo's words. He didn't fully understand them at the time, but they stirred something within him. One day, it hit him, when he was nineteen, standing at Father Milo's grave. He wondered who would harvest all those oranges at the Sanchez house now that Father Milo was gone. Dante remembered the shriveled orange that had so disturbed Father Milo. He said a prayer that more men would become priests. As a soft breeze blew past, a picture of Father Milo juggling oranges materialized before Dante's eyes. He was juggling for a young raven-haired girl in a white smockish dress. Dante wondered how the girl could see the vision too and repositioned himself closer to her in order to catch her eye and perhaps share some sort of silent acknowledgment between them that Father Milo was really, truly among them. But as he approached, both she and Father Milo vanished.

Father Dante bit into the other half of Mrs. Trendle's orange, scraped out all its goodness with his front teeth and chucked the remains in the garbage pail in the sink. He picked three more oranges, all of the same size, out of the bag and threw them, one at a time in the air, catching them in a perfect cadence, one after another. He was impressed and surprised that he was able to juggle even after all these years. He caught them all at once and held them into his cassock as he reached into the bag to get a fourth.

"You going to give four a try?" Father Francis asked.

"Uh-huh." He got three of the oranges airborne again, but they all flew in three different directions when he tried to add a fourth. "I used to be able to do this. Father Milo taught me." He left the fallen oranges to roll on their varying paths, sat down at the kitchen table, propped his elbows and put his face in his large palms. He wiped at his eyes with his first finger and thumb.

"It's OK, son," Father Francis said, laying a hand on his shoulder. "Wait on the Lord. He is always at work. You might not see the fruit of His labor today. Or tomorrow. But you will see it. In the meantime, Father Dante, you need a restoration of faith. You have lost confidence, and your vocation suddenly seems too large for you. It is not, Father Dante. Your heart is large enough to hold it all."

⁚✄⁝✄⁚✄⁝✄⁚✄⁝✄⁚✄⁝✄⁚✄⁝✄

The phone rang at 9:05, just as Father Dante returned from Daily Mass.

"Uh, Lawrence Crenshaw here. I need to talk to you. It's important."

"Yes, of course, Mr. Crenshaw."

"The DNA test."

"Yes. You took it? That's, that's wonderful."

"Well, probably not so wonderful for you."

"What do you mean?"

"Can we meet?"

"Of course. When?"

"I've got a doctor's appointment tomorrow at ten and then I'm free. Can we meet at noon?"

"Sure."

"I'll come to the Church."

"Yes, yes. That will be fine. I'll meet you in the rose garden out front."

A half an hour later, as Dante was ironing his week's worth of clerical shirts, trying to take his mind off the mystery that would loom before him for the next twenty-six hours, the doorbell rang. Dante hugged Sylvie and kissed her on the forehead, scooped three-year-old Claire into his embrace and kissed her little brother Joey, who smiled in his mother's arms.

"Uncle Father Dante," Claire blurted out. "Can we have cookies?"

Father Dante poured two cups of coffee, one with cream and two sugars, one black. He gave the babies each two Chips Ahoy cookies, one for each hand, and settled everyone in the living room.

"Is the coffee all right, Sylvie?"

"You always get it perfect. You always remember how much cream and sugar to put in. You're the only one in my life who does."

"How's the house hunting?"

"The hunt goes on."

Claire made her way around the living room, picking up saint statues and crucifixes and clunking them back down again.

"Not finding anything?" Father Dante asked.

"Well, we did find the perfect house, but someone out-bid us."

Claire settled on two saints, who were now having a conversation in some sort of gabble that only toddlers understand. Two half-eaten cookies lay beside them.

"God has a different blessing in store, Sis." Father Dante said.

"It's all for the best. That house was too close to the mailboxes."

"Too close?"

"Yeah. The mailboxes were only like three houses away."

"Why is that a problem? You got something against postal carriers?"

"No, no. It's just that going to the mailbox is the only thing I do alone. It's my one moment of solace during the day, and three houses is not enough. I want the walk to the mailbox to be as long as possible."

"Ah Sylvie. You give virtually everything you have to your children. It's really quite beautiful to watch. But you are holding something back. You really must learn to let go of that ninety seconds it takes to retrieve your mail."

"You're kidding, right?"

"Of course."

"OK, because I didn't see you begging for more time with the kids the last time you babysat. I just about ran you over as you bolted out to greet me in the driveway."

"Aw, I love those kids. You know that. And I am happy to watch them any time. When you going to give me another one to baptize?"

"Oh sure, you can just pour a little holy water on them and slather them up with oil and leave the hard work to me and Paul. If I don't find a house with a ridiculously inconvenient mailbox, there won't be another one. Please pray some rosaries for what's left of my sanity, Father Dante." She rubbed at her temples. "You're the one who prayed me into this world. It's your responsibility now to make sure I have an exceedingly happy life."

Mateo and Elina had intended to have a house full of children, but for years after Dante was born, none came. Elina didn't want Dante to be an only child. She had always herself wished for a sibling, but her parents never saw the need. Elina, all by herself, had already made them parents, allowing them to count parenthood among their many achievements.

About two years after they married, Mateo and Elina sought the help of a fertility doctor. The cause of the infertility was never identified, but genetic testing did reveal that they both had a recessive gene for Cystic Fibrosis. That would mean each pregnancy carried a one in four chance that the baby would have Cystic Fibrosis.

"See, my darling," Mateo told Elina, hugging her in tight to his flannel shirt. "God has His reasons for sometimes denying us our heart's desire."

Elina wept for a good twenty minutes into Mateo's embrace and never shed another tear after that. They decided to be careful not to have relations during what would be Elina's fertile time, just in case conception might occur.

Of course, Dante knew nothing about all of this. One day, after coming home from Mass, he told his parents he had made a special request of God. He had been inspired by the homily, in which Father talked about the many miracles associated with St. Philomena. On numerous occasions, she has interceded before the throne of God, on behalf of infertile couples. And babies result. Dante told his parents he had placed his request at Philomena's feet. He wanted a baby sister.

Elina and Mateo looked at each other, concerned on a number of levels. First, they didn't want their Dante to be disappointed when God failed to fulfill his beautiful request. Second, they worried that Dante would experience a deep loneliness at the absence of a sibling. And Mateo didn't want him to lose faith in the intercessory power of the Saints.

All their worries proved to be unfounded. St. Philomena came through. As careful as Mateo and Elina were to avoid conception, the Author of Life had an alternate plot.

Elina spent the entire pregnancy worried about Cystic Fibrosis, a difficult disease of the lungs and digestive system that often takes its victims at an early age. Mateo spent the entire pregnancy reminding Elina that God is with them. As is St. Philomena. So there is nothing to fear.

"But a 25 percent chance, Mateo."

"God is not a God of statistics, Elina. He gives each soul what it needs. If it needs health, He gives it health. If it needs trials, He lets trials come."

"Are you sure this is the right thing, Mateo?"

"What is the right thing?"

"To have this baby."

"That decision has already been made, my love. And it wasn't by us."

"What about the suffering? CF is brutal, Mateo."

"It is not for us to decide, my love."

"Then why does God give us the knowledge and the ability to determine what will happen?"

"He wants us to trust Him. That's all we can do now, Elina. Trust Him. God does not make mistakes."

"Well, genetics do."

"This baby is a direct answer to the prayers of an innocent soul. How can we deny this is the will of God?"

Seven months later, a hearty cry rang out in the delivery room as Sylvie Lucy entered the world with not a shred of defective genetic fiber.

᠙᠙᠙᠙᠙᠙᠙᠙᠙᠙᠙᠙

Father Dante was in deep REM, dreaming he was at the L.A. County Fair. He was, of course, dressed in his cassock, holding a gun, trying to win one of those large, awkward-looking 36-inch penguins, whose head was molded askew like all other fair animals, which are stuffed with sawdust and who knows what, rather than the more "quality" polyester fiberfill. The object of the game was to shoot the target with the water pistol and make the bell ring for as long as possible, racking up 100 points before the dreaded buzzer. Dante was trying to win the prize for his sister Sylvie, an avid fan of the arctic birds ever since *March of the Penguins* came out. So, Dante was getting increasingly excited as the water propelled from his pistol and hit the bull's-eye spot on center, setting off the crisp, harsh ring of the bell necessary for victory. Dante was congratulating himself internally on being such a great shot -- much better than he'd remembered. Several children had gathered to cheer him on. And then, he realized the bell was coming from his nightstand and he was awakening in his own bed. He groped for the phone, knocking his reading glasses to the floor. It was the answering service, calling to tell him of a parishioner in need of anointing.

When he arrived at the hospital, he found Mary Lou Martin, face full of lesions and bruises, right arm wrapped.

"You were right," he told her.

"Yes, Father," she whispered, reaching for him with the hand that wasn't wrapped.

She had flagged him down after Mass several days earlier and told him she had a terrible feeling something bad was going to happen on the way back east for a family reunion.

"Oh, I feel like that every time I'm going to travel," Father Dante told her to ease her mind. "I think a lot of people do."

"No, this is different," she insisted. "I've never felt like this before."

"Well, let me give you a blessing," he said, extending his hand. He prayed that nothing would happen to her or her family that lay outside the will of God.

Several days later, with a feeling of deep foreboding, she and her three daughters loaded up the car and began the road trip to Wisconsin. They hadn't even gotten out of California when a semi changed lanes, displacing their vehicle into another lane, which collided with three cars, scaled the median and ended up on the other side of the freeway. Somehow, their car was spared another hit from the oncoming traffic.

"How are your daughters?"

"Debbie is in ICU. She was thrown from the vehicle, but they are hopeful she will recover. The others are in stable condition."

"It's a miracle you are all alive. I will go anoint your girls now, OK? You rest." He squeezed her hand. "I'll be back."

"Father, don't be surprised if Fiona refuses the sacrament. She is fallen away."

"Don't worry, Mary Lou," Father said. "I've had people refuse to baptize their children. I've known couples who refuse to get married in the Church. I've known many Catholics who refuse to go to confession. But I've never met one person yet who turned down an anointing."

Fiona didn't either, though she did make it clear that she had no plans to die. All she needed was a surgery or two to repair some broken bones. Her internal injuries were few, compared to others in the car and there was minimal trauma to the head.

On the way out, Father Dante smiled at a couple, sitting together in the waiting area, holding hands – a white woman and a Hispanic man, about his own age. The image of them, leaning into each other, pressed itself onto his mind and remained there as he drove back to the rectory. He stopped at Circle K, and John Cohen's *Ravens and Doves* played on the speaker as he pumped gas. All the way home, he contemplated how the lyrics applied to his parents. It was their song.

Baby, I know life with me
Is not exactly what you might see
On the pages of Modern Bride
Who could predict that you and I
Would find a love to deepen any sea
Would find a love to make demons flee
Some days fly like ravens
Some days fly like doves
Everyday I'm flying
Deeper into your love
Maybe it hasn't always been this way
But it will surely always be
No force in this world
Could come between you and me

Father Dante retired early that night, but he had trouble falling asleep as he tried to imagine what bad news Larry Crenshaw could have about the DNA test. His mother couldn't have been mistaken could she? A picture of the couple in the waiting room floated before his closed eyes as Cohen's song returned to him. He was glad for the distraction.

And then one line of the lyric insisted on repeating itself like a scratched LP. *Some days fly like ravens.* He remembered the one and only time he had heard his parents purposefully hurt each other.

"I don't want him to go," his mother insisted.

"Elina, the risk is really quite low."

"But why take the risk at all? It's unnecessary."

"You've got to let him live a little, Elina. You can't keep him in a bubble."

"Not letting him fly to a third-world nation in a puddle jumper is keeping him in a bubble?"

"Third-world nation? Oh, Elina, the drama. They do have airports, you know. And even runways."

"I just don't like those little planes, Mateo."

"I understand. I know why you have such worries. But, really, I would never do anything to put our son in danger. And he's been begging me. It would be such a wonderful experience for him. It's the Virgin's Shrine, Elina. Think of it. What an experience for him."

"Would you have let Raquel go?"

"You mean, do I love our son any less than my own flesh and blood?"

"No, I didn't mean that."

"Flesh and blood does not make a bond. People have been known to kill their own flesh and blood. Sometimes before they are even born. Or at least contemplate it."

It wasn't until Dante read his mother's letter after her death that he understood the contents of this conversation. Now he knew what the reference to flesh and blood was all about. Now he knew what it meant that people kill their own. Or at least contemplate it. Now he knew the cruelty of his father's comments and why it sent his mother to their room in a door-slamming rage like Dante had never seen before and why she didn't emerge until the following morning, despite Mateo's profuse apologies through the locked door. And why Elina got her way and Dante never did board a puddle jumper with his father.

14

Walking on Cereal

Larry Crenshaw showed up ten minutes early. Father Dante knew this because he himself took a seat in the rose garden fifteen minutes before their agreed upon meeting time. The garden always relaxed him, though lately, the angels had remained silent. He was counting on Larry Crenshaw being a bit late and thought he might finish a rosary. But he only got to the visitation.

Larry Crenshaw looked different somehow. A little thinner. A bit older. His jowls hung a little looser. He was wearing a yellow polo and white shorts. His legs looked spindly. He wasted no time getting to the point of his visit.

"Well, I've got some bad news, Father." He said it before he had even sat down.

"What is it, Mr. Crenshaw?"

"I had a sudden cardiac arrest. They resuscitated me and found out I have Brugada Syndrome."

"Brugada Syndrome. What is that?"

"It's a congenital heart condition, often with no symptoms. Your heart just skips a beat or two one day with no warning and bam, you're dead. There is a genetic component. So my doctor asked me if I have kids because they all have a fifty percent chance of also having this condition. So, of course, I thought, 'No, I don't have kids. Well, that's good.' And then I thought, 'Or do I?'"

"So you got the test so you could let me know if I have a genetic heart condition?"

"Yes."

"Well, that's great news!"

"How is that great? Your ticker has a fifty percent chance of being defected, and that's great?"

"That I can deal with. What makes me so grateful is that you would take the test in order to save my life. And I'm really nothing more than a stranger to you."

"Yes, a stranger. Which brings me to my next point. I would like to make peace with my past."

"Of course. Would you like me to hear your confession?"

"No, I don't want to go to confession. I haven't been to confession since I was a kid. I just want to tell you, as one human being to another, that I am sorry. I mean no offense. If I did want to go to confession, I wouldn't be lacking in things to confess. I could start with a tally of the number of times I took advantage of a business associate or cheated on my income tax. I could talk about the times I lost my temper with my employees or the years I refused to pay a little more for better quality health insurance for the families of the people who worked for me. I could ask forgiveness for hoarding my money and spending it on extravagant luxuries while the bank repossessed homes of the people I laid off in an effort to make the share holders happy with the quarterly profits. I could recount the multitude of women I slept with, without ever intending to give them any part of myself. But all this is eclipsed by the one thing that is the greatest regret of my entire life." He rubbed at his eyes.

"It's OK, take your time."

"You know what I'm going to say, don't you?"

"I do."

"Then I don't have to say it. We understand each other."

"Yes, but if you say it, it will lose its power over you."

Larry Crenshaw stared into the sky. "I could have lived as a rich man. Instead, I lived as a man with a lot of money. There is a difference, you know."

Father Dante nodded.

"The man who raised you – he was a rich man."

"And I am his heir. My father left me many treasures."

Larry Crenshaw checked the time on his Baume & Mercier. "Listen, I've got to get going. I've got an appointment at one-thirty." He stood, and Father Dante stood with him. Both men made their way across the rose-flanked path that lead from the courtyard to the parking lot. "Just get your heart checked out, huh? If you need a good cardiologist, call my secretary and she will put you in touch with mine." Crenshaw got into his black and red Bugatti Veyron and paused before closing the door. "Oh and my estate. I'm leaving it all to you."

Father Dante just stared for a moment, stunned at the weight of that statement. "I am very grateful for your generosity to me," he said finally. "But, you are aware that I will not keep it."

"I am very much aware." He put on his seatbelt. "Do whatever you'd like with it."

As he watched his father drive away, a number of causes came into Dante's mind and he silently scolded himself for spending money belonging to a man not yet dead. Not that Dante at all looked forward to Lawrence Crenshaw's demise. He dreaded it. There was so much ground to cover between him and the father he barely knew. But even more important, between Crenshaw and eternity. Father Dante considered it no accident that the faithless man's son turned out to be a priest. A priest who wouldn't be here if it weren't for his mother's ability to peer inside her own womb and determine there was an actual person within. It must mean something in the grand design. Dante prayed he'd have enough time.

Then, the thought of the money flooded in again. It would, undeniably, be a blessing. He couldn't help but think of all the good he could do for people he had watched suffer. His heart beat hard, especially, for Camp Shadowfax.

Dante was acutely aware that cancer causes great suffering. He understood that his mother never did fully recover from his grandmother's untimely death. And his sister had died of cancer before he was born. So it didn't take much for Jewel Cob, a parishioner who had lost her daughter to cancer, to convince Father Dante of the need for a horse camp for kids with cancer. Especially since the girl who was his occasional and fleeting visitor had come to him in his dream the night before, riding a pure white horse with her white flowing dress billowing around her and her black shining hair streaming behind. And so, Father Francis approved an annual parish dinner auction to benefit the cause, and Father Dante worked the camp into several of his homilies.

One day, while Father Dante stood outside in the courtyard, shaking hands with parishioners after Mass, a boy about seven ran to him and pressed something into his hand.

"Here, Father. This is for Camp Shadowfax."

"Thank you, son," Father Dante opened the crumpled dollar bill and winked at the boy's grinning father.

"It's no fun being sick or having no hands or fingers, or having just one leg," the boy said. "Or having three legs if you're a horse. You can't run and play."

Jewel Cob came up with the name Camp Shadowfax in honor of her daughter's horse, who was named for the *Lord of the Rings* snow-white stallion who carried the wizard Gandalf into battle to defeat the evil that was bent on destroying the world.

"Run, Shadowfax," her daughter would exclaim, as she squeezed her heels into her horse's sides. "Show me the meaning of haste." Shadowfax's hooves would kick up clods of wet sand as he carried the elated girl along the shore, occasionally chopping at shallow waves that lapped into their path.

And so, each participant left camp with a drawing of themselves at the Pacific, riding a horse whose mane is blowing wildly in the wind, and whose rump bears the brand DdL, which happens to be the artist's initials.

It was always a great treat to the children (and the horses) when Father Dante visited. He would have sugar cubes in one pocket and chewing gum in the other.

One day, a little girl about seven years old took him by the hand and pulled him to the arena, begging him to watch her ride. A riding instructor walked beside her while a volunteer held the reigns. On her second lap, she was joined by another rider – the shiny-haired girl with the billowing white dress on a white horse. Both of the girls smiled at Father Dante as they passed the corral gate where he stood, nodding his approval at their great riding skill and indomitable spirit. And then, the girl who always vanishes did vanish. And the other took a few more laps before suddenly slumping over and falling into the arms of the riding instructor. She went into a coma and died two days later.

ಬಿ⅜ಌ⅜ಬಿ⅜ಌ⅜ಬಿ⅜ಌ⅜ಬಿ⅜ಌ

Father Dante hated the once-a-month trips to Costco to stock up on canned goods, coffee and frozen orange juice. The fluorescent lighting was so bad for his mood – the antithesis of the lighting in the place he loved most. Never had he seen a church or chapel with fluorescent lighting, and for that, he was grateful. He counted himself among the blessed who never had to pass an entire day in an office. When he was in high school, he worked at a sandwich shop, building subs under halogen lamps. In college, he worked at a construction company building houses under the sun. And now, for the rest of his days, he would work at building a little corner of the kingdom under the unsurpassed brilliance of the Light of the World.

As he stood with his head inside the freezer, deciding whether he should buy canned corn or splurge on frozen this time, a familiar voice came from behind.

"Father Dante."

It was the man with the vocation and leftover resentment. He was sitting in a motorized cart with five dozen eggs and a carton of yogurt.

"Well, hello," Father Dante said, putting the corn back in the freezer and rubbing the cold briskly off his hands. "I've been thinking about you."

"I've been meaning to come see you. It's been crazy with finals and everything."

"Anything new in your life?"

"You could say that." The man's face was suddenly beaming.

"Well, what? What is it?"

"I'm engaged to be married."

"You are? Well congratulations. Who's the blessed girl?"

"She's a psych student. She helped me through a lot of stuff. She's a really great girl. And a very good Catholic. She is even a catechist."

"Well, that's wonderful."

"Thank you."

"So did you ever figure it out?"

"What?"

"When you came to talk to me about becoming a priest, I challenged you to go figure out what that driver gave you."

"Yes, I figured it out." A smile grew wide across his face. "He gave me my beloved Michelle. If I hadn't been in the accident, I never would have met her. I would have walked right past her. Actually, I would have rushed right past her. I rushed, rushed, rushed everywhere I went. I never would have noticed her. And she's the most beautiful creature God created, second to the Blessed Mother, of course. She is a paraplegic. She was also in a car accident – at the age of 17. But I've never met anyone so full of, of–. I'm not sure how to describe it really. She's angelic. Have you ever known anyone like that?"

Dante smiled. "Just one."

A vision of his mother dressed in a long flowing pink dress hovered before the interior of his eyes, in a place only he could see. She smiled large, like the day she came to pick him up early from school. The radio station had just given her a raise, securing the De Luzes' spot in the middle class. She wanted to go to a nice restaurant and celebrate – a place with white tablecloths and food that looks as much like fine art as a form of sustenance. A place that six-year-old Sylvie would have hated because it would have required her to sit in a seat for more than twenty minutes in a place that does not offer chicken nuggets shaped like dinosaurs or an elaborate labyrinth of tunnels and slides for post-meal recreation. That's why 12-year-old Dante, dressed in knee-length khaki shorts and a green polo shirt, ended up with his mother at Christoph's on a school day, amid the businessmen in Italian suits and ladies in high-heeled strappy silver sandals and tight fitting pencil skirts.

Elina and Dante smiled at each other over virgin Daiquiris, both missing Mateo as much as anyone has ever missed anyone in all the history of mankind. But grateful, oh so grateful, for each other. Elina couldn't imagine where she would be without children to love. And Dante knew all-too-well that parents do not live forever. So the remaining De Luzes spent a great deal of time cherishing each other.

Truth be told, Dante would have rather had the dino-bites that are his sister's favorite than the petite filet smothered in wine-sautéed mushrooms, ordered at his mother's suggestion. But he savored every minute of that lunch just the same.

"Ooops," Elina said, looking under the table. "There lies my napkin. Not very proper of me, is it?"

Dante rushed out of his seat, around to her side and disappeared from the waist up under the linen table cloth. When he had retrieved the napkin, he unfurled it with a smile and placed it on her lap. "Madame," the boy said with heightened eyebrows in fairly authentic French.

"Just like your father," Elina smiled and grabbed his hand, squeezing it tight. "You are turning into a great man like him."

Dante was proud to have Mateo's blood coursing through his veins. He was certain it carried greatness, not in the way the world sees it, but greatness in the ways of love.

"Excuse me, please." A woman with two toddlers in the front of her grocery cart and a third child hanging off the back smiled at Father Dante as he and his parishioner blocked the door to the frozen vegetables with their conversation about true love.

"Sorry," Father Dante smiled back at her, moving to the center of the aisle.

"I am happy you have found someone so special," Father Dante told the man. "When do I get to meet her?"

"Well, we're going to be starting our marriage prep classes soon. We've been going to her parish for Mass, so I'm not sure where we'll end up."

"Wherever the good Lord leads you." Father Dante held out his hand. "Congratulations again. May your love be fruitful and your home blessed with divine grace."

"Father, do you think God is OK with this?"

"Do you?"

"I hope so. I don't want to disappoint Him."

"True love is a gift from God. Just like a calling to the priesthood. You could have gone your whole life without finding someone like Michelle. But you found her."

"So it's OK with Him."

"It's His gift to you and your beloved. True love bears much fruit. Who do you think raises holy priests?"

Father Dante thought about how different he might have turned out if he had been raised by his biological father. He almost certainly would not have been a priest. Would he have had any faith at all?

He decided canned corn would be wisest. He picked up a case and headed for the coffee. He read the fine print on the shelf tags to figure out which brand was cheaper per ounce. Had he been raised as Larry Crenshaw's son, he thought, no such decisions would have ever been made.

He chose the three-pound store brand and headed for check out. Behind him in line happened to be the newly-engaged, helplessly in love man.

209

"Why do you think God didn't want me to be a priest, Father? Do you think it is because of my speech impediment?"

"How do you know He doesn't want you to be a priest?"

"He brought Michelle to me."

"I am quite certain God could have worked with any weakness of yours within the vocation of the priesthood. He has sure worked with mine. The vocation of marriage is no less demanding than that of the priesthood. If you really want to know your weaknesses, you will enter into marriage. There's nothing like a spouse to make your faults perfectly clear. When you are apt to focus on hers, she will show you a mirror. Your spouse will be the first one to point out your shortcomings, either by verbal complaint or silent example. And children – they will illuminate your flaws like pores in a make-up mirror."

"Sounds fun and rewarding."

"It's a glorious vocation. But it's not for the faint-hearted. And neither, come to think of it, is the priesthood."

Father Dante stopped into the parish office to drop off the three-pound bag of Roaster's Choice coffee and eighteen rolls of paper towels.

Music director Rosemary Bromwell followed him into the supply room

"Father, while you're here, do you mind if I get your opinion on something?" For Rosemary Bromwell, getting your opinion actually meant giving you hers. "We really need to have a talk with the altar boys. That one, what's his name, I can never remember. Always moving. Twitching his foot. Twiddling his fingers."

"Jared."

"Yes, you've noticed. I hate to bother you about it, but I've spoken with Sister about it several times and she hasn't done anything to remedy the situation."

"Exactly what needs to be remedied?"

"He's never still, not for a moment."

"But always has a smile on his face."

"Yes, but it's like he's waiting for a ride at Disneyland. Doesn't he understand the seriousness of what's happening at the altar?"

"I actually find his joy quite refreshing. We have too many sour-pusses around here. He can infuse a bit of holy joy into our parish."

"But, it's distracting. I've heard parishioners talking about it – how the boy just can't sit still."

"Well, we could put ankle weights on him under his cassock. And wrist weights too, so he can't fidget."

"Oh, Father, you know I don't mean to sound harsh. I think he's a fine young boy, but like I said, he just needs a few pointers on what to do with his hands and feet – and the rest of him for that matter – while serving at the altar. And Father, I think an announcement needs to be made, from the pulpit, that if people have crying babies, they need to take them out until the baby settles down. We have a cry room for a reason, but nobody seems to want to use it."

"Is the noise of youngsters drowning out your music, Rosemary?"

"I was more worried about your homilies, Father. And the liturgy."

Father Dante smiled. "Have you ever been a parent, Rosemary?"

"No."

"Me neither. But I've heard enough Confessions to know it ain't a cake walk. We, at this parish, are not going to make it any harder."

"Why is it hard to pick up your child and take him out when he's screaming and then come back in when he's calm?"

"That's not the hard part. The hard part is how my announcement from the pulpit will be interpreted. No matter how I choose my words and how nicely I say them, some parent will hear me say that children are not welcome here. And that parent won't come back the next Sunday or the next. And maybe not until their children are all grown up. Or maybe never."

"I can't imagine anyone would take it that hard, Father, just because of a simple request that they not let their children ruin Mass for 500 other people."

"When I was a kid, I attended a parish where there were signs on every door 'No food, No drink, No chewing gum inside the Church.' Everyone ignored those signs. Toddlers were always stuffing their mouths full of something their parents had brought in little zip-loc bags to keep them quiet, and it never worked anyway. Babies make noise, no matter where they are, or what is in their mouths, except of course, when they are hiding in a rack of clothing in a busy department store and they hear their mother frantically calling out their name. Anyway, one day, Father Milo decided he was going to say something. 'As I came down the aisle today,' he said, 'I was walking on Cheerios.' Everyone knew what was coming. He was going to scold parents for bringing snacks for their babies. 'It is, to me, like walking on rose pedals,' he said. 'Children are the future of this church. Never let it be said that any of us here ever glared at a crying baby. Children are completely welcome here. The Kingdom of Heaven is probably littered with Cheerios too.' See, Rosemary, Father Milo taught me just about everything I know about being a priest. So I can pretty much guarantee you that, if there is an announcement from the pulpit about the noisiness of babies at our parish, it will not be from me."

On his route back to the rectory, Father Dante noticed a larger than normal number of roses whose lives had been spent. Maybe it had been too long since he pruned. He couldn't remember the last time. He also couldn't remember the last time he had heard a song coming from the garden. Father Dante and his mother would often sit on the concrete bench and listen to the far-off choirs of celestial voices. Occasionally, she would hum along as she dreamily rocked to and fro, in rhythm with the music.

Father Dante grabbed clippers from the shed and found Sylvie at his front door when he came back around.

She had come by to drop off paperwork for Veronica to make her first Holy Communion in the spring. And to voice her latest struggles with mothering six children under the age of nine.

"Who let you out of the house by yourself on a Saturday," he asked, kissing her on the forehead.

"I needed to escape. Don't ask me how I did it. The other day, I needed coffee, so I told them I'm going to go get coffee, and they whined at me: 'But we want you to stay and cuddle up with us and watch *Tangled*.' So I told them 'Daddy's here and he can watch it with you.' So Paul gives me one of those looks that says: 'If I have to watch that movie one more time, I'm logging onto SpouseBeGone.com and will be serving you with divorce papers upon your return.' And the kids are just as unhappy about it: 'But daddy doesn't really watch it with us. He sits there and watches sports on his iPhone while he's supposed to be watching the movie.' To which, Paul and I are both thinking: What grown man in his late thirties is *supposed* to be watching a movie about a Disney princess with magical hair? For the *seventh* time.'"

"I haven't seen it yet," Father Dante said, snipping dead roses off the Bob Hope rose bush. "I would have come over and watched it with them."

"So instead of feeling grateful for the love these little people engulf me with all day, I began to feel trapped and suffocated."

"I heard it has a good message. Self sacrifice."

"So, then I snapped at them and went on a mini-tirade about how they never give me a moment to myself."

He moved on to the John Paul II rose bush. "I'd really like to see how Rapunzel compares with Belle on the self-giving love scale."

"The other morning, my kids are hanging on me and begging me for food, and I actually had to start my coffee to brewing before I put their toast in the toaster.'"

"Belle, as you know, is my favorite Disney princess. Not only because of her willingness to give up her life for her father and see right through to the wounded heart of the Beast, but because of her love of books too."

"Have you heard a word I've said, Dante? Ugh! You men are all alike."

"Why don't you try giving up coffee for a day, Sis." He snipped a perfect pink rosebud and handed it to her. "Sounds like you've got a monkey on your back."

"Awe, but it's Mystic Monk Midnight Vigils blend. I just got it. I ended up mail ordering three pounds so I wouldn't have to desert my children to go get coffee anymore."

"Well, that was good problem solving."

"It's for a good cause. Supports a monastery. Maintains my sanity."

"Those are good causes."

"I better go." She picked up her purse off the concrete bench and slung the strap over her shoulder.

Father Dante put the clippers down and walked with her toward the parking lot.

"Dante, have you ever heard those European sirens in those movies about someone getting kidnapped in a foreign country. You know what I'm talking about." She made the sound to demonstrate, her voice oscillating slowly between a high and low pitch. "That's what Joey sounds like when he calls my name. We all call him the mommy siren."

"Well, I know what to get you for Christmas."

"You can cross European squad car off the list of possibilities."

"I was thinking ear plugs."

"Wisdom, I need wisdom, Dante." He opened the door to her mini-van for her.

"Then, stay and pray in the chapel."

She got in and put the keys in the ignition. "I need toilet paper too."

"Off to Wal-Mart, then huh?"

"I've got to get my shopping done and get home and get the kids ready. Joseph is serving at the Vigil Mass. Thanks for the rose." She laid the flower on the passenger seat and picked up a piece of folded, wrinkled paper. "Oh, here, this is for you."

Father Dante opened it and found drawings of round, puffy creatures with large eyes and antennas, one colored pink, one purple and one with an orange and yellow swirl.

"It's from Katherine. She told me to tell you, and I quote, 'They're all fuzzy and everything. They have cute powers. When you rub their bellies, cute powers come out.'"

"I will cherish it." Father Dante smiled and stooped into the car to kiss his sister on the forehead. He closed the door, and she turned the key and opened the window, staring into his face.

"Dante, are you OK? I'm sorry. We spent the whole time talking about me. But you have something on your mind, don't you."

Father Dante didn't think he had acted any different than usual, but Sylvie always had been quite intuitive.

"I'll tell you about it sometime," he said. "When you have a few minutes."

"What is it?"

"It's a little complicated. When are you coming over again?"

"Well, now you've got me in suspense. How can I leave now?"

"It's not urgent. Go run your errands and we'll talk tomorrow. I'll call you."

"You're putting it off. It's something big. You're afraid to tell me."

"It's nothing earth-shattering, Sylvie." He folded Katherine's drawing of the fuzzy creatures with cute powers. "Go get those kids to Mass. I've got to go hear some Confessions. Pray for me, Sylvie, and tell those little ratfinks of yours to do the same."

ℬ❳❲❳ℬ❳❲❳ℬ❳❲❳ℬ❳❲❳ℬ❲

Father Dante sat in the Confessional, saying the prayer he prays each time he enters.

Give me wisdom, Lord. Let all who enter here see the face of mercy and hear the voice of compassion.

He opened the door and sat back down.

A small woman in her late 30s peeked into the Confessional, around the screen that allows penitents to remain anonymous.

"Welcome," Father Dante said.

"Thank you." Her voice was frail, like an elderly woman, and her demeanor was old and tentative. She wore a white polo shirt, blue slacks, blue socks and brown penny loafers, which probably could have been purchased from the children's department. She stood uneasily, stooped as if she would go unnoticed if she made herself very small.

"Welcome. Please, come sit down."

She moved slowly to the chair.

"May the Lord bless you and help you make a good confession."

"Bless me Father, for I have sinned. It's been two years since my last Confession. I have missed Mass a number of times."

"Uh-huh. How many?"

"Um. I guess about a hundred."

"So you haven't been to church in two years."

"No. I watch the Mass every Sunday on TV."

"Have you been ill?"

"No."

"Is there anything else you would like to confess?"

"Well, I have not always been kind to others."

Father Dante nodded.

"Anything else on your mind?"

"No."

"Well, you know, the televised Mass is only for those unable to attend in person. You are doing yourself a great disservice by not receiving our Lord in the Eucharist. He is longing to be united with you."

"I know Father."

"Have you missed Him?"

"Yes."

"Why have you not come?"

"I can't. I want to, but I can't."

"Because..."

"I can't be around that many people. I start to feel like I can't breathe."

"Do you feel like that in other places?"

"Yes. I only go to the grocery store in the middle of the night. When there aren't so many people."

"Have you told a doctor how you are feeling? There are ways to treat what you are going through."

"Yes. I was on medication. But I began to have suicidal thoughts, so I quit taking it."

Father Dante would have liked to tell her that crowds are nothing to fear. That most strangers would never harm you and, in fact, would come to your assistance if you need help. But, he remembered little Wang Yue, a 2-year-old toddler hit by two trucks in a Chinese marketplace and left bleeding in the street. No one stopped to help. A surveillance camera revealed that many altered their path to avoid her, even as life slipped from her suffering body.

"I know the world can seem a cruel place," Father Dante told the penitent. "But we are all in God's care. He never forgets us for a second. He cares about the smallest details. I would like you to go read Matthew 10:30."

When Father Dante thought of that scripture, he always remembered how Elina used to enlist him to pull out her gray hairs. There came a day when they both realized there were just too many. The task was taking too long and Elina was risking the thinning of her hair. So she began to color it instead of remove it. She kept that up until she became ill and was unable to do it anymore. Seeing his mother go gray was unsettling. He hadn't realized how Clairol had hidden the passage of time.

"Have you ever had a panic attack at church?" he asked the woman in the confessional.

"No. But other crowded places, I have."

"What's the worst that could happen to you at church?"

"I don't know. Maybe I'll have a panic attack and disrupt everything."

"Tell you what. You come to Mass tomorrow. Daily Mass has a much smaller crowd. Sit up in the front. I'll be watching out for you. I'll be praying for you. The whole time. You'll see, nothing will happen to you."

"Is that my penance? To come to church?"

"No, no," he smiled. "It is your salvation."

෫ ✣ ෬

15

Secret Recipe

On Fridays, Father Dante takes only bread and water. A number of people know this, either because they have witnessed it or they have heard it in one of his homilies. But the difficult penance is the one no one on earth knows about. It provides a constant reminder of the Lord's sufferings. And that, of course, is why it is so beautiful. A tiny, tiny thing: so beautiful. Father Dante wears a pebble in his left shoe. It is the perfect penance for him. Ever since he was a kid, he had been hyper-sensitive to every small matter. He could not stand tags in his shirts or a drop of water on his pants. The thing he hated most was the way his socks bunched up inside his shoes. His mother tried to choose thin socks with very discreet seams, or at least seams that did not end right at the small toe. But even that did not always prove satisfactory.

His poor mother had put up with it since he was eighteen months old and had rarely done more than gripe under her breath that he was picky and difficult to please. One day, when Dante was seven, the poor woman had had enough. It was as if all her patience on the issue had been used up. She knew she had to break him. And she knew there was a perfect way to do it.

"OK, Dante," she told him. "These are the only socks that are laundered and we need to pick up your father at the airport.

So, you need to put them back on and just ignore the seams." If he would wear the white crew socks just this once, she theorized, he would see that he would soon forget about the alleged agony they caused his toes. Elina thought that going to see his father would be incentive enough. He had been away for two weeks.

Dante wanted to comply. He wanted desperately to see his father. He wanted desperately to please his mother. But his toes would not allow it. The very thought of putting the seamed socks on made him feel like he was being imprisoned or drowned or shackled.

"No, Mama, I can't wear these," he whined. "I just can't!"

"You mean you won't."

"No, *I can't.*"

"Then, you can't come with me to get your father. Because you can't go barefoot."

"Please, Mama, where are my other socks – the black ones?"

"They are all dirty, Dante. You need to wear these." She picked one up and gathered it into an accordion up to the toe. "Come on. Sylvie's all strapped into her car seat already."

"No, Mama," he said, sitting on his feet. "No, not those."

"Dante, Papa's plane is landing. We need to go. Put these on." She grabbed his ankle and tried to muscle the sock onto his toe, but he wriggled so fiercely, her efforts were fruitless.

"OK, then," she said, standing up and dropping the socks in front of him. "I'll see you in a little while."

"No, Mama. Please, I can just wear my other socks." He went to the bathroom to dig them out of the laundry.

"No, Dante," she said, putting her purse strap over her shoulder. "I'm not taking you to the airport with dirty socks. You'll stay here." She opened the door. "I'll be back in just a little while."

"No, Mama," he cried, grabbing onto her, tears now streaming down his cheeks. "Don't go. Don't leave me here. I don't want to be alone. I want to see Papa. I want to see the airplanes."

"Then put on your socks and shoes," she said. "I'll wait for you in the car. I'll give you five minutes and then, I will leave."

"No, Mama! Don't leave."

"I'll wait five minutes."

When the allotted time had elapsed, Elina quietly opened the door and snuck in to find Dante sitting on the floor in the family room, hugging his legs into his chest, with the socks still untouched by his side. She snuck back out, started the car and pulled out of the driveway. She saw his panicked, tear-streaked face contorting in horror and his tiny hands pressed against the glass of the family room window as she pulled away from the house. She drove around the corner and parked, gave it thirty seconds and then returned home, all set to tell him she'd decided to give him one more chance. He would know she means business and the fear of being left alone would surely overshadow the fear of sock seams. But as she walked in the door and his trembling body dissolved into her embrace, she fell to her knees and wept right along with him.

"I'm sorry, Dante," she said. "You know I would never really leave you. I was pretending to go so you would put on those blasted socks."

She wished she could erase the abandonment she had inflicted upon him. She had been left too as a child, by her mother, but not by her mother's choice. Her mother would have never made the decision to leave as she herself had just made Dante think she'd done. No cure for any obsessive-compulsive behavior could justify that kind of trauma.

And so, Elina and Dante, the little one wrapped in his mother's embrace, made their way into the bathroom to dig through the dirty clothes.

It was, finally, a case of good old-fashioned peer pressure that cured Dante of his aversion to gym socks. He didn't want to be the only one on the high school basketball team wearing black dress socks. During the games, he was usually distracted enough not to notice the horrid seams.

The irony is that black dress socks are about the only kind of socks suitable for a cassock or clerics, so his discomfort all but ended when he was ordained.

Until, of course, the idea of the pebble came to him. Maybe he should add an extra one for a while, he thought, as he finished his slice of Wonder bread. One in each shoe. An extra for Larry Crenshaw.

ෞ♋ඎ♋ෞ♋ඎ♋ෞ♋ඎ♋ෞ♋ඎ♋ෞ♋ඎ

Sharon Perry, minister of the sick, who usually brought communion to those who cannot make Mass, was herself ill, so Father Dante got Mrs. Crowe's address from the office. When he arrived at the small, one-bedroom apartment, there was a note: *Sharon, come on in.*

Father Dante knocked and cracked the door slightly. "Mrs. Crowe, it's me, Father Dante. I brought Communion. Sharon's not feeling well."

"Come in, Father," came a faint voice from the bedroom.

The sheet was off, crumpled at the bottom of the bed. The blanket was half on the floor and half rumpled over the woman. A thick layer of dust coated the dresser and certain portions of the nightstand, in the few places not occupied by tissues and nearly empty drinking glasses. A line of balled up tissues was wedged between the mattress and the headboard.

Dante picked up the sheet. "Mind if I fix this a little?" he said. With as limited as the woman's mobility was, Father Dante wondered how the bedcovers could have gotten in such a disarray. It must have taken quite some time. Father read to her from the day's Scriptures and gave her Communion.

"Who's been taking care of you while you've been sick?" Father asked after they had taken several minutes for silent prayer.

"My daughter comes by from time to time to bring me something to eat. She stocked the pantry with some cans of soup."

"Would you like me to make you something before I leave?"

222

"No, thank you, Father. I can't eat anything."

"Some tea, then?"

"No, no. I don't want to trouble you."

"It's no trouble. Just point me towards the tea bags."

"Far right kitchen cabinet."

When he opened the cabinet door, Father Dante's eyes fell on a bottle of prescription medicine on the second shelf. He read the label as the mug of water went round and round in the microwave. Through the amber-colored plastic, he could tell there weren't more than maybe seven to ten pills left.

The tea seemed to take an eternity to infuse to the proper color brown, and Father Dante wondered if he had gotten the water hot enough. "Would you like sugar, Mrs. Donnelly?" he called in to her as he dunked the tea bag up and down.

"No, thank you, Father."

"How about some dry toast? Or some crackers?"

"No, thank you, Father. I don't even know if I can keep black tea down."

He set the steaming tea on her nightstand and adjusted her pillows, holding her head, with its soft cottony hair, in his large hand. "Here, I'm going to prop you up a bit, so you can drink your tea."

"Thank you, Father."

He sat on the edge of her bed. "Are you taking Propofol?"

"Oh, my medicine?"

"Yes, I saw the bottle out there when I made the tea."

"Yes, it helps me sleep. I've been in such pain with my arthritis, it keeps me up nights."

"Propofol is a very strong drug."

"Nothing else seemed to work."

"Your doctor prescribed it?"

"It's a prescription drug."

"It has someone else's name on it."

"Oh, yes. That's my daughter. She gets the prescription from her doctor so I don't have to get out and go to mine. It's painful for me to even get into the car."

"Does your doctor know you're on it?"

"I'm sure he does."

"When is the last time you went to the doctor?"

"I can't remember. One day runs into the next, you know, when you're sick."

"Especially when you're having trouble sleeping."

"Well, I don't have much trouble now. The medicine does the trick. My daughter calls me each night and makes sure I've taken it. My memory is so terrible, I wouldn't even remember to take the medication if it wasn't for her. She calls and reminds me."

"Mrs. Donnelly, Propofol is the medication that killed Michael Jackson."

"Really? I thought it was dope or something."

"That's what Propofol is. You shouldn't be taking it unless your doctor specifically prescribes it for you. And even then. What if you took too much?"

"I think it's pretty harmless, Father. My daughter tells me I can even take a second dose if the first one doesn't make me sleepy enough. She takes double all the time."

"How are things between you and your daughter?"

"Well, it used to be kind of tense. She has a lot of resentment, for what reason, I don't know. Well, I suppose I was never the model mother. But since I got sick, things have been a lot better between us."

"Your house plants look like they could use some attention."

"Too late for that, Father. They're deader than a doornail. Don't have the energy to get up and water them."

"Your daughter doesn't have much of a green thumb?"

"No, never has. She doesn't pay them any attention."

"How often does she come?"

"Maybe once or twice a week, I suppose."

"Not on a specific day?"

"No, no."

"Too busy with work?"

"No. She doesn't work. She's on disability herself. Threw her back out. So she doesn't have a set schedule or anything."

"Mrs. Donnelly, I don't want you to take any more of those pills."

"How will I get to sleep?"

"You know, sometimes insomnia can be used for a great spiritual benefit. Say prayers. Turn on EWTN and see what Mother Angelica or Father Groeschel have to say." He pulled a card out of his pocket and laid it on her nightstand. "Or call me. I'll pray with you. But please don't take any more of that medication. I'm afraid it might be the end of you."

"I don't think I would mind that all too much, Father. God forgive me. I don't think I would."

"Well, I would mind, Mrs. Donnelly. And so would all the other people who love you. Please, for our sake, don't take any more. We need your prayers. Middle of the night prayers are very powerful. If you do happen to suffer insomnia, would you mind offering a prayer for a man named Larry? And for me, so I will know how to reach him."

ಬುೋ೫ಆಬುೋ೫ಆ೫ಆಬುೋ೫ಆ೫ಆಬುೋ೫ಆ

When Father Dante returned home, there was a message on his answering machine. "Dante, call me." There was desperation in those three words, so he picked up the phone right away.

"Sylvie, what's up?"

"Dante, I haven't been able to sleep. Will you please tell me what you needed to talk to me about?"

"I'm sorry, Sylvie. I didn't mean to keep you hanging. I shouldn't have said anything."

"You said you would call."

"I'm sorry, Sylvie. I've had so much on my mind."

"Well, please, just tell me now."

"OK, Sylvie. It may come as a bit of a shock to you." He paused to deeply inhale. "Mom left a letter after she died. It had some information in it that I found very surprising."

"What was it?"

"Papa was not my biological father."

"What? What do you mean? Was Mama married before?"

"No. She was not married. And she nearly had me aborted. But then, she met Papa. And I know that's a lot to process, but here's where it gets really crazy."

"Crazy?"

"My biological father is billionaire Lawrence Crenshaw."

"Your father is a billionaire?"

"My biological father is a billionaire." Long silence. "Sylvie, are you OK?"

"I can't believe Mom kept this secret all our lives."

"Well, you yourself told me all parents keep secrets."

"Yes, Dante. But I didn't mean this. I was talking about keeping private stashes of Cheetos and sneaking into the bathroom to eat them while making your kids sit at the table and eat carrots. Or, maybe at the very worst, lying to them about how far you used to go on the first date. I wasn't talking about hiding a billionaire father from a kid."

"Why are you so upset by this, Sylvie? I think this is rocking your world more than mine."

"I'm just trying to imagine, Dante, what it must be like for you, finding out our father was not your father."

"He was my father, Sylvie. *Is* my father. I would have very much loved to have his blood coursing through my veins. And, all my life, I believed it did. But his love still does. That's what counts, isn't it?"

"Yes, of course, that's what counts."

"I couldn't have asked for any more of that. Our parents knew how to love."

A long silence.

"Are you there, Sylvie girl?"

"Yes, I'm here."

"Are you alright?"

"Yeah. It's just – our mother, Dante. Who was she? Who was our mother?"

"She was Elina De Luz. A loving mother and devoted wife. A woman of faith. A good and compassionate soul. And yes, a woman with a past. Without which, I would not be here."

"So, have you met him? Your billionaire father?"

"Oh yes."

"What's he like?"

"Well, he's not like Papa."

"Well, what's he like?"

"Remember how Papa had that way about him, every time you were in the room, every time you wanted his attention, any time you wanted to talk to him, there was nothing else in the entire world at that moment. Just you and him."

"Yeah, I remember."

"Well, with Larry Crenshaw, there are a million other things: tee times, power lunches, board meetings. The latest exotic car, the next mansion location. And soon, these things are going to pass away. His eyes are going to have to turn to something else."

‽)❇(❧❇)❧❇)❧❇)❧❇(❧❇(❧

When Father Dante stopped into the parish office late afternoon of the following day to pick up his messages, there were five from Stephanie Jansen, in parentheses, "Joyce Donnelly's daughter."

She had no polite greeting for him when he returned her call.

"Did you tell my mother not to take her medication?"

"Yes."

"Why? She had a horrible night last night."

"Ms. Jansen, do you know anything about Propofol?"

"Yes. Probably more than you do. I am a nurse. And I have read the package insert cover to cover."

"Then you know it's a very dangerous medication."

"No, it is a safe medication."

"It killed Michael Jackson."

"An overdose killed Michael Jackson."

"And how do we know that won't happen to your mother?"

"She is not mentally impaired. She knows how to take her meds."

"She said you told her she could take a double dose." The line was silent. "Did you tell her that?"

"No."

"Then she is not capable of administering that medication to herself. Because it is her understanding that you did."

"That medication has relieved my mother's suffering. I'm not going to take it away from her."

"And if it ends up killing her?"

"What is life if all it consists of is suffering?"

"So you're OK with that."

"With what?"

"If the medication kills her."

"OK with it? Of course I'm not OK with it. She's my mother. But there comes a point when the person you love is in such agony–"

"That it is better for you if they just cease to suffer."

"Better for me? I don't know what you're implying, but I do know that you have thrust yourself into a matter that is not at all your business. It is beyond me that you would want to take something away from my mother that would relieve her pain and make her last days on earth at least somewhat tolerable."

"Last days on earth? Your mother is only 64. Right now, she's recovering from a stomach virus or food poisoning or something. And she has some Arthritis, which is miserable, but not fatal. I have many, many parishioners who live with chronic pain. There are ways to manage that pain besides giving them dangerous drugs that aren't even prescribed for them. I happen to know your mother is on a number of other medications as well as Propofol." Father Dante didn't, in fact, "know" this, but he surmised it. "And I'm afraid the combination might prove lethal."

"She takes the pain meds during the day and the sleeping meds at night."

"And her doctor said that was OK?"

"It is safe."

"Your name is on the prescription, Ms. Jensen. Not hers."

"I don't want to make her go to the doctor. She hates going. And it's hard for her to get out."

"And inconvenient for you too, I'm sure."

"This is not about me, Father De Luz. This is about what's best for my mother."

"I'm glad to hear you say that, Ms. Jensen. So you will take your mother to her doctor, then, and let him prescribe the proper medication?"

"She has an appointment for next Wednesday."

"Great."

"Just out of curiosity, what brings you around to visit my mother?"

"She asked for someone to bring her Communion."

"Oh, OK. Well, I don't think she is going to be needing those services anymore."

"If she tells us to take her off the Ministry of Care list, of course, we will."

"You can go ahead and take her off."

"She would be the one to tell us, Ms. Jensen."

"Then, I will have her call."

"Ms. Jensen, I know what you're going through. My mother was ill for quite some time before she died. I sure wish I had her back. I miss her terribly. I still feel like an orphan. Cherish your mother while you still have her, Ms. Jensen. Time passes and takes away what we love most. And what we will miss more than we could have ever imagined. Every passing day brings us closer to that day when it just might be too late."

൬✂ൔ✂൬✂ൔ✂൬✂ൔ✂൬✂ൔ✂

Since Larry Crenshaw had not returned his calls, Father Dante decided to show up unannounced the Friday before Thanksgiving. He had a tin of candied figs for Roberta and one for Larry Crenshaw and a third for whatever downstairs receptionist would let him through.

The candy within the dollar store tins (adorned with artistically unimaginative horns of plenty) was no ordinary thing. Father Francis had made it. He got the recipe from a parishioner who once worked at Aunt Felicity's Fudge Shoppe in Nantucket, which might possibly sell the best fudge known to man. It also offers customers a heart-smart, fat-free alternative in candied figs. The parishioner gave Father Francis the secret recipe with the understanding that he would never give it to another soul. To Father Francis, a promise is a promise, so no matter how many times recipients of the luscious confection begged him for the recipe, he told them kindly but firmly that he would go to his grave with the little scrap of hand-scrawled paper that no one else on earth had ever read. Not even Father Dante knew where Father Francis kept it. The elderly priest guarded it faithfully, even as he prepared the candy, making sure no one (like Father Dante) was reading over his shoulder or watching too closely. He went about it as a dog with a bone, placing his body between the onlooker and the treasure in danger of being snatched.

Larry Crenshaw seemed grateful for the figs. But he had something on his mind.

"I keep awaking to the sound of knocking. Several times, I got up and went to the door. No one there. I wondered if it was somebody playing tricks. By the fourth or fifth night, I stopped checking the door. I knew it was just in my dreams. But I still lie awake wondering what it means. Who's trying to get in?"

"The knocks of St. Paschal."

"Hmmm?"

"It is said that the sound of knocking came from St. Pachal Baylon's tomb for years after his death, and later, his pictures and relics. The mystic friar, who lived in the 1500s, still comes to warn people with the sound of knocking."

"Warns people of what?"

"In Spain and Italy, it is said he warns them of their impending death."

"And in America? What does it mean here?"

"Likely, the same."

"What's the point of being warned? Is there anything you can do about it?"

"He warns them so they can receive the Sacraments before they die."

"Last rites?"

"Yes. Confession, anointing of the sick, Communion."

"Am I going to die soon?"

"Only God knows that."

"And St. Paschal apparently."

"Do you want me to hear your confession? Just in case?"

"Nice try." He opened the tin of figs and held it out to Father Dante.

The priest smiled and took one. "Thank you."

Larry Crenshaw picked up a fig and bit into it. "Now, I have a question for you."

"Sure. What is it?"

"Do I call you 'Father' or do I call you 'son'?" The words came out slightly muffled through the fig.

"Whichever you prefer."

"They're both going to take some getting used to." He offered the figs again.

"And, uh," Father Dante chewed, "what do I call you?"

Larry Crenshaw reached into the tin and popped another perfect confection in his mouth. "Keep bringing me these and you can call me whatever you want."

ಬ❌ೞ❌ಬ❌ೞ❌ಬ❌ೞ❌ಬ❌ೞ❌ಬ

Father Dante waited in the narthex, vested in a purple chasuble. It was his favorite color to wear. Not because he particularly liked purple, but because it is worn during Advent, his favorite time of the year. It was a season of quiet waiting, longing for Light to come into the world. Longing for goodness to dawn.

The hyperactive altar server shuffled into the narthex, watching his feet move across the tile. Strangely, there was nothing hyper about him.

"Jared, I haven't seen you serve for a while." Father Dante shook his hand.

"I'm not an altar server anymore."

"Why not?"

"They said I am not reverent enough. They told me to sit still, and I tried. I really tried. But I just couldn't." The boy blinked to dam back his tears. "I don't think altar serving is my calling. They told me maybe I should serve the church in a different way."

"Like what?"

"They mentioned ushering or helping with the decorations or something."

"Do you want to do those things?"

"I don't know. I guess so."

"Are those things as important as serving at Mass?"

"Um. I don't think so."

"You are right. They are not. Serving at the altar is the highest privilege. And it will not be taken away from you. I will see to that. Did you bring your alb?"

"No."

"Bring it next time."

"Really? But Miss–"

"We will implore Heaven's help. If you've been given the desire to serve, there must be a way."

"Who's the patron saint of sitting still?"

"Don't know off hand," Father Dante said, rubbing his chin. "But let's put St. Francis in charge. Maybe he can help instill in our congregation the joy you feel at Mass."

The boy smiled wide.

"Now," Father Dante said, "as for today, I have a different job for you."

"What?"

"See that woman in the front row? To the left there. Sitting by herself."

"Yeah."

"She needs prayers. Can you pray for her during Mass?"

"Sure. How come?"

"Just lift her up to heaven, Jared. Lift her up."

"OK, Father, sure."

"And while you're at it, can you pray for a man named Lawrence? There's something wrong with his heart. It has to be fixed before it's too late."

The woman with agoraphobia made it through the Mass without incident. Maybe Jared's other prayer would be answered as well.

Father Dante could only hope. He wanted to find out if St. Paschal had made any progress, but Lawrence Crenshaw had not returned his half-dozen calls.

ಬ)ჯ(ಞ)ჯ(ಞ)ჯ(ಞ)ჯ(ಞ

Elina held the tiny animal in her hand. "OK, kids. This is the first installment."

"What's an installment?" asked 4-year-old Sylvie. "Is that a type of sheep?"

"No, no. This is the first of the pieces of the nativity. By Christmas Eve, Mr. Hornbecker will have received the entire set. One piece at a time for eleven days."

"Aw, cool!" exclaimed Dante.

"And do you know what piece he will receive last – on Christmas Eve?"

"Which one?" asked Sylvie.

"Baby Jesus," Dante guessed.

Elina gave her son directions how to sneak up to someone's door, hang the organza pouch containing a portion of salvation history on the door knob, ring the bell and run fast.

"Can I come too?" asked Sylvie.

"You'll be too slow, and we'll get caught," Dante said. "Maybe you can do it next year."

"I think we should let her try," Elina said.

"But what if we're discovered? It will ruin the whole thing. What if she shrieks or giggles?"

"You have to be very quiet and very fast, OK Sylvie?" said Elina. "You can do it."

And indeed she did. Every day Dante and Sylvie would make it back inside the house and watch out the window as Mr. Hornbecker collected the treasure from the door knob, stepped out onto his porch and looked both ways down the line of bungalows. Then he would shake his head, turn and, fumbling his fingers inside the bag with great effort, remove the newest acquisition and place it with the expanding manger scene, which he kept on his porch railing. Dante and Sylvie would watch as he paused there, looking on at the tiny figures, standing there still as a statue in his baggy gray slacks and maroon suspenders. It seemed to them that his head was bowed at the scene, but it was hard to tell really because the years – and probably the grief – had already bent him. When the children rang the doorbell and personally presented the baby Jesus to him on Christmas Eve, his eyes grew moist and he reached out his boney, wrinkled hand and grabbed Dante's forearm, opening his mouth to speak, but nothing could squeeze out past the emotion collecting in his throat. So he just nodded his head and Dante noticed that the old man was so stooped, that the two were on eye level. Then he took his hand off Dante and stooped even lower to grab Sylvie's hand. "Thank you, little one," his voice trembled.

"You're welcome." She rushed him and grabbed him around the legs, knocking him a bit off balance. He loved it.

This is where Father Dante got the idea how to win back Mrs. Granger's soul for God. It would be a perfect tribute to his mother on his first Christmas without her. Mrs. Granger had lost two sons, a husband and a sister within a two-year period. The first son was diagnosed with cancer. The second died two months later in a car accident. A few weeks later, their father died of a heart attack and the first son lost his battle with cancer a few months after that. From all of this, Mrs. Granger, a life-long lukewarm Catholic, got the impression that there must not be a God. Father Dante made it his business to convince her that indeed there is and indeed He is madly in love with her.

She seemed mildly annoyed at the first few pieces of the nativity – the lamb, the shepherd, the first wise man. The second two wise men, the ox and the donkey were met with apathy. When Mrs. Granger received Joseph, she studied him and ever so slightly shook her head. Father Dante had no way of knowing what was happening to the nativity pieces because, unlike Mr. Hornbecker, Mrs. Granger did not keep them on her porch. Father Dante watched her go inside with the Joseph and then remained at his window, praying a decade of the rosary for his neighbor. On the fifth Hail Mary, Mrs. Granger drove past. The following day, the widow was outside, sweeping her front step, looking up and down the street, then piddling around in the geraniums in the small flowerbed that lined her porch, looking down the street again, then sweeping the walk one more time, looking up the street, and then watering the geraniums with a slow-flowing garden hose. When she had finally given up her watch, Father Dante made his move and was able to accomplish the drop-off seemingly without being noticed. Mrs. Granger looked down at the figurine of Mary and nodded her head. Father Dante was again watching from his window and began praying his decade. This time, on the seventh Hail Mary, Mrs. Granger backed out of her driveway.

Father Dante decided to hold fast to his family tradition and, on the ninth day – Christmas Eve – reveal the identity of the giver of the gifts.

"Yes, hello Father," Mrs. Granger said skeptically. "What brings you here?"

Father smiled and held out his hand toward her, flat like a table, the baby Jesus placed on top.

Father thought he detected a faint smile on Mrs. Granger's leathered face, but then her mouth turned to stone again. "So you're the one who has been stalking me with little trinkets."

"Yes, it's me." He smiled warmly, still holding the Christ Child.

"Well, thank you, Father," she said flatly, taking the baby off his hand. "It was very thoughtful."

Suddenly, a wave of longing washed over Father Dante and he wanted to be a child again. A child at Christmas. It was Mrs. Granger's perfume. She was wearing Cachet.

Every year, Elina would find Prince Matchabelli's Cachet in her stocking. She had Lucy to thank for that, although Mateo was the one who bought it. Soon after they got married, Mateo and Elina were at Walgreen's in the middle of the night looking for cough medicine to bring over to Lucy and, passing through the cosmetics, Mateo stopped to spray Elina's wrists with a selection of four or five scents. Cachet was the only one that neither of them found offensive, so that's the one that made it into her stocking two weeks later. Elina learned to love the scent because it was soft and because Mateo loved it. She would use only a tiny squirt each day to make it last all year long. In her single life, she had worn Les Larmes Sacrées de Thebes of Baccarat, which came in a mirrored pyramid bottle with a purple crystal stopper. She never actually liked the scent, but she wore it because her father spent $3,800 on it and she figured it must, therefore, be good. And she never had any trouble getting a date, so it must have, in actual fact, been good.

"Well, Merry Christmas, Mrs. Granger," Father Dante said as he swiveled toward the sidewalk.

"Merry Christmas, Father," she called after him, with limited emotion.

He heard the door shut behind him. Then, open.

"Father, do you want to see what I've been doing with the nativity?"

"Well, sure."

"Let me grab my purse. I'll open the garage and meet you at my car."

They drove in silence for several blocks. Father Dante was thinking of something to say. He usually had no trouble making conversation, but he had a feeling that, in that car, at that moment, every word counted. Something very big was at stake.

Not that the wrong words could do harm. But the right ones had the potential of doing so much good.

"We're almost there, Father," said Mrs. Granger, eyes glued to the road. "It's a short drive."

"You've got me in suspense, Mrs. Granger. But that's quite all right with me. I like surprises."

"You don't seem like the type that can be surprised by much."

As they stopped at a red light, Mrs. Granger stared at Denny's restaurant on the corner. Father Dante joined her in looking in the window. There he saw a younger Mrs. Granger, with her husband and two boys about 10 and 12 years old. The boys stuffed large amounts of food into their mouths, nodded wildly and smiled wide. Their parents shot knowing glances at each other. Dante remembered those glances shot from his own parents' eyes. They always filled him with a certain amount of comfort. Knowing his parents could communicate without words. It was a secure feeling, proof that, in an ever-changing and unpredictable world, some things were invincible and everlasting.

Mrs. Granger pulled into Ascension Cemetery and led Father Dante on a short, silent walk to a headstone that read *George Granger, beloved husband and father*.

"This is where your nativity ended up, Father," said Mrs. Granger.

"It's a wonderful place for it."

The woman placed the baby Jesus in the manger, which was set up in the grass in the shadow of her husband's gravestone.

"It's the only place for it. I really have no use for it. But George loved Christmas. When he was alive, we'd set up six or seven nativities around the house. We had one that was not breakable that the kids could play with when they were little. And we had a great big plastic one in the front yard." She bent down to fine tune the placement of the nativity's characters, putting the donkey outside the stable and placing the sheep close to baby Jesus, maybe so its breath could keep the baby warm. "He would have liked this nativity, Father. And I thank you."

"You are welcome."

She stared at the scene, lost in her memories of Christmases past when everyone she loved was still alive.

"You know," Father Dante said, "it would do a great honor to George's memory if you would embrace the Christ child, just as he did."

"I can't, Father. I'd like to. But I just can't believe in a God who would take away everything I ever cared about. God is supposedly love, right? Where is the love in that?"

"You are enfolded in God's love."

"I can feel no love. All there is is suffering."

"Are love and suffering incompatible? Why can't they be one and the same?"

"If you'd ever suffered as much as I have, you'd know the answer to that. I feel-" She swallowed hard. "I feel no more love. I just have pain."

"Why do you come here?"

"Why do I come here?"

"Yes. Why do you come to your husband's grave?"

"Where else can I go? There's nothing left for me anywhere else."

"Isn't all this nothing more than dirt and stone? Or is your husband looking on from somewhere? And your sons too."

"To tell the truth, I'm hoping to find them. I know I won't. But I hope. When I come here, I'm hoping to feel something brush past my cheek. Or hear a faint voice inside my head. It will all be my imagination, of course. The wishful thinking of a lonely old woman who is desperate for the ones she loves. It will all be fantasy. But I hope for it anyway."

"And do you find it?"

"No."

"But you still hope."

"I suppose."

Father Dante stooped down and picked up the baby Jesus. "That is what He's all about." He passed it to Mrs. Granger, who hesitated and then took it from him. "Hope."

The woman looked at the baby lying in her hand.

"See, if you have hope," Father Dante said, "you have Him."

She kept staring. Dante stared too. He wondered why it was so easy to say those words and so hard to believe them. Truth be told, he had also lost hope, though he never would have admitted it to another living soul. He could not imagine Larry Crenshaw ever coming around.

"I'll bet it seems like only yesterday," Father Dante told Mrs. Granger. "That your boys were babies. I'll bet it seemed like a miracle. Having something so precious in your arms."

She nodded.

"That's what Christmas is, Mrs. Granger. Having something precious to hold onto."

She burst into tears, and he hugged her close into his clerics.

"Hold onto it, Mrs. Granger. Don't let go."

The clouds moved over the sun and a gust of chilled wind swirled around the two of them. Then the sun reappeared and they were warm again. This is what Christmas always felt like for all his years growing up: the cool, heavy air, the genial sun and the gentle movement of souls toward God.

239

16

The Torch

A small boy, about seven years old, but too small to be seven, sat before him in the confessional. Father Dante smiled at the boy's large brown eyes, rimmed in a fringe of thick eyelashes. He had seen those eyes somewhere before. Which parishioner does this child belong to?

"Hi Father. I came to tell you my sins."

"Wonderful. Have you been to confession before?"

"I don't know. I don't think so."

"So, just say 'Bless me Father for I have sinned.' And then tell me what you feel sorry about."

"OK." He fiddled with a rosary. Blue glass beads with a gold-tone crucifix.

"How old are you?"

"Eight."

"Wonderful."

"My Grandma goes to confession every week. She told me to ask my Mom to bring me. She said it would make me feel better about all the things I do wrong and it would help me not to do those things again."

"She is right."

"So I begged my mom to bring me."

"Wonderful. So say, 'Bless me Father for I have sinned.'"

"Bless me Father for I have sinned."

"And now, what's on your heart?"

"Jimmy and me have a lot of fun with violent vegetable games."

Father Dante still could not figure out where he'd seen those eyes before. "Violent vegetable games? What is that?"

"We throw Jimmy's little sister's play vegetables at each other."

"Do you hurt each other?"

"No."

"Then why do you feel bad about it?"

"Jimmy's mother told us not to. It chips the paint and it makes Jimmy's little sister cry."

"Oh, I see. Did you say sorry to Jimmy's mom and sister?"

"I don't know."

"Well, next time you see them, why don't you do that, OK?"

The boy nodded, looking down at his hands, his eyelashes casting shadows on his cheeks below them.

"Is that all you wanted to talk about? Do you have any other sins you would like to confess?"

"No, that's all."

"Do you listen to your mother always?"

"Well, no, not always. But a lot I do."

"Are you sorry for the times you have not?"

"Yes."

"OK, now I will give you a penance. That is something you must do to make up for the wrong you have done."

The boy looked up at him intently.

"For your penance, go out and give your mom a big hug and thank her for bringing you to Confession. Then go kneel down in the front row and thank Jesus for forgiving you."

"OK."

"Do you have any questions for me?"

"Like what kind of questions?"

"Anything. Any kind of question."

"I can ask you anything?"

"Sure. I might not have the answer, but I can tell you where to find it."

"Like Siri?"

"I actually even know a little bit more about some things than Siri does. So what's your question?" Father Dante could tell the boy had a lot of them. He was trying to prioritize and pick the one most pressing.

"Why are there always more white gummy bears than any other color?"

"You don't like white gummy bears?"

"No. They're gross."

"You know, I think you stumped me. But I do know this: If you eat them with chocolate chips, even the pineapple ones are good."

"Chocolate chips?"

"Uh-huh."

"Thanks, Father. I'll try it."

"By the way, what is your favorite flavor?"

"Strawberry."

"Mine too."

The boy smiled and nodded.

Father Dante gave him absolution, a smile and a handshake and waited for the next penitent. An unusual amount of time passed, maybe forty-five seconds. For some reason, (maybe it was all the talk of gummy bears) Father Dante thought of eating figs with Lawrence Crenshaw. Then, a woman entered and solved the mystery of the familiar eyes. Roberta. Wonder of all wonders, it was Roberta. She sat on the edge of the chair, back perfectly straight, stiff for even her.

"I did not come here to confess, Father," she said. "But my son wants me to go to Confession, so I'm going to sit here for a minute, if that's OK."

"Sure. What would you like to talk about?"

"I don't know. What does one talk about in confession when they are not making a confession?"

"I don't know. The only people who usually sit in that chair are the ones who want to confess their sins."

"I don't believe in sins."

"What do you believe in?"

"I don't know. But if I were a god trying to win people over, I would not go about it the way your God does."

"Really? How would you do it?"

"I would not stand by and watch people suffer. That's for sure."

"You would answer every prayer. With a yes."

"Well, not every prayer. But the good ones."

And in the next three minutes, Father Dante learned why Roberta had left the Faith and abandoned hope. She had asked God to fix something and He had not.

She had suspected for some time, but confirmed it by searching history on her husband's computer one day. He had been a regular visitor to at least a dozen porn sites. When she confronted him about it, he was relieved. He had wanted for some time to share his discoveries with her and petitioned her to help him live out the perversities that he had adopted as his own fantasies. She was repulsed by the idea and suggested therapy. His refusal angered her and she made it a condition of her fulfillment of their wedding vows. He begrudgingly agreed, and she prayed incessantly for his healing, though she had never before been highly religious. Therapy seemed to be working, though their marriage was still strained from the memory of his betrayal and her threats of leaving. There was a distance between them that she hoped would recede with time. Her husband had come to look forward to his therapy. The prayers seemed to be helping. She was becoming closer to God as she realized her indebtedness. But then, one day, her husband told her he had fallen in love with his therapist. She fulfilled him in a way his wife never could. And now that broken woman was sitting before Father Dante demanding to know what virtually every person who suffers demands to know. Why.

For this, Father Dante had no specific answer. Only that it is somehow necessary for the greater good or a great battle is still being waged, both answers that do little to satisfy the person submerged in grief.

"Why were you so upset at the pornography?"

"It's offensive to women."

"Who taught you that?"

"I don't know. Nobody taught me. It just is what it is."

"Isn't that a moral judgment? Pornography is offensive?"

"It's a problem because it sets up unrealistic expectations for women to live up to."

"Why shouldn't men be able to look at whatever they want?"

"What are you getting at?"

Ever since Roberta told Father she was unaware that angels could have thumbs, let alone green ones, he knew she had been well educated in the Catholic faith. She knew her Catechism. Angels are pure spirit. They do not have bodies.

"You learned a moral code from somewhere," Father Dante said. "If there is no God, then there is no sin. But isn't there a right and wrong – as it relates to the treatment of other human beings?"

"Yes."

"Then, there is a failure to live up to that, right?"

"Quite often, yes."

"That is what we call sin. And that is why Confession should be so popular."

"Shouldn't they be telling the person they offended they are sorry."

"Yes. And God. If someone does something to offend you, God is offended too. That's how much He loves you. That's how much He wants to protect you."

"But He didn't protect me."

"He betrayed you?"

"Yes."

"Why did He set it up so that pornography is a sin? Wasn't that to protect you?"

"It didn't work."

"People choose to live outside of God's will. How is that God's fault?"

"Why didn't He hear my prayer? I wanted my husband back."

"What did your husband want?"

"Someone else, I guess."

"And God should have forced him to stay with you?"

"Isn't that what God Himself ought to want?"

"Unfortunately, because of man's selfishness, God doesn't always get what He wants."

"The all powerful, almighty God not get what He wants? What kind of a God is that?"

"A God that will suffer and die for us." Father Dante looked up at the crucifix hanging on the wall between them. "Do you think He wanted to go through that?"

"Maybe He has a different definition of the word *want*."

"Now, that is a very intriguing idea."

They both sat in silence for several moments, Father looking at his shoes, one hand on each knee and Roberta looking up at the crucifix.

"So what exactly does God want?" Roberta broke the silence.

"He only wants our love, but He often doesn't get it. There are too many lesser gods competing for it. And people choose to love them instead."

"That's exactly what my husband did to me. He chose the cheap. He forsook the real thing. I will never understand that."

"I'll bet if there was one thing the all-knowing God could not understand, it would be that, Roberta. But why blame Him for something someone else did?"

"Am I supposed to come and sit in Church and listen to them telling me that God answers our prayers when I know full well, He doesn't? Am I supposed to sit next to all the phonies and smile and pretend it's all true? Do you know my ex- and his new wife go to Mass every week? Are those the kinds of people I'm expected to spend my Sundays with?"

"No, you don't come to spend the hour with them. Or even the parishioners living saintly lives. There's only one thing that draws us. And once we've found it, nothing and no one can keep us from it."

"Well, I guess I haven't found it yet, whatever 'it' is."

"Did you ever remember who your confirmation saint was?"

"Actually, to tell you the truth, I never have forgotten. I just didn't want to tell you."

"Why not."

"You were annoying."

"I'm sorry. Am I still?"

"Yes. But I don't hold it against you."

"You don't?"

"No. It's your job."

"To be annoying?"

"To be relentless."

"Like God is in His love."

Roberta flashed Father Dante a skeptical smirk.

"So," the priest said, "who is it?"

"Who?"

"Your Confirmation saint."

"St. Dominic."

"You're kidding."

"No."

"Really? You've got to be kidding."

"No. I'm not. Why is that shocking?"

"Dominic is *my* Confirmation saint."

"Well, I suppose we will have to share."

"Yes, how wonderful, Roberta. How wonderful."

"These are the kinds of things that make you happy?"

"Yes, oh, yes. These are the things."

She stared at him, and he thought he could see, in the swirling contents of her soul, a longing for that kind of happiness.

"How did you come to choose St. Dominic?" he asked her.

246

"Nothing overly deep. Something about his symbol or something that I liked, but for the life of me, I can't remember now what it was."

"A dog with a flaming torch in its mouth."

"Yes." There was, for the first time, a hint of excitement in her voice. "That's it. I was a real dog lover in my youth. I chose him for the dog."

"I chose him for the torch."

"You were a pyromaniac?"

"No, no, but I did want to light the world on fire. When Dominic's mother was pregnant with him, she had a dream that her unborn child was a dog who carried a torch in his mouth that would set the world ablaze."

"When I was pregnant, I dreamed I was eating that fish from Dr. Seuss' *Cat in the Hat* between two slices of bread. But, listen, I think I've taken up enough of your time. I'm sure that line out there isn't getting any shorter."

"Why don't you go ahead and make a Confession. That way when your son ropes you into going to Church this Sunday because your mother put him up to it, you can receive Communion."

"Well, I don't think you'll see me in Church any time soon. But I'll tell you my sins, just so I don't have to lie to my son about going to confession. Anyway, what harm could it do?"

Now, if only he could get Roberta's boss to start thinking the same way.

17

Inheritance

The sky threatened a light drizzle as Dante set up his easel at the corner near the dry cleaners with the missing decimal point. He hadn't come in a while, but he needed to accomplish something. If he couldn't do anything for the soul of his own flesh and blood, maybe he could do something for a stranger's. But if it was going to rain, the harvest would have to wait for another day. Not that Father Dante would mind getting a little wet. But the ink would run.

And then, there he was. Just getting off the bus across the street.

"Hey, brother," Father Dante called across the street. "We missed you and your Mama at dinner."

"Oh yeah, sorry about that. Something came up."

"That's OK. Maybe another time, huh? This time, we'll bring dinner to your Mama."

The man crossed the street. "My Mama died."

"Oh, I'm so sorry," Father Dante said. He made the sign of the cross. "Eternal rest grant her, oh Lord."

"And may perpetual light shine upon her," the man mumbled, head down, hands in his pockets.

Father Dante doesn't find himself shocked very often. But he was, indeed, shocked. And the man must have known it too, because he explained, "My Mama used to say that all the time."

"You're Catholic?"

"My Mama was."

"She had you baptized?"

"Yup."

"Then you are too."

"Not so much anymore. My life hasn't been what you might call holy."

"Once Catholic, always Catholic. Baptism leaves an indelible mark. And if you let me draw you again, it just might show up on the drawing. Like a tattoo. On your soul."

Father Dante had known that since he was in third grade Catechism class. He had tried to picture what the mark would look like. The only thing that came to him was a dove, but he was pretty certain he was probably wrong. He was so intrigued by the indelible mark, he decided it would be the first thing he would look for when he got to heaven. He would look for it on the first soul he met there. When his mother told him in her death-bed letter that Larry Crenshaw was a baptized, non-practicing Catholic, he pictured the mark as a triangle. That's the way he would draw it, if the man whose mother loved shrimp would agree to a new sketch.

"No thanks, Father. I've got somewhere I gotta be."

Father Dante knew he would never see that man again. He prayed several Hail Marys for him until a boy about eleven scooted by on his skateboard, made a U-turn and agreed to a caricature. The kid was dressed in all the usual attire of a generation robbed of hope – excess amounts of clothing and metal, all black and silver – but there was a faint optimism in his eyes. Father Dante embarked on a predominantly one-sided conversation, talking as he sketched, about his own youth, the difficulty of being a kid, the pitfalls of growing up, the hope that lies in the future if only you believe hope can change the future.

"How come you're not in school?" Father Dante asked, sketching out the boy's eyebrows.

"I dunno."

"You don't know?"

He silently watched Father Dante sketch for a few minutes. "How'd you learn to draw?"

"Correspondence course. You interested in art?"

"I like to draw."

"Here," Dante ripped off the sheet with the boy's face on it and handed it to him. Then he turned the easel and handed the boy a marker. "You draw me."

"Oh, I don't know if I can do that. I don't draw people."

"What do you draw?"

"Dragons, snakes, skulls."

"Well, just draw a skull with some meat on it."

The boy smiled.

"Come on. No one has ever drawn me before."

The boy squinted at the priest and placed the pen on the paper. Soon, the pen started to move. "This is weird drawing with a pen. You can't make mistakes."

"You can. You just have to incorporate them into your design."

The boy placed his tongue between his lips and continued to work.

"So how come you're not in school?"

"Got kicked out."

"How come?"

"Brought a gun to school."

"Whose gun was it?"

"My mother's. She always told me it wasn't loaded."

"But it was?"

"Yeah."

"Are you the one I heard about on the news?"

The boy nodded. "Probably."

"The gun went off on the school bus."

"Yeah."

"Why did you bring a gun to school?"

"For protection." The boy cocked his head slightly as he sketched.

"From other kids?"

"Yeah. They think they are tough. I wasn't really going to use it. I was just going to scare them."

There was only one time in Dante's childhood when he felt unsafe. It was the morning that Elina woke Mateo up for Mass and Mateo rolled over and went back to sleep. She nudged him again and stroked his sideburns, tracing a circle around his ears with her long fingernails.

"Come on, sleepy head," she said. "You don't want to be late."

"I'm not going," he murmured.

She put her hand on his forehead. "Are you sick?"

"No. I just want to sleep."

"Did you not sleep well?"

"I'm just very tired."

"Well, we already missed the early Mass, Darling. Don't you want to get up now? You can always take a nap when we get home."

"I'm going to skip today."

"Skip?"

Though not yet Catholic, Elina knew enough about Catholicism to understand the gravity of the decision Mateo was making. For her to skip Mass was one thing. But for Mateo–.

"Sweetheart," she coaxed. "I know you. You're going to regret not going. Come on, get up and I'll make you a strong cup of coffee and some toast while you hit the shower."

"I'm not going, Elina."

"Do, do you want me to take Dante and Sylvie and go without you?"

"Whatever you want to do. I'm not going to tell you not to go to church, but we could all use some down time."

"I thought church *was* your down time. You've always told me that's where you get rejuvenated."

Dante listened from the bedroom doorway.

"Well, today, I'm getting rejuvenated right here in my bed." He rolled over and pulled the blanket over his shoulders. "I don't want to hear anything more about it."

To Dante's surprise, Elina got down on her hands and knees, lifted the orange-flowered bedspread and fished her black suede boots from under the bed. "Go fix your hair, Dante," she said, moving the zipper up the full length of her calf. "We don't want to be late."

"We're going without Daddy?"

"He's coming," she said. "It only takes him a minute to get ready. Now go wet down your hair and comb it." Dante was already in his church clothes. Every Sunday, he woke up knowing it was Sunday and, unlike on school days, never had to be told twice – or even once – to get out of his pajamas. As Dante made his way down the hall to the bathroom, he heard his mother say, "Come on, Mateo, you don't want to disappoint Dante. You know how much he loves going to church."

He wasn't sure if his father did not reply or he just couldn't hear him because the reply was too soft, but that was the end of what he heard. He turned on the water and looked at himself in the mirror. His mother had told him several weeks ago that he needed a haircut, but he begged her to put it off for awhile so he could grow hair like his father's. Mateo had a large amount of thick, wavy hair that he wore past his ears. Dante's was lighter in color and texture, but it had some wave, so he thought it might look somewhat like his Dad's if it was allowed to reach the proper length. Sister Teresa, who was in charge of the altar servers had never said anything specific about the appropriate length of hair, but his mother, the non-Catholic, had always told him it looked nicer to be clean cut at the altar. His father, the Catholic, never weighed in one way or another. Dante figured his Dad did not want to be a hypocrite. That's one thing his father could not be accused of. He had his faults, but that was not one of them.

"Come on, Dante," Elina said, passing by the bathroom, holding Sylvie in her arms. "We're going to be late."

"Daddy coming?" Dante dried the back of his neck.

"No."

"Why?"

"He's not feeling well."

Dante remembered his father telling his mother that he felt fine, but he knew it wouldn't be a good time to say so. He decided to wait until they were at least half way to church.

"Why do you think Daddy doesn't want to go to Church today," he asked as they waited for the light to turn green.

"Poor Daddy sick," piped Sylvie from the back seat.

"Don't worry, Dante. I'm sure this is an anomaly." Elina glanced over at his furrowed brow. "Do you know what an anomaly is?"

"No. Not really. Is it something to do with the weather? A natural disaster? Like a Tsunami?"

"No, it's something that doesn't happen very often."

"Tsunamis don't happen very often, but boy, when they do..."

His mother smiled. "Yes, but an anomaly means something out of the ordinary has happened and probably won't happen again. It means that next week, your father will be waking all of us up to go to church."

Dante could tell his mother wasn't completely convinced of her own words. But they brought him some comfort anyway. A parent's optimism always does, even if it is shrouding doubt.

"I miss Daddy," Sylvie said.

"I'm going to light a candle for him," Dante said. They rode the rest of the way in silence.

One of the readings at Mass was about Jesus predicting Peter's martyrdom.

I tell you the truth. When you were younger you dressed yourself and went where you wanted; but when you are old you will stretch out your hands, and someone else will dress you and lead you where you do not want to go. Jesus said this to indicate the kind of death by which Peter would glorify God. Then he said to him, "Follow me!"

Dante pictured his father in place of Peter, requesting to be crucified upside down because no man is worthy to suffer the same death as his Lord.

After Mass, the children who normally run around the courtyard playing tag asked Dante to join in.

"Can I, Mama?"

"Sure," she said, seating herself on a concrete bench. "Just for a few minutes."

Little Sylvie toddled after him.

Elina was expecting to have to call Dante from the game several times because children's games usually don't end unless an adult has an idea to end them. But this time, it did, about five minutes later, when Elina was just about to give Dante a two-minute warning to wrap it up.

"We better go, Mama," he said, running past her. "We need to check on Daddy. But I'm going to go light a candle first."

A large statue of the Sacred Heart of Jesus stood on a high platform, which also supported a large basin, where people pushed, into the sand, their prayers, lit onto long, skinny, beeswax candles.

Dante imagined that the candle stood in for him at the feet of Jesus and that his prayer went on, without stopping, until the last drop of wax melted into the sand and the flame went out. He viewed the candle as a very effective means to reaching the ear of God because it would last much longer than he himself could ever pray. The longest he'd ever prayed for anything was when his friend Lonni's parents said they were getting a divorce. Dante wasn't sure exactly how that would change Lonni, but he knew it would, in some profound way. He couldn't imagine living without both of his parents, so he hit his knees for an entire hour and twenty minutes on behalf of his friend. About a month later, his friend told him he was moving away. His dad got transferred to Austin and now the whole family was going to make a new start.

When Elina and Dante got home, Mateo was watching a football game, a bottle of Coors Light propped in the arm of his recliner. It was 11:30.

Dante ran to his father and hugged him around the middle.

"How was church, Mijo?"

"Good. I lit a candle for you." He looked at the TV and sat rigidly on the arm of the chair, the one opposite of where the beer was sitting. "Who's winning?"

"Broncos."

"The reading was about Jesus telling Peter he was going to be crucified."

Elina came to the recliner, rubbed Mateo' shoulder – the one on the beer side – and kissed him on the top of the head. "We missed you."

There was seldom ever any kind of anything between the two of them. No kind of obstacle, seen or unseen, that ever robbed them of their oneness. But on this day, Dante looked into his mother's face and saw the distance. She got up and went into the kitchen to do dishes. She did them with a steady stare into the sudsy water.

The following week, Dante broke down in tears because he was scheduled to serve at the 10 a.m. Mass and his parents were still in their pajamas at 9:30. Elina had told Mateo that she would not be taking Dante to church alone, so if he wanted his son to remain Catholic, he would have to step up. So, no one took Dante to church. His father watched football again and his mother stayed in bed reading *Vogue*. She apologized to Dante for having a headache. Dante sat on the couch near his father's recliner and watched football, thinking between plays about what part of the Mass was being said three miles away. Dante thought he knew the moment when the host was elevated in Father Milo's hands. He whispered along with Father, "My Lord and my God."

"Good grief!" Mateo exclaimed. "What a stupid play that was! Can't these guys get it together?"

At that moment, Elina emerged from the kitchen, where she had taken a break between fashion articles to pour herself a cup of coffee, and, cloaked in her pink chenille bathrobe, turned that little knob on the TV.

"What are you doing, Elina?" Mateo demanded. "I'm watching the game."

"What am *I* doing? No, Mateo. What are *you* doing?" She glanced at her son. "Dante, go play."

"Come on, Elina, this is an important game."

"You've been preaching to me for years how church is the most important thing in your life. And now, what are you doing? What are you doing to your son? He can't get there by himself. And if you think I'm going to take him, you're wrong. You're the one who's Catholic. I'm not taking him alone. So, make your choice. Faith or football. And then just let me know and I'll try to fill our son in on the philosophy de jour."

"What's this sudden interest in church, Elina? Last time I checked, you weren't even sure there was a God."

"That's not true."

"It is true. And now you've got me convinced. I'm not so sure either."

Dante felt the world end as he sat in the hallway outside his bedroom door, hugging his knees into his chest, vaguely rocking back and forth.

He heard his mother's voice soften as she said, "Oh, Honey. I'm so sorry. I'm sorry I haven't been with you in this."

"I just don't understand, Elina," he heard his father say, in a voice shaking with tears.

"What don't you understand?"

"Anything. I don't understand anything."

"All the loss. You don't understand all the loss."

"My children. So many of them perish."

Dante knew of one child his father had lost, but what other children? He would not find out until his mother died and left him a letter that his parents had suffered three miscarriages, at fairly early stages of pregnancy.

"God has given you Dante and Sylvie," Elina reminded Mateo.

"Yes, they are great gifts. And a great comfort. But why the rest, Elina? Why? Why has God taken so much from me?"

"I once asked you the same thing, Mateo."

"And what did the wise Mateo say?"

"What *did* he say?"

There was a long silence.

"And there's no more grant money, Elina. It's all dried up."

"So you can't continue your research? When did you find this out?"

"A couple weeks ago. The grant ends at the end of the year. I'll make the best of what time I have left with it."

"Maybe it's time for you to write."

"I have nothing in me. Besides, no one will pay me to do that."

"Not yet. But maybe someday."

"In the meantime, we will starve."

"Come on, Honey. Let's get dressed. We can still make the eleven-thirty. We're going to place all of this at His feet."

"That's what the wise Mateo said. I remember now."

Dante heard the lever of the recliner pop, and he scurried into his room.

After Mass, Dante asked his mother and father if he could light a candle. There was only one candle already burning. It was in the exact place he had left his and it had a black speck amongst the cream colored wax, about an inch from its base. Just like the one he had lit for his father the week before.

A drop of rain landed on Father Dante's left hand as the expelled boy continued his sketching.

"Why does your Mom have a gun? Does she need protection too?"

"She's got a crazy ex."

Father Dante nodded. "It's a crazy world sometimes. Not the way God intended it."

Another rain drop hit the paper, just missing the sketch of the priest's beret.

"You could change that, you know. You young people. You have the power to change things."

"No one around here ever changes anything. It's always the same."

"Really? Did you think when you woke up this morning you would be sitting on a street corner drawing the ugly mug of a Catholic priest?"

The boy flashed a reluctant smile, igniting that bit of optimism Father Dante thought he had detected upon first laying eyes on him twenty-five minutes before.

"Sometimes, life surprises us," the priest said.

Still retaining his smile, the boy turned the easel.

"Ah, a very fine first effort at a living human," Father Dante exclaimed.

"Thanks. Wanna see my dragon?" The boy pulled his pant leg up to reveal a dragon drawn in blue ink on the inside of his lower leg.

"You drew that?"

"Yeah. I wanna get a tattoo. I'm designing my own."

"I prefer artwork on paper or canvas, or even on walls or a bus stop bench, but that's a very good dragon."

"Thanks."

"You know," Father Dante said, rubbing his chin as he looked at the portrait the boy had drawn, "all you need is a few pointers about perspective and you'd have it down. The trick is proportions. See, your eyes are just a little too high here. You want them to be midway between the top and bottom of the face." Father Dante drew an oval and divided it to demonstrate. "Then you divide the bottom half of the face in two and that's where the tip of the nose goes. See?" He handed the paper to the boy. "Here, you can keep this."

"Thanks."

"Sure."

Several more rain drops.

"You got a Dad?" Father Dante asked.

"Nope. Don't even know who my father is."

"Well, I know who mine is, but he won't return my calls."

"How come?"

"Guess he doesn't want to talk to me."

"How come?"

"Not sure. But remember how I said you can change things?"

"Yeah?"

"Will you pray for my father?"

"Sure, I guess."

"I'll pray for yours too."

"Like I said, I don't even know who he is."

"Then he doesn't know what he's missing." Father Dante smiled at the boy and held up the drawing he had given him. "Thanks for this." He closed the cover on the drawing pad and put the tablet in his duffle bag. "Better get packed up before it starts really coming down."

The boy looked a little sad.

"Keep drawing, OK?" Father Dante twisted the nut to collapse the easel. "You've got talent."

"It's all I want to do. It's all I've *ever* wanted to do."

"You've heard of Secretariat."

"World's fastest racehorse."

"Uh-huh. Legendary. Watching that horse was like watching a Pegasus. He didn't run. He flew. No horse has even come close to accomplishing what that horse did. Even to this day. But you look at him, he looked like any other horse. On the *outside*. Well, when Secretariat died, they did an autopsy. And you know what they found inside him?"

"What?"

"A heart two and a half times the size of a normal horse's heart."

"Wow."

"That's what carried that horse. His heart. Not his legs. On the inside, he was different. On the *inside*."

The boy nodded. "Are you going to be here tomorrow? Maybe you could show me some more about drawing."

"Not tomorrow, but sometime next week, God willing."

Father Dante saw, in his mind, a large door opening and light pouring in. He had a flash-forward in which he is surrounded by a half dozen kids, all anxious to learn how to draw. He thought about St. John Bosco, who back in the 1800s, surrounded himself with troubled youth, teaching them the faith and skills they would need to turn their lives around. Unlike John Bosco, Father Dante would not have to beg for funds for the boys. He said a quick prayer to the saint and put his easel into the duffle bag. So many of the boys that crossed Father Dante's path were fatherless. He knew what that was like. And he knew, too, what it was like to have a father. So, he knew exactly how large the void is. He could be a father to the fatherless, he thought.

Who better for that role? Dante had learned it at home. With Mateo gone, Sylvie needed a father. Dante stepped up and quite enjoyed the role. Most of the time.

The year before he finished college and went off to seminary, Dante was awakened in the middle of the night by his 15-year-old sister Sylvie. She had her hands placed on his shoulders and her face right in his. The smell of alcohol gust into his nostrils, jarring him from his drowsiness.

"Dante, Dante, wake up." She shook his shoulders and looked into his opened eyes. "Wake up. Mama says I'm drunk, and I say I'm not. She told me I had to prove I'm not drunk, by coming in here and telling you I'm not drunk."

Dante sat up and put his hands on her shoulders. "Sylvie, I hate to break it to you. But mom is right. You are drunk. Quite so, actually."

"Not you too, Dante," she whined. "The whole world is against me." She sat down on the edge of his bed, folded herself in half and put her head in her hands.

"Well, if you don't believe us, wait until morning and see what your own pounding head tells you."

"Actually, I'm not feeling so well right now," she said, curling her upper lip. "I think I'm coming down with something. I think I'm going to be—"

And with that, Sylvie rushed to the bathroom and got more acquainted with the porcelain throne than she had ever been before. Elina, who had dragged herself out of bed with a temperature of 103, gathered Sylvie's long brown hair into a bundle behind her and held her forehead, assuring her it would all be over soon. Sylvie vowed through her tears and in between heaves that she would never drink beer again.

"What kind was it?" Dante wanted to know.

"Coors." Another heave.

"Coors?" Dante was aghast. "Ughck."

"I know you're a beer snob, Dante, but Heineken doesn't sound much better right now." Another heave.

"Here, Mama," Dante said, placing his hand on Sylvie's forehead. "I'll take over from here. You go back to bed. I'll let you know if we need you."

Elina reluctantly agreed. The flu had gotten the best of her.

"I'm just going to sleep here tonight." Sylvie curled up in the fetal position on the linoleum.

"No, Sylvie girl, come on." Dante placed his hand in her arm and nudged it gently. "I'll get you to bed. I'll get a bucket."

"No, Dante, I can't. Will you just get me a blanket and my pillow?"

Dante did as she asked, tucked the blanket around her shoulders and brushed the straggles of hair from her face. This he did about a half dozen times, after each session of retching.

When the gastronomical storm had finally passed, Dante sat over Sylvie, rubbing her temples until she fell asleep. Then he lay down beside her and drifted off. Their mother found them there in the very early morning after coming to look about her daughter and finding her bed empty. She fetched the blanket from Dante's bed and covered him up. And then, as she liked to tell it, she smiled up at Mateo, who smiled back, delighting in the gift they had given each other. Two beautiful children asleep together at the base of the toilet.

Father Dante opened the paper and found a familiar face inside the community section. It was the man whose mother loved shrimp. He had been shot and killed during an altercation at a party. Both men wielded guns and about a half-dozen shots were fired. No one else was injured. Father Dante felt a deep sadness that he never was able to convince the man to confess his sins. What if time were to run out on Lawrence Crenshaw as well? Father Dante tossed the paper on the coffee table and walked out into the soundless rose garden.

He looked up into the sky, blue with mere thoughts of white wisps.

"Why can't I hear the singing anymore," he whispered. No one answered. He spoke again, this time in a full voice. "Why don't they sing anymore?" He kept his neck craned like that, standing there looking up into the far distance, for over a minute. Then, with all his throat could muster: "I *want* to hear them!"

He sat down on the bench and hung his head. "Why won't they let me hear them, Mama?" he whispered. "Ever since you've been gone–" His throat dammed back a torrent of tears, and no more words could pass through them.

And then a soft, sublime sweetness – like what the smell of a rose would sound like if it were possible to hear a scent – wafted into Father Dante's ears, forcing his knees to the brick pavers, bursting the dam.

He clutched the rosary from his pocket and began a Divine Mercy Chaplet for the soul of the man who was killed at the party. By the third decade, his tears had ceased, and he was sitting quietly on the concrete bench, his prayer streaming into eternity just above the cadence of voices.

Suddenly, something harsh from this world pierced through. Caller ID said Cedars-Sinai Hospital. Another parishioner needing anointing, no doubt.

"Hello, it's Lawrence Crenshaw."

"Oh, hello."

"I'm going in for surgery in the morning. They're putting in a cardioverter-defibrillator implant, but there are some complications."

"I'll be right there. Just– just hang tight."

Father Dante sat at a stoplight and watched the people pass. The little girl with the raven hair crossed with the rest of the crowd. She looked through the windshield at him for just a second or two and then scurried to the sidewalk and disappeared around the corner. When the light turned green, Father Dante moved into the intersection and craned his neck to see if he could get a glimpse of her. She was gone.

When he reached Larry Crenshaw's hospital bed, Father Dante was surprised how old and frail the man looked. His pale skin hung loose on him.

A shapely woman in her late 30s with long layers of blow-dried blond hair sat by his bedside, rubbing his lower arm, a fuchsia smile painted on her face.

"Hello, I'm Father Dante." He held out his hand. She brushed her hair out of her face and shook his hand.

"I'm Laura."

"Nice to meet you."

"Laura is one of my old friends," said Larry Crenshaw. His voice had a mild tremble that Father Dante hadn't noticed during their short phone call.

Laura stood and leaned into Crenshaw's face. "I'm going to take off now, OK?" She gave him a kiss on the lips. "I'll see you a little later, Sweetheart." She put her purse strap over her arm. "Call if you need anything, Larry, but I'll be back tomorrow before your surgery. Nice meeting you, Father."

"Good to meet you."

Larry Crenshaw watched her leave and then turned his gaze on Father Dante. "Thank you for coming."

"Of course." He took a step closer. "May I sit down?"

"Please."

"So, how are they treating you?"

"Well, it's not the Cirigan Palace. But it's a well-run establishment. How are things back at the parish?"

"Well, the staff and customers can be a bit difficult to deal with at times, but the boss makes it all worth it."

"Oh yes, Father– Father– What's his name?"

"Oh, Father Francis. Yes, he is a wonderful mentor. But no, I was referring to the CEO." He raised his eyebrows and glanced toward heaven and then back at Larry Crenshaw, widening his smile as he settled into the man's pondering brown eyes.

"I've heard He can be pretty demanding."

"Oh, yes. But He only asks for what we are able to give."

"Wish I could say the same for the stockholders. I've put a lot of food on a lot of tables. And not one of them knows I'm lying flat on my back waiting to have my chest sliced open."

"Well, you have your friend Laura."

"My friend Laura is just hoping to get me to hobble down the aisle before I meet the reaper. I've got about a half dozen friends just like her. None of them knows I've already had the papers written up to leave my fortune to a parish priest. Wait until the press gets that story. You're going to be famous. Sorry to do that to you."

"No apology required. I'm not going to accept the inheritance."

"Now, don't be crazy. I'm sure you have a number of causes you'd like to fund."

"I'll only accept your inheritance if, in the end, I'm successful in persuading you to accept an even larger one."

"What inheritance is that?"

"The Kingdom."

The two sat in silence for a few minutes.

"Don't you want it, Mr. Crenshaw?"

Larry Crenshaw shook his head. "So many years gone."

"God stands outside of time. Maybe we can too. For whatever time is left." He reached out and touched Lawrence Crenshaw's veiny hand. The old man pulled it away, subtly as if he didn't notice he had been touched, lifting both hands over his head to smooth his salt and pepper hair.

"St. Paschal has been relentless," Larry Crenshaw said.

"Has he?"

"I don't think I'm going to make it out of surgery."

"Many people feel that way when they're headed for the O.R."

"And they don't all make it out."

"The vast majority do."

"They've found a number of aneurisms. They're not sure what surgery will mean for those."

"And they determined it prudent to proceed with the surgery?"

"I don't know about prudent. But necessary."

"It's all in God's hands then."

"About that." The man looked down at his bed covers and smoothed out the wrinkles as far as he could reach.

"About that." Father Dante smiled in agreement.

"I know this will come as a shock to you, but–" He looked out the window and drew a deep breath, as if attempting to inhale some fresher air from beyond the pane. "I'd like to make a confession."

"Praise be to God." Father Dante would have rather not admitted to himself that he was indeed shocked. He would have liked to have thought he had more faith than that.

"Can you get me a priest?" Larry Crenshaw glanced quickly into Father Dante's eyes and then back at the window.

"Of Course, I can call Father Francis. Or–" Father Dante fixed his gaze on his own hands, folded in his lap. "Or, I did bring my purple stole. You know. Just in case."

"Hmmm." Larry Crenshaw drummed his fingers lightly on the bed sheet and looked into Father Dante's face. "Why doesn't that surprise me?"

The priest smiled.

"But the thing is," Crenshaw said, "there is something I can't tell you. A family secret. Of sorts."

Dante's heart began to race, and he felt the muscles in his face collapse.

"Just kidding, Father." The old man smiled weakly and winked. Then he turned his head away and cast his gaze toward the window, though there was still nothing but white sky to view. He closed his eyes, and his smile slowly faded. A tear squeezed past his tightening eyelids, and a heavy sigh pressed from his frail body. "On second thought–" He seemed to be gripped in a sudden snare of fear. Or weakness. Or maybe both.

Father Dante had witnessed a number of these bedside battles. He closed his eyes and prayed that Larry Crenshaw would not lose his courage to confess – that he would fight for it, with all the dogged tenacity he had employed throughout his life in pursuit of burgeoning fortunes. *Please, St. Joseph, patron of a good death, who had Jesus by his side when he died. Please.* The priest desperately wanted to give his father the Body of Christ, which hung at his heart, under his cassock, in a golden pyx within a brown pouch.

When Father Dante opened his eyes, he saw the raven-haired girl, standing beside the bed with a soft smile. Never before had he seen her like this. She was wearing a purple sash around the waist of her billowing white dress.

"On second thought, Father," the old man said, reaching for the priest's hand. "I think, if you don't mind, I'll call you 'son.'"

About the Author

Sherry Boas is author of the highly-acclaimed Lily Trilogy: *Until Lily, Wherever Lily Goes* and *Entwined with Lily's*. She began her writing career in a hammock in a backyard woods in rural Massachusetts when she was eight years old, writing a "novel" about the crime-fighting abilities of her Cocker Spaniel. Fourteen years later, she would draw her first writer's paycheck for a very different kind of story when she landed a job at a newspaper in Arizona. She spent the next decade as a journalist, winning news awards, but her heart still belonged to fiction. So, after twelve years at home with her four adopted and highly inspiring children, she entered the ranks of contemporary novelists and enjoyed immediate success for her subtle, faith-based literature available from Caritas Press. *Wing Tip* is Boas' fourth novel. She is also author of *A Mother's Bouquet: Rosary Meditations for Moms*. Find her work at www.LilyTrilogy.com or CatholicWord.com.

Also available from *Caritas Press*

The Lily Trilogy
By Sherry Boas

Until Lily   **Wherever**   **Life Entwined**
                Lily Goes   **with Lily's**

A tender and gritty account of the truths underlying the human condition and the inalienable value of every human soul, even if it can do nothing more than love or be loved.

A Mother's Bouquet   **A Father's Heart**
Rosary Meditations   Rosary Meditations
for Moms   for Dads
by Sherry Boas   by Father Doug Lorig

Other rosary titles and works of fiction coming soon.

Visit www.LilyTrilogy.com

www.ingramcontent.com/pod-product-compliance
Lightning Source LLC
Chambersburg PA
CBHW020550180626
46810CB00007B/2453